THE OLD
CAPE MAP

BARBARA EPPICH STRUNA

Cover Designers: Timothy Graham, Michael Struna
Edited by Nicola Burnell
Author photo by Michael Struna

Print ISBN: 978-0-9976-5667-1
Ebook ISBN: 978-0-9976-5668-8
Library of Congress Control No. 2023919973

This is a work of fiction. Names, characters, places, brands, media, and incidents are either the product of the author's imagination or are used fictitiously. Any resemblance to similarly named places or to persons living or deceased is unintentional.

No generative artificial intelligence (AI) was used in the writing of this work. The author expressly prohibits any entity from using this publication for purposes of training AI technologies to generate text, including without limitation technologies that are capable of generating works in the same style or genre as this publication. The author reserves all rights to license use of this work for generative AI training and development of machine learning language models.

To the search for adventure and a creative mind

ALSO BY BARBARA EPPICH STRUNA

The Old Cape House

The Old Cape Teapot

The Old Cape Hollywood Secret

The Old Cape Blood Ruby

Family, Friends, and Faith

ADVANCE PRAISE FOR
THE OLD CAPE MAP

"History meets mystery in this twisty page-turning tale, a suspenseful journey over the beaches, through the woodlands, and across the decades on old Cape Cod. We all know there's gold on that sandy peninsula. Let Barbara Eppich Struna and her beloved sleuth, Nancy Caldwell, lead you to it in *The Old Cape Map*."

-- William Martin, *New York Times* Bestselling author
Cape Cod and *December '41*

"*The Old Cape Map* by Barbara Struna is a gem of a book. It's a mystery tale about the search for a long-lost stash of pirate gold. It has murder and mayhem and villains and more than one treasure map. But it is also a historical novel about family and friends, and how an act of kindness by an elderly man with a colorful past, changes the lives of two young girls and their descendants.

"Struna does a masterful job of weaving the stories of amateur sleuth Nancy Caldwell and her niece with those of an immigrant Hungarian family at the turn of the century, shifting easily between the quiet back roads of Cape Cod and the burgeoning industrial area around Central Massachusetts.

"In the process, we are drawn into the lives of these believable characters, root for them to overcome seemingly insurmountable obstacles, and cheer at their ultimate triumph."

--Paul Kemprecos, *New York Times* Bestselling author

"You're sure to enjoy this ride from 1900 to present day with believable characters. The historical elements were accurate, and the immigrant Hungarian family, with all the trials and tribulations of people of that era, proves interesting. The ending hints at the next novel in the series. A great read."

--Iris G. Leigh, author, *Liza's Secrets*

"This is Struna's fifth book in her Old Cape Series. In *The Old Cape Map*, as in all the others, the author weaves the reader from past to present and back again ever so gently, intertwining characters with one another as they try to untangle the web of intrigue that surrounds a long-lost map and its supposed treasure. Another page turner."

--Anita A. Caruso, author, *Brayden's Magical Series.*

1

Present Day August
BREWSTER, CAPE COD

AN EARTHY SMELL from the hot kitchen crept through the tiny house as a grease-laden window fan struggled to pull the acrid smell out of the Brewster half-cape home. The clock was nearing high noon. A dense liquid from cooked leaves, stems, and roots was set aside, and then the discarded mash of vegetation was stuffed into the garbage disposal. The gray aluminum pot was washed and rinsed.

A bottle of cheap Cabernet Sauvignon sat on the chipped, white-porcelain counter, next to a medicine bottle of triazolam, prescribed for Marty Horvath's insomnia. By the time Marty's car pulled onto the shell driveway, the mixture of aconitum napellus and three tablets of medicine had been blended into a second pot containing Marty's favorite afternoon drink – a soothing Hot Toddy made with wine and rum.

"Hey, Marty. Where you been?"

Marty hung his cap on a peg near the back door. "Saw an old fishing buddy down at the pier and got to talkin'. You know how it is."

"How about something to drink?"

"Sure." Marty made his way to his favorite chair in the living room.

A steaming mug was delivered to a TV tray beside the bay window. Within the hour, Marty was asleep. Any leftover poisonous concoction was removed and returned to the kitchen. The aluminum pot was emptied into the drain, rinsed twice, and then stashed back under the sink. The mug was thoroughly washed, dried, and replaced in the upper cabinet. Inside a brown bag, which would be tossed into a dumpster behind the local grocery store, was the leftover lemon, tea bag, and paper towels that had been used to prepare the toxic drink and clean the counter of any evidence.

Marty would be dead in three to four hours. The cleaning lady wouldn't show up for another week. Outside, a big smile grew across the man's face from behind the wheel of the SUV. He hoped the lovely purple monkshood flowers that grew along the fence on the shady side of the house would get rid of his cousin for good.

2

June, Present Day, Eleven Months Later
BREWSTER

THE SMALL PACKAGE addressed to me, Nancy Caldwell, sat unopened on the kitchen counter. I knew what was inside. I couldn't open it.

My dear friend from Ohio, whom I had not seen in over five years, was finally here, or at least what was left of her. I recalled the call from her daughter asking me to scatter some of her ashes across Cape Cod. This tiny peninsula had become her mother's favorite place to be. She loved the beaches, marshes, and our two-acre property, which dated back to 1880. I, of course, had said yes.

I took the small box out to Paul's art studio, which was connected to the rear of our home and housed in an old barn. "Look what came in the mail today."

I walked over to my talented husband, who was standing at his easel, adding the finishing touches to his latest landscape.

He looked over to me. "Is that Mary?"

"Yes." I placed the package on his drawing table.

"When are you going to scatter her ashes?"

"I just checked the weather, and it's going to be clear and calm over the next few days, except Thursday, when the wind should be around ten to twelve miles per hour. Bearberry Hill in Truro will be the perfect spot for the wind to take Mary out to sea."

Paul smiled.

"Want to come?"

"Sure." He reached out to give me a hug.

I accepted his loving gesture with eagerness. We held each other for a while.

"Don't be sad."

I nestled my face into the crook of his neck.

"Can't help thinking about my own mortality at a time like this."

The following morning brought a cool, sunny day. After my coffee, I carefully picked up Mary, grabbed a small shovel from the garden shed, and ventured down the hill behind the house to the farthest corner of our property, our pet cemetery. I smiled, thinking of the old pup we had brought with us when we'd moved to the Cape from Ohio, over thirty years ago. This spot was where he would often escape into the back woods. In fact, on the many visits that Mary made to the Cape, she had always liked his escape route.

"This is a good spot for my ashes," she'd said, and I'd laughed at the time, never thinking I would actually have to do the spreading.

My next stop was an area nestled beneath the old oak tree on the western side of our house, where Mary would collect acorns for her crafting. She was a quilter and used the acorn tops to make little fabric pincushions. I dug down about six inches, near the base of the tree trunk, and then sprinkled a few ashes into the hole. Hopefully, Mary would nurture this big tree so it remains strong and steadfast in its future life.

I stood up to gaze at the overgrown lot next to our property line, beyond the old oak. Rumor had it that an old man had died in a fire on the property back in the early 1900s. I whispered a short prayer and hoped he had been loved. I then wondered if his ashes were somewhere among the ivy, wildflowers, and scrub.

After dinner, Paul and I drove to a small, secluded beach near Breakwater, where I added some of my friend's ashes to the coastline. Mary's last trip would be on Thursday, to Truro.

It was another beautiful morning. I packed coffee, water, and a few snacks for our ride to Truro's Bearberry Hill.

"Thanks for coming with me," I said, taking a sip of coffee as Paul drove onto the Old King's Highway.

He rubbed my thigh with a reassurance that he'd always be with me. "I don't mind."

"I'm happy this solemn journey will be over before the girls fly in from Ohio." The small plastic bag holding the last of Mary's ashes was cradled in my lap. "I don't want to make the visit with their aunt and uncle a weird event. I can hardly wait to see them."

"I can't remember the last time I saw Jane and Madeline." Paul switched lanes to pass a truck.

"I think Jane was only ten. Everything seemed to stop so abruptly when the pandemic hit us. Has it been almost four years?"

After about an hour's drive, we arrived in Truro and parked on the road that ran next to the path that would lead us up to the top of Bearberry Hill. We hadn't visited this bucolic vista for quite a while. The landscape was magnificent, an unobstructed 360° view of sea and land. I spun slowly around to take it all in.

When I opened the little bag, my friend's ashes flew out and were caught up in the gentle wind that blew across the hilltop. "Look down upon us with care, Mary. Watch over all those who loved you."

Back home in Brewster, a car followed us as we pulled into our driveway.

"Who's that?" I stretched my neck around to see who was in the car. "It's Smitty. I forgot she was dropping by today."

"I'm glad you called Martha to help you. I mean, 'Smitty.'" It will be good to see her again." Paul parked toward the back of the house.

I climbed out and hurried toward Smitty. "How are you doing?"

She looked the same, except her hair was now dyed jet-black. A far cry from years ago, when it was red. She also had a new name. In her last Christmas card, she had explained that she'd met someone. Apparently, he'd had a bad experience with a woman called *Martha*, so Smitty had decided to use her last name as a nickname, which was Smith but with a twist. Typical of my old friend.

"Mrs. C! Good to see you."

I looked forward to catching up with her. "How about a cup of coffee?"

Paul waved hello and headed toward his studio.

Smitty waved back at him, then she turned to me. "I'd love some coffee."

We walked into the house.

"Before we discuss business, let's share."

Time felt like it had stood still. Our conversation fell into step, as if our youngest, Danny, was still five years old and Molly, his sister, was arguing with him about something or another.

"Can you believe Danny graduated from college and is on his own now? And Molly is a teacher, living with her boyfriend in Millbury, Massachusetts?"

"Time sure goes by fast. Nancy, I was so pleased to hear from you and thrilled that you want me to give the old house a once-over. All your remodeling looks wonderful."

I smiled. "Yes, I want some help before my two nieces arrive from Ohio for a few weeks' stay with us."

"Well, I haven't done much cleaning since last summer." Smitty fidgeted with her fingers.

"Oh. Is something wrong?"

"Not physically. I'm doing great. Lost a few pounds. It's a good thing I met Johnny. He's always so supportive of me. My head just needs some more time to heal."

"What happened?"

"Maybe you haven't heard? I was the woman who found that old man dead in his house on Brier Lane last summer." Smitty took a sip of her coffee.

"I remember reading about that in the police log. There weren't many details. I had no idea it was you who discovered the body."

"My identity was never mentioned." Smitty gazed out the kitchen window. "You know, the whole scene really bothered me. The smell was awful! He must have been dead for over a week."

I reached to hold her hand. "If I recall, Cape Cod was in an August heat wave. I'm so sorry that happened to you."

Smitty covered her mouth with her hand. "Sometimes, I wake up screaming... remembering those disgusting flies... the maggots..."

I shook my head in mutual disgust.

"I don't take on any more jobs for elderly people who live alone." She pushed her unfinished coffee cup away. "I just can't."

Eager to change the subject, I stood up to start the tour of the house. "Let me show you around, so I can tell you what I need cleaned."

As we reached the top of the stairs, Smitty turned to me. "Do you think you could do me a favor? I don't like to ask, but I know you're a whole lot more adventurous than I could ever be."

"What is it?"

"The day I found the body, I went to the back shed, as usual, to get the spare key. That's when I noticed that several of the purple monkshood flowers had been cut away from the fence. I stepped into the garden to get a closer look at the cut stalks, and then I tripped on some garden clippers that were lying on the ground. I caught myself on the fence. That must have been when my ring slipped off my finger. It was an antique ring that I'd found at a yard sale. Not very expensive, but I really liked it. I'd planned to go back to look for it among the flowers, but I never returned, because I found poor old Marty Horvath dead in his chair by the bay window. Then, the police showed up and everything went downhill."

"What do you want me to do for you?"

"Do you still have that metal detector?"

"Yes."

"No one is living there now. Maybe you could try to find my ring for me?"

"Are you confident it's empty now?

"Yes.

"Okay. I just want to make sure there will be no problems."

"It's also off-season, so the street is very quiet."

I patted Smitty on her shoulder. "I'll be happy to help you out." It had been a long time since I'd done anything with my metal detector. I hoped I would be able to find her ring.

"Mrs. C, it's good to be back in the Caldwell home." She gave me a big hug. "Meet any pirates lately?"

We both laughed as she followed me into the first bedroom.

3

1898
BREWSTER, CAPE COD

ROSALIA KALMAR'S NOSE prickled at the smell of smoke. She quickly sat up in bed. Little five-year-old Anna lay sleeping next to her, lost in childlike innocence.

The small, sparsely furnished room that was their home looked clear of any burn. Rosalia's bare feet touched the cold, wooden floorboards as she hurried to look through the closest window for the direction where the smoke might be coming from. A foreboding, willowy column of dark smoke twisted high into the eastern sky. She held her heart and bowed her head in thankfulness that the fire wasn't close.

Her body froze when horses' hooves pounded the dirt road outside of the main house. After a few seconds, she dared to look again. Two men on horseback were racing toward Orleans. Rosalia whispered a silent prayer for their safety. She recalled the terror of being a small girl in Hungary, when Russian Cossacks had ridden down from the mountains and raided their small town of Pápatérzer. This memory had stayed with her. She closed her eyes and remembered hiding under the kitchen table, shaking with fear that they would spear her as they ransacked her sleepy village.

Rosalia sat on the bed beside her daughter. "Jó reggelt."

Anna stirred under her covers.

She stroked Anna's silky brown hair and smiled.

A voice hollered down the hallway. Catherine, the head housekeeper, appeared at their doorway in the rear of the Freeman House, where the two new immigrants lived. She called out again, "Laundry today! Crisp collars!"

The two recent arrivals from Hungary scurried to dress for their daily work schedule. First, some oatmeal and then tea, finishing with drawing the water for the household laundry. Anna followed in her mother's steps, never leaving her side.

Rosalia supported the clothesline with long wooden poles. Soon, the clean sheets billowed in the sea breezes. Anna played on the grass with her cloth doll, pretending the small figure was her best friend. When Rosalia saw Mr. Freeman walk toward her, she smoothed her apron and pulled Anna close.

"Rosa?" The master of the house puffed on his morning cigar.

Rosalia stood as tall as her slim five-foot body could muster and repeated her name to her new employer. "Mr. Freeman, my name... Rosalia."

"Of course. Of course." Mr. Freeman bent over to pat Anna's head. Then, with a broad smile, he turned to his newest employee. "Welcome to our home, Rosa. I hope you are comfortable." He turned on his heel and headed for the house. "I expect crisp collars."

"My name... Rosalia," she whispered under her breath as she lifted the clothes poles higher.

A few mornings later, an older man approached the new laundress as she smoothed the wet sheets across the clothesline.

"Mornin', ma'am." He tipped his hat as he came closer.

Rosalia kept working.

"Might I trouble you for a minute?"

The young woman stopped and stared at the man. He looked tidy but a little rough, and he was higher in years than her young age of twenty-one.

"Is Mr. Freeman at home? I'd like to speak with him. My name is Wilkins."

Rosalia heard the familiar word, *Freeman*. She answered with a heavy accent, "No speak English. Mister no home."

Anna walked over to a pail of soapy water.

Rosalia yelled at her daughter to stop, "Álljon meg!"

The stranger smiled and then called Anna a sweet girl in Hungarian. "Kicsi édes lány."

Rosalia's eyes opened wide with surprise. She turned and thanked him, "Köszönöm."

Catherine came out of the kitchen. "Mr. Wilkins, how are you? Mr. Freeman is not at home today. May I help you?"

"Just wondering if he might be interested in adding to his coin collection?"

"Well, I don't know, sir."

"I see you have a new laundress. Doesn't speak much English?"

"No, I'm afraid not. And she isn't interested in learning, either. The Mister is doin' a friend from back East a favor by letting her come to Brewster. Of course, he was in need of a new laundress anyway."

"I see." Mr. Wilkins scratched his chin. "Back in the day, I sailed with a Hungarian. Maybe I could help her with a few words."

"I'll tell the Mister you stopped by." She glanced at Anna and then back to Mr. Wilkins. "Teaching the young one might be a better idea. They always learn quicker." Catherine returned to the kitchen.

Mr. Wilkins tipped his hat once more at Rosalia then waved goodbye to Anna. "Vizsla!"

4

June, Present Day
BREWSTER, SEA PINES INN

"TOMMY, DID YOU get that information I asked for?" Maxwell D. Appleton barked into his cell phone, then leaned back when he heard the answer he wanted. "That's great. I'll meet you at the Snowy Owl Café tomorrow. 11:00 a.m."

Max placed his yellow pad filled with scribbled notes into his briefcase and then locked it. After a quick look around his room upstairs at the Old Sea Pines Inn in Brewster, he went downstairs for dinner.

By early evening, Max was driving east down Main Street, looking for the property his Grandma Anna had so often talked about. He stopped across the street from an overgrown lot. Through the car's window, he could see a fixer-upper house on the empty property's left side.

On its right side was an old Greek Gothic summer house with a sign out front that read, *The Caldwell Art Gallery*. That piece of woods in the middle has got to be it, he thought.

The following day, Max waited outside of the Snowy Owl for Tommy Smith. His phone showed 11:05 a.m.

He didn't like people who were late. At 11:15 a.m., he started to pace in front of the café, then went back inside to order another coffee. As he turned around to leave, a short, muscular young man with blond hair appeared behind him.

"Hi, boss." Tommy stepped up to the counter and ordered himself a latte.

With a scowl, Max replied, "I'll be at the picnic table out front." He grabbed his second cup of coffee. "Hurry up."

Within a few minutes, Tommy joined Max outside.

Max was scrolling through his phone. Without looking up, he said, "You're late. What did you find out?"

Tommy took a sip of his latte. "It took me some time, but I found a few things."

His boss raised his eyes.

"That property you've got your eye on was taken by the town for non-payment of taxes."

Max looked up from his phone and slapped the table. "Shit!"

Tommy straightened his back in surprise at his boss's angry response. He tried to placate him, saying, "There's something else. I found an article about a big fire in the same area of that property in an old newspaper from 1908. It was owned by a Mr. Wilkins."

Max's eyes opened wide in excitement. His knee bounced faster under the table.

This time, Tommy spoke up. "Boss, are you okay?"

Max took a deep breath to steady himself. "Of course."

Tommy stirred his drink and continued. "According to the article, this old guy was reclusive. He died in the fire with no immediate family or distant relatives to mourn his death. The article stated that the cause of the fire was unknown. It also said some locals thought the property was cursed, because the house had been built on sacred land."

Max still looked troubled. "So, who owns the property now?"

"The town does, I believe. Probably no one was interested in buying into its bad karma. Back then, people could be real superstitious."

"You've had a week to find what I'm looking for." Max leaned closer to Tommy. "I'm paying you well. You need to give me more." He stood to leave. "I don't like to be disappointed."

"Don't worry, boss. I'm on it."

Tommy recalled those same words coming from his father. *I don't like to be disappointed.* He hated his father. He had been mean and abusive to him as a kid. He'd stay out of sight of him as much as he could.

On the short ride back to the Sea Pines Inn, Max knew he was on the right trail based on some ramblings from his Grandma Anna about a man named Wilkins. Maybe it was the same man from the news article. All he wanted was a little more proof that he had the right location.

Max still needed Tommy. The kid had a short fuse, but he could keep his mouth shut, and he knew his way around the Internet. Besides, he was going to be very busy as soon as he picked up the key to his cousin's house over on Brier Lane, or should he say, *his* house now.

Later, as the skies got darker and Max grew tired in his upstairs room at the Old Sea Pines Inn, he went to bed but couldn't sleep. He watched the clock creep toward midnight. Restless, he eventually climbed out of bed and sat down at a small wooden table lit by a green desk lamp.

He leaned back and recalled how his mother always said their family had a secret. Something about hidden treasure and a missing map. It all had to do with an old house in Brewster. But which house? His cousin's place? Or the one that had once stood on that deserted, burned-out property beside the gallery?

From his briefcase, Max withdrew a small, weathered leather pouch. He closed his eyes and revisited the day he'd gone to see his Grandma Anna with his mother, back in 1972. She had been recovering from a stroke, and his mother had insisted they visit her.

Almost seventy-seven years old, Grandma Anna still lived by herself in a small 1880 house in Millbury, Massachusetts. It was old, in need of a coat of paint, and smelled of cooked cabbage. His grandmother's favorite meal was stuffed cabbage rolls. His mom would usually prepare her mother's favorite dish and then set up a snack for him at the kitchen table, before she disappeared into the basement to do Grandma's laundry.

Grandma looked pale. Max felt sorry for her. She hadn't been the same since the stroke. Sometimes, she was okay, but other times, she appeared to be far away in her thoughts, and she didn't make sense when she talked. He recalled the day his mother was interviewing someone to look in on Grandma. As soon as he'd finished his Yahoo drink and chips in the kitchen, he'd joined his grandma in the living room.

She smiled at her only grandson. "You're a smart boy. I know that because you're always reading when you visit."

Max smiled back at her.

"I would like to give you something."

He remembered Grandma's touch. Her fingers had felt skinny and weak as she grabbed onto his hand to lead him into the tiny room where she slept.

She faced the dresser's mirror and gently touched her wedding picture. "Oh, how I miss that man."

"Grandpa Eddie?"

"He was so kind and loving." She slowly opened the middle drawer of her bureau.

Max sat on the bed and waited to see what she was going to give him.

She pushed her hand deep into the drawer, under her nightclothes and handkerchiefs, and pulled out a small pouch. Her hand shook as she handed her gift to him. "Like I said, you're a smart boy. You'll know what to do with this when the time comes."

"Thank you, Grandma." Confused, Max wasn't sure what he was supposed to do.

She tapped the top of the faded leather. "No one, not even my Eddie, ever believed me when I told them about this. Except, perhaps, my little brother, Louis."

Max cradled the pouch in his hands.

With Max's help, Grandma Anna slowly walked back to her lift chair in the living room in front of the television. Once settled, she pulled her grandson closer and whispered, "There is a map… somewhere… Maybe for more treasure." She shook her head. "I just can't remember where it is." She adjusted her robe underneath her hips as she whispered, "I think Louis may have taken the map and hidden it somewhere. Back on Cape Cod. For safekeeping. Oh, I do miss my little brother."

As he was about to open the pouch to see what was inside, his mother appeared in the doorway. "Max, I could use some help in the kitchen."

Grandma Anna shushed him and gave him a wink; her signal that this was to be their secret. "Don't let your cousin, Marty, get his hands on this. I don't trust him."

Max's lips went from a smile to a serious stare as he hid the pouch under his bulky sweatshirt. "Coming, Mom." That was fine with Max, he never liked his older cousin anyway.

He turned around to glance at his grandma. Her eyes were closed, but she was still talking. He could barely hear her words as she mumbled, "Mr. Wilkins was a kind man." A smile grew across her face. "He gave Ellsbeth and me such a fun treasure hunt."

"Who is Mr. Wilkins?"

Grandma Anna opened her eyes. "He had a big, old, brick house. I used to clean for him." She drifted off again. "What a nice man he was. Too bad he…."

His mother called again, "Max, I need you! *Now!*"

Max's head fell forward and woke him up. The digital clock showed 2:00 a.m. He must have dozed off. Max still held the old pouch in his hand. He gloated to himself, thinking of all the years he'd kept it hidden from everyone. Always dreaming of finding more treasure.

He sat straighter, opened the pouch, and carefully unfolded a yellowed paper from around one gold coin. He gently held the treasure between his fingers then returned it to the safety of the pouch. Under his breath, he whispered, "Wilkins. Mr. Wilkins."

Then, he thought, *this man has to be the same Wilkins whom Tommy told me about.*

A quick glance at his phone messages made him grimace. There was a new voicemail from a business partner. He knew what it was about, so he deleted it. He'd get the money owed to his partner in good time.

5

February 1900
BREWSTER

TWO YEARS HAD PASSED since Rosalia and Anna arrived in Brewster. The young mother did her job well and kept to herself. She never minded the process of starching and ironing Mr. Freeman's collars. There were days when she took pleasure in seeing the stiff white of the freshly ironed neck pieces. Anna, now seven years old, was becoming proficient in speaking English, with the aid of Mr. Wilkins.

Letters from a Michael Horvath had been arriving once a month, addressed to Rosalia care of the Freeman house. Michael and Rosalia had met on their way to America. He was also from Hungary but lived in a different village, north of Pápatérzer. He could speak and write English.

While they'd steamed across the waters and travelled closer to their new American homes, the two passengers had grown attracted to each other. By the time they'd landed in New York, they had exchanged addresses and vowed to write as they departed for their new homes. Michael had stayed in New York and Rosalia had left for Massachusetts.

Today, the sight of Michael's handwriting made Rosalia happy. She secluded herself under a tree in the back of the house to read his letter. He had held true to his promise of keeping contact with her, even after she had confided in him her tragic story of being raped by her employer at just sixteen years old. Michael had told her he admired her for keeping the child and for being so responsible. He was kind to Rosalia, and little Anna liked him because he had played hide-and-seek with her across the deck of the large steamer and entertained them with his flute.

As time passed, they grew closer through their written words, even though they were separated by hundreds of miles, Michael in New York City and Rosalia on Cape Cod. The young laundress stayed faithful with her return letters to Michael. Always written in Hungarian, she needed help only in addressing the envelopes in English. Catherine, who was very fond of Rosalia and Anna, was always willing to help.

Michael's last letter stated that he had finally saved up enough money to travel to Cape Cod. He enclosed a separate paper, written in English, stating his intentions toward Rosalia.

In broken English, Rosalia asked Catherine if she would speak with Mr. Freeman about Michael and the possibility of finding a job for him.

"Of course." Catherine sat down to read the letter written in English. "Now, mind you, I can't promise anything."

Rosalia smiled and pointed to Michael's letter.

Catherine read Michael's letter once more, this time out loud. "So, it seems that your Michael is coming to Brewster."

Rosalia nodded.

"And he says here that he will marry you." She gestured to her ring finger. Rosalia smiled.

"Let me see what I can do. Say a prayer." She stood. "Maybe Mr. Wilkins could help you with your English? Anna is doing so well." Catherine disappeared into the kitchen.

6

June, Present Day
BRIER LANE, BREWSTER

MY NIECES WOULD SOON arrive for their visit. I figured I had time to try to find Smitty's ring, so I dusted off my X234 Bounty Hunter and checked that the battery still had a charge. I was good to go.

Recently, life had interrupted my usual wanderings for adventure. Today, I was eager to get my hikers muddy.

Brier Lane was an old road in the middle of Brewster, near the Brewster General Store, and Smitty had given me a pretty good description of the house. I pulled onto the weed-covered shell driveway and parked halfway toward the back of the house, which definitely looked abandoned. The shed door was leaning half open.

I grabbed my metal detector and headed for the rear fencing. I could see the tall monkshood flowers growing on the shed's side and noticed a few empty spots where some of the plants had been dug up. Strange, I thought, but Smitty had said it looked odd to her, also.

After donning my headphones, I started swinging the detector side to side, listening for any pings or dings. Within minutes, I felt a hand on my shoulder. I jumped and quickly turned around to see a man standing behind me.

With a scowl on his face, he yelled, "Can I help you, lady?"

I lifted one of my earphones up. "Sorry." Then, I turned off the detector.

He shouted, "What do you think you're doing?"

"I'm really sorry, but I didn't think anyone was living here. I was—"

"I don't care what you think. I want you off my property."

"Of course." Embarrassed, I fumbled with the detector and nearly dropped it. "May I explain myself?"

"Some other time, lady." The man was clearly agitated. "Right now, I want you off my property." He glared at me.

"I'm sorry. I'll leave. You see, my friend lost her ring in this area about a year ago. She was the woman who found—"

He quickly cut me off again. "You should leave now!"

I watched him turn away from me and enter the back door of the weathered house. I guessed I'd better get going. No need to pursue this detecting any longer. Poor Smitty would be disappointed. I gathered my paraphernalia and retreated to the car.

The man's black SUV was parked so close, I could barely open my car door for fear I would scratch his vehicle. After I squeezed inside, I cracked open the window for some cool air. That's when I heard loud banging coming from inside the house. I carefully backed out of the driveway, wanting no more trouble.

Driving away from the house, I kept wondering what an idiot that guy was. Granted, I was on private property and shouldn't have been there. At least he could have given me a chance to explain myself. I realize Brewster is a safe place but it's not totally exempt from crime.

By the time I arrived home, Paul was closing the gallery. I waited in the driveway for him to bring the *Open* sign to the gallery porch. I called out, "Hi honey."

I was comforted to see him as he came closer. His lovely, graying beard made him look so handsome. I leaned nearer to give him a quick kiss on his cheek.

"Did you find anything?"

"No. Only a nasty man who probably owns the house."

"You've got to be careful."

"I know. I left pretty quickly. No harm done."

"Want to sit on the porch for a minute?"

"I'd love to. I'll get a coffee and meet you outside."

With my drink, I took a seat in one of the old oak rockers next to my husband of almost fifty years. We both rocked for a few moments as we looked out over the front of our property.

Paul sighed. "It's been quite a journey for us."

"A real adventure." A soft breeze stirred the porch chimes.

Paul looked over to me. "And we're still here, through all the renovations, two more kids, and, thanks to you, a lot of surprises."

I smiled. "I know sometimes things didn't go our way, but we eventually got through it with a lot of tears and laughs together."

"All the kids are doing well and seem happy."

"That's the most important thing for me. If they're happy, they can stand up to anything that comes at them."

"So, are we ready for another wedding?"

"I think so. Casey, being an artist and a gallerist, and her fiancé, a graphic designer, are a perfect match."

"I love you, Nancy." Paul took hold of my hand.

We rocked in silence again.

I stood up. "You hungry?"

Paul grinned.

"Give me a few minutes. I'll come up with something delicious."

"You always do."

7

June, Present Day
BOSTON

THE FOLLOWING MORNING, Jane Jackson adjusted her wireless headphones and mask from her window seat. Her sister Madeline settled into the middle seat beside her.

The stewardess stopped by their row. "How are you girls doing today?"

Jane pulled out one earpiece. "Pardon me?"

"Just checking to make sure you're comfy."

Madeline looked up from her iPad and smiled at the woman.

Jane replied, "We're fine. Thank you." She knew her mom had asked the airline to keep an eye on them, because they were travelling without an adult. She'd reassured her mom that she could handle anything that went wrong—after all, she was fourteen and Madeline almost thirteen. Embarrassed at the attention, she hoped no one else had noticed as she settled in for the quick flight from Ohio to her Aunt Nancy and Uncle Paul's home in Brewster, on Cape Cod.

Jane grabbed her phone and read in her notes app that they should catch their bus at 1:30 p.m., outside of door C110. She'd be fine. Madeline was another story; her sister liked to roam.

The terminal was bustling with people hurrying to make connections and finding their baggage, plus others just looking lost. Jane asked a security guard if they were going in the right direction, and he nodded, "Yes."

"Thanks." She confidently pulled her carry-on case down the long corridor, with Madeline following behind until C110 appeared on the sliding glass doors. Once outside, at the Plymouth and Brockton bus stop, Jane calmed, knowing everything was on schedule.

She pulled her mask down and sat on the bench to browse her phone, feeling very grown-up. Out of the corner of her eye, she saw Madeline sit next to her and mimic her big sister's actions, crossing her legs and bobbing her foot up and down.

This trip was going to be so awesome. In only a few hours, they would be lounging on a Brewster beach, sipping ice-cold sodas.

8

Present Day - Three Hours Later
CAPE COD

THE TREES FLEW BY us as we traveled from the Hyannis bus station to Brewster. From the rearview mirror, I caught quick glances of my two nieces in the back seat. It had been a long time since I'd seen them. They looked tired. Jane had a pensive gaze on her face. I hoped they'd have a good time with us over the next several weeks.

As soon as we pulled into the driveway, Jane glanced to her left and asked, "Do you own those woods?"

"No. We own the woods on the other side. You're looking at an overgrown piece of property."

"Who owns it?"

"I really don't know."

The car pulled to a stop.

"Aunt Nancy, everything looks just like I remember it. The gallery and flowers are so pretty. Where's Uncle Paul?"

"He's in his studio, as usual. Let's go in, and I'll show you where you will be sleeping. I'm afraid you'll have to share a room. The new floors in the other two bedrooms were supposed to be finished by the time you arrived." I looked over my shoulder. "Sorry, girls. Don't worry, you'll still have fun."

I watched Jane carry her backpack up the stairway, with Madeline right behind her. The smallest bedroom upstairs had twin beds on opposite walls and a plaster-covered old chimney between them. I stood at the foot of the stairway in the dining room and overheard them talking.

I heard a bed scrape across the floor. Jane spoke up. "I get dibs on this bed."

Madeline laughed. "You're too funny."

"I don't care. If I'm close to a wall, I'm afraid of hitting myself when I'm sleeping. I need to stretch."

I took a few steps up to a short landing to peek at which bed was chosen.

Madeline was standing with her back to me. Then, she jumped on the other bed to her right and lay on top of the blue-and-white bedspread.

They looked happy. Each bed had a window behind it. They could look out and see the empty, wooded lot beneath, with its old trees that edged our property line. I was always fond of those ancient hardwoods, covered with green ivy that wrapped around their trunks and branches, almost all the way up to their tops.

Before I turned to leave the girls alone to get settled, I saw Jane kneeling on the bed by her window. I overheard her say, "I wonder if we could go over there and explore?"

Madeline replied, "Why? It's just a bunch of old trees."

Jane placed her backpack on the floor in front of her bed. "I'm hungry. I'm going to find some snacks."

I quickly turned and stepped down to the first floor. As I entered the kitchen, I heard Jane's foot land on the wooden floor of the dining room, with Madeline close behind her.

At the bottom of the stairway, the girls found the bowl on the dining room table filled with goodies. I met them with a welcoming smile. "Help yourself."

Jane chose a bag of chips and some M&M's. Madeline picked her snacks out, and the two sisters asked to see my office.

"Follow me."

As the girls nibbled on their treats, they browsed the walls filled with photos of the family and seemed interested in the memorabilia depicting my not-so-illustrious escapades. One wall was covered with framed newspaper and magazine clippings about some of my adventures in treasure hunting. Another wall held several framed pictures, including one of me, then pregnant with Danny, standing near their cousin, Jim. Next to that was a close-up of Brian and me in Antigua, plus Molly as a young teen with Casey in front of her gallery in Chatham.

"Is that the necklace that caused so much trouble for you?"

"Yes, but it wasn't the necklace's fault. I was the one who wanted to wear it so much. It was so beautiful. I thought it would bring me good luck because I was frightened of flying."

Jane took a closer look at the piece of jewelry around my neck. "Are you still afraid of flying?"

"Not anymore."

Jane moved near the front bay windows. Pictures of more of the eighteenth-century jewelry I had found, when I dug up the pirate cache in our woods, only added to the whole image of my mysterious exploits. She stopped in front of my favorite portrait and asked, "Who's that?"

"Maria Hallett Ellis. It was painted in the mid-1700s. Wasn't she beautiful?"

"Wow, look at that red ring on her finger."

"That is a Pigeon Blood ruby. It was a gift to Maria from the pirate Sam Bellamy around 1720."

"Why is it called Pigeon Blood?"

"The red color represents the finest in rubies, the first drop of a pigeon's blood."

Jane looked away. "That's kind of gross."

"Not everything from our past is beautiful and romantic." I shooed the girls out of my office. "Let's get dinner going."

After hamburgers on the grill, we went for a sunset stroll along Crosby Landing Beach on Brewster's bayside. The tide was out, leaving the ocean floor exposed. As always, anyone who wanders out across the wave-rippled sand during low tide is always amazed at how far from the shoreline they can walk. The girls were no different. They couldn't believe how much of the ocean bottom was exposed underfoot and how far away the water was.

I picked up several scallop shells. "The tide goes out almost two miles here. Isn't that awesome?"

Everyone's bare toes squished in the damp sand as we made our way farther and farther out across the sandy bottom. Jane pretended she was flying. Madeline flew right behind and around her as the two girls soared across the rippled sand. Once the no-see-ums appeared, the tiny bugs forced the fanciful adventure to come to an end.

On the drive home, I asked the girls, "You want to do some exploring on that empty lot next door tomorrow?"

Jane answered first. "Sure. What are we looking for?"

"There are some wildflower plants that I'd like to dig up and transplant into our yard."

"Oh." My niece sat back in her seat, looking very disappointed.

I whispered, "You know… a few years after we moved in, an older man stopped by and said he used to play with one of the boys who had lived in our house a long time ago. The two boys would explore an old brick foundation that's in the woods next door." I could see Jane become more interested. "And he said they always thought the whole property was cursed, because someone died in a big fire there around 1908."

Madeline piped up, "I don't want to go explore there. What if it's haunted?"

I reassured her. "Madeline, whatever spirits that might be out there are friendly."

Jane joined in and teased her sister. "Don't be such a baby."

9

Monday, June, 1908
BREWSTER, CAPE COD

UPSTAIRS IN THE BREWSTER house her father had built on Main Street, Ellsbeth Doanne reread the letter of acceptance from the Sea Pines School of Personality for Girls. It was signed by the school's principal, Miss Bickford.

She heard her mother crying downstairs.

A few months ago, after she had submitted her scholarship application to Sea Pines, she'd overheard her parents yelling at each other. She knew her mother and father were not getting along. In fact, they always disagreed. But Ellsbeth never expected her mother to come to her room later that day to explain the reason behind some bad news. She recalled what her mother had told her.

"Your father and I are going to separate."

"Why?"

"We have grown apart. You and I are moving to New Hampshire to live with a dear friend of mine. Your father will remain in Brewster."

"I don't understand." Ellsbeth sat on her bed and wrung her hands together. "Don't you love each other anymore?"

Bessie gave her daughter a hug. "Oh, my dear, we still care about each other, but now it's different. We're not happy."

Ellsbeth started to whimper. "Well, I'm not happy now."

With another embrace, Bessie tried to console her daughter with, "It will be like an adventure. You'll meet new friends and see new places."

"But I don't want to leave Brewster, and I don't want to go on a stupid adventure!"

"Everything will turn out fine. You will see, in time." Her mother had kissed her on the forehead and gone back downstairs.

Ellsbeth had a restless sleep that night. When she'd applied for the scholarship, the young girl, at fourteen years old, had never dreamed she would be accepted. Now, they were leaving Brewster. She would not be able to go to the school after all. She wanted to go to Sea Pines! This was very unfair!

After dressing, Ellsbeth shoved her acceptance letter into her desk drawer and stared out the window.

From her second-floor bedroom, she noticed that Mr. Wilkins was working in his garden next door. He was always digging holes, even though it didn't look like anything new was growing. Some townsfolk thought he was crazy because he had built his house on sacred grounds. They also thought he was unfriendly, so they stayed away from him. Ellsbeth liked Mr. Wilkins. He always told her such interesting stories about the things he'd done and the exotic places he'd seen. They'd even shared a few secrets.

She was going to miss his stories. She recalled that, sometimes, Mr. Wilkins would begin his tale with, "Now mind you, this one is between you and me. Don't tell no one." Then he would give her a wink. Maybe today he would tell her one of his secrets.

She ran down the stairs, out the side door, and crossed over onto Mr. Wilkins property.

She found her friend on the front porch of his brick house. Ellsbeth pulled up a wooden rocker next to his. "Hi, Mr. Wilkins. Is Anna coming to clean today?"

The old man puffed on his pipe. "Maybe."

"I hope so. I'm going to miss her when I move to New Hampshire."

He rocked a little. "Your mama told me you'll be leavin' soon."

"I don't want to go."

Well, it might be a good thing. You're young."

"I don't think so. I'm so sad."

After a few seconds of silence, Anna Horvath appeared in the distance. She ran across an ivy-covered mound in front of Mr. Wilkins brick house and then called out, "Did you start the story yet?"

Ellsbeth waved at her friend and yelled, "Not yet. Hurry up!"

Mr. Wilkins rocked at a steady pace. "How about one last story, Ellsbeth, before you leave?"

Anna reached for her best friend's hand. "My mother thought something was wrong at your house. She told me you might be leaving." Anna took her seat in the rocker on the other side of Mr. Wilkins. "Could you tell one of your secret ones?"

He relit his pipe, leaned back, and began, "Now mind you, this one is between you two and me. Don't tell no one." Then he winked. "I was young, maybe twenty or so, and I had an itch to travel."

Ellsbeth leaned closer. "Where did you go? How long were you gone?"

Anna piped up. "Did you meet any dangerous people?"

"Hold on... Stop asking me so many questions."

Ellsbeth quickly forgot she was angry about leaving Brewster and focused on his every word.

"I went all the way to San Francisco. Unfortunately, I got crimped."

Anna leaned back in her seat. "What's *crimped*?"

"If you keep asking questions, I'm never going to finish." He puffed on his pipe. "You see, crimped means I was shanghaied onto a ship. A bad guy, or a crimper, put something in my drink, and I woke up the next morning sailing on a ship bound for who knows where."

"Were you scared?" Ellsbeth asked.

"Of course. But I discovered, if I worked hard and didn't complain, I'd be all right. The captain was a one-eared pirate called Bully Hayes."

Both girls gasped and covered their mouths in shock.

Mr. Wilkins smiled at their reaction. "Soon, I got to be friends with the captain. He wasn't a good person, tricking people out of their money or their ships, but I paid no mind, as long as I got rewarded for my loyalty." He showed Ellsbeth his gold pocket watch and then Anna. "One time, we dropped anchor in Australia, and before you knew it, Bully had sold the very ship we sailed on! The next day, we boarded a new ship with plentiful cargo that was worth a lot of money."

The girls said in unison. "Then what happened?"

"We eventually set sail for New England. The farther we sailed, the crazier Bully got. He picked up some female passengers at a small port, and I didn't like what he wanted to do with 'em. Me and some of the other crew decided to put a stop to his bad behavior. One night, we overpowered him, dropped him on an island in New South Wales, and skedaddled home. Once we got into Boston Harbor, we sold the ship with all its contents and divided everything up."

Anna sat on the edge of the rocker's seat. "Are you rich?"

"Maybe I am." He relit his pipe.

Ellsbeth looked up at the cloudless blue sky. "I wish I was rich. I would give it to my mother, so we could stay on Cape Cod."

Mr. Wilkins stopped rocking and leaned back. "I guess I'm goin' to miss you, Ellsbeth."

The young girl sat quietly with a frown on her face and her chin in her hands.

Anna glanced over to her friend. "So, it is true. You're leaving?"

Ellsbeth looked down at her feet.

"I'm going to miss you, too, Ellsbeth." Anna picked at her fingernails.

"Cheer up, you two. I'm working on special gifts for both of you. Ellsbeth, come by tomorrow for yours."

Ellsbeth perked up at the thought of a gift from Mr. Wilkins. She turned to leave. "Bye. See you tomorrow."

Anna stood up. "I'll get started." She opened the screen door, walked to the kitchen closet, and began to fill a pail with water.

The kitchen didn't look that unkempt. Anna thought she'd be done with her weekly clean in no time.

10

1908
BREWSTER

MR. WILKINS WATCHED Ellsbeth leave for home on her regular path. She walked around the big oak tree and then crossed over and back onto the Doanne's family property.

Once Ellsbeth disappeared behind a door, he went inside to find Anna. Before he started down to the cellar, or what he called his "fancy root cellar," he gently reminded her not to disturb him. "Don't worry, Anna, your surprise will be waiting for you the next time you come to clean."

"Okay, Mr. Wilkins." Anna began to wipe down the furniture and wood trim in the front of the house. "You've been tidy this week. I'll not be too long." She wondered what Wilkins had in store for her.

Mr. Wilkins watched his footing as he descended the last of the narrow steps then turned left toward his work bench. The high, wooden table held a locked strong box and had a stool tucked under its top. Next to the workbench stood his long-handled shovel. He began to hum an old sea ditty to himself as he unlocked the box to reveal a large cache of gold coins, parchment, pen and ink, and several small leather pouches. "Heave ho... Across the sea we go..."

After he had filled four of the pouches with four gold coins, he grabbed his shovel to bury two of them in the cellar's dirt floor. He set aside the other two pouches. When he'd finished his task, and before he went back up the stairs, he marked a paper pad with two more slash marks after the word *Basement*.

His list included other locations: Garden #1, Garden #2, and other gardens numbered all the way to #10. They all had marks after their names. Garden #7 had an exclamation point after its label. Seven was Mr. Wilkins's lucky number, so inside that particular leather pouch was a very special coin.

His thoughts distracted him as he reminisced about a poker game, many years ago, in Boston. It was the same night he and the crew had sold the spoils from Bully Hayes's ship, including the ship itself. They had all celebrated at the nearest saloon. That's when he'd won the most beautiful gold coin he had ever seen... the Brasher Doubloon.

He gave a nostalgic sigh then pulled open a drawer under the tabletop. Inside it lay two maps that were drawn with the position of his house in relation to the road out front. Also drawn on the maps were circles to denote trees, and Xs for all the locations where the pouches were buried. Mr. Wilkins knew he might become forgetful and need reminders to show him where he had buried them. They were crude drawings, but they looked good enough to him. He added the locations of the newly buried pouches.

As a sign of his friendship for his two favorite girls, these maps would be given to them after he was gone. One map had Anna's name written on the top, and the other bore Ellsbeth's name. With a smile, Mr. Wilkins wrote his name at the bottom of each map but upside down, to trick them, making them work to figure out how to read the map. What fun, he thought.

Old man Wilkins had no kin, and he wasn't getting any younger. His thoughts crossed over in his head to the local barrister, Samuel Cowes. He would seek counsel from his old friend and put something in writing. He wanted the girls to be well taken care of after he passed.

It would be a shame if his secret pouches were found by some bad people or they were just lost forever. He was also concerned that someone might come after him, looking for the loot. Bully Hayes would still be angry for leaving him on that island. Even "King Phillip," a fellow pirate from Bourne who had helped overthrow Bully, could show up at his doorstep, looking for more of his share of the profits. The half-blood never could hold onto his money.

Well, Mr. Wilkins would be ready, with everything safely stashed and kept secret.

With a sigh of relief about making everything legal at the end of the week, he returned to the gift of a special treasure hunt and map for each of his two young friends. Two more smaller parchments were drawn with the house and the road, but he added only one X location on each map. Two treasure hunts for two friends. He'd give a map to Ellsbeth tomorrow and the other to Anna at the end of the week, when she came to clean. It would be fun.

It was getting close to supper. Anna called down the basement stairs, "Mr. Wilkins, I'm leaving now. Need anything else?"

"Nope."

After Anna left for home and he was alone, Mr. Wilkins hurried up the cellar stairs carrying his shovel along with Ellsbeth's and Anna's filled pouches. He headed to the left backside corner of his house and began to dig the first hole to replicate the location of the 'X' on Ellsbeth's map. Then he moved over to the right backside corner of the house; the second hiding place, for Anna's map.

Tuesday, June, 1908

The following day, Ellsbeth crossed over the property line. "Mr. Wilkins?" She knocked against his front door. "Mr. Wilkins?"

Ellsbeth slowly opened the screen door and walked in. She found him in his rocker, sound asleep. She shook his shoulder. "Mr. Wilkins?"

The old man remained quiet.

She saw his pipe on the floor next to the hearth. She picked it up and shook him again.

With that, he opened his eyes. "Ellsbeth! What time is it?" He sat a little straighter.

"Almost noon. Are you all right?"

"I guess I fell asleep after my supper last night. I was busy most of the day, doing something very important."

Ellsbeth sat in a chair opposite him and waited.

Mr. Wilkins smiled and looked straight at her. "Want your surprise?"

She sat taller and nodded her head.

He pulled himself up and stretched. "Well, let's get a move on." He walked to the back yard with Ellsbeth following.

Mr. Wilkins took a small, rolled parchment out of his vest pocket. "This here's for you."

Ellsbeth beamed. She unrolled the map and began to study it. "What's this for?"

"I'm goin' to make some coffee. I need to wake up. You figure it out, my girl." His last words trailed after him as he opened the back door and disappeared into the kitchen.

Ellsbeth whispered to herself as she looked at the map, "Let's see. Here's Mr. Wilkins house and the big oak I walk past when going home."

She turned the map upside down, then right side up. She looked up at the back corner of the house furthest away from her, and then to the map. There was an X in front of that corner. She looked down and across the dirt; it was covered with leaves. As she walked closer, she kicked away some of the dry, curled tree droppings. She noticed fresh-dug dirt.

After brushing away the debris, she grabbed a stick and started to poke at the ground. Within a few minutes, the top of a leather pouch appeared. She scraped at the black dirt with her fingertips and smiled as she pulled out the small pouch. Ellsbeth grabbed at its leather ties to open it. Inside, she found four gold coins.

"Mr. Wilkins! Mr. Wilkins!" She ran into the house and found him sipping his morning drink.

"You did well. Show me what you found."

Ellsbeth was giddy with her newfound fortune. "Thank you. Thank you." She spilled the treasure across her one hand and gave him a hug.

Embarrassed at her spontaneous affection, Mr. Wilkins returned to his coffee. He looked over to Ellsbeth. "Those are real pirate coins – Spanish – worth a lot of money." He gave a few puffs on his pipe. "Now, be off with you. I got work to do."

Ellsbeth turned to her friend and gave him a wink, then ran out the door.

11

Tuesday Afternoon, June 1908
BREWSTER

THE SAME DAY ELLSBETH found her treasure, Anna was returning from another cleaning job at Mrs. Davis's house on Lower Road. When she reached her tiny family home on Brier Lane, her mother had the dinner started for the family.

Her father worked as a carpenter, making repairs and building new additions across the Lower Cape. Today, he was late getting home. The kitchen clock struck 5:00 p.m., and her mother looked worried. He was always home by 4:30 p.m.

As the oldest, Anna had a lot of responsibilities. Helping care for her three siblings, who ranged from ages seven to three years, was no easy task for a young girl. Besides cleaning for others, she ran errands for those who needed her time. Usually, she was paid in cash, but occasionally it was in trade for food supplies, wood for heat, apples, and lots of fish. Whatever extra money Anna earned was given over for household expenses.

The clock approached 6:00 p.m. Now, Anna was worried. She began to help her mother finish folding clothes. Rosalia still did the laundry for the Freeman house. Only now, so she could care for the children, she took it home on Mondays and returned it all on Fridays.

A wagon pulled up outside the front door. A knock and a yell sounded in the evening air, "Mrs. Horvath! Come quick! It's your husband!"

Rosalia ran outside to find Michael sprawled on his back across the open bed of a work wagon. His clunky boots weighed down his feet, which dangled over the edge.

"Michael!" She grabbed his clammy hand and pleaded to the two men up front. "Please. *Please*." She touched her husband's chest and waved her hands at the men motioning them to help her carry Michael inside. "Please. Please."

Rosalia followed the men as they carried Michael into the house. "Anna! Take children outside. They eat outside."

"Yes, Mother." The children followed Anna as she led them out the back door and to a safe place, away from the drama unfolding in her parents' bedroom off the kitchen.

Anna remembered her father had been nursing a cold for the past week. She also knew a common cold could turn into pneumonia and kill within days. She silently prayed.

12

Present Day
BREWSTER

THE FOLLOWING MORNING, after breakfast, the girls gathered around in the kitchen to hear what our plans were for the day. I began with a caution. "We're going to explore next door, so wear some long pants and don't forget to tuck them into your socks, in case there are ticks." Before the girls left Ohio, I had warned them during a Zoom meeting about the tiny insects that could burrow into their skin and give them Lyme disease.

They ran upstairs to change.

The grass, wet with morning dew, was slick as we tramped across the wooded lot. Each explorer carried a small trowel. Jane followed behind me, pushing a wheelbarrow.

I stopped, turned, and pointed to my left. "Be careful. Over there toward the road is a big hole exposing a set of steps. I think it was an entrance to the basement from the house that burned down."

"What are we looking for?" Jane asked.

"I'll know it when I see it. It's a green plant in early summer and looks almost like weeds." I stopped and bent over to inspect the stems in a mound of green. "Here it is. In the spring, beautiful yellow flowers bloom all over these plants." I grabbed a shovel and carefully dug into the ground.

Madeline watched from afar. "Can't you buy these at a store?"

I smiled at her as I added a wedge of the plant into the bottom of the cart. "These wildflowers are called aconite, and they are what I consider to be ancient plants. They are very difficult to cultivate, yet they grow naturally in the woods. The birds spread their seeds."

Jane crouched down. "How much do you want us to dig up?"

"Not a lot. We don't own this property, but the wildflowers are like God's gift to us. I want to save them because I'm sure whoever buys this land will clear-cut everything to build a house."

Madeline joined her sister as I began to carefully arrange the clumps of green so as not to damage the treasured slices of nature.

After the wheelbarrow was filled, I announced, "That's enough, girls. Let's get home for a snack of some apple fritters."

Jane added, "One more, please. This is fun." I watched as she positioned her trowel flat on the dirt and pushed it forward for her last slice. The trowel stopped short. She pushed again. The small shovel would not slide underneath the layer of dirt and plant. She knelt down to get into a better position. Again, the point of the tool stopped short.

"Everything okay, Jane? Did you hit a stone or a root?"

"Not sure." Jane picked at the dirt. Her fingers touched something flat. "That's weird." She pulled at the piece. "It feels like leather." Within seconds, she caught sight of the edge of a yellow metal-looking piece. She reached for it.

I leaned over Jane. "What is it?"

"It looks like gold!"

"What?"

I watched as Jane's blackened fingertips dug into the forest floor.

She cried out, "Here's another one!"

Within a few minutes, she had found two more golden coins for a total of four.

Madeline knelt down, excited to brush away the dirt within her reach.

I crouched nearer and started to slowly push the dark soil in circles, trying to find more coins.

Dark clouds formed above our heads, and a few sprinkles of rain began to drop. None of us noticed. We remained on our knees, sifting and searching through the dirt.

Once the sun had completely disappeared, the heavens opened up in a fast summer shower. Everyone grabbed their tools. Jane gripped the wheelbarrow and pushed it behind us, running for cover across the green forest floor and into the safety of our garage.

"Whew," Jane said as she brushed the rain off her T-shirt with one hand. The garage door slammed behind us. The other hand quickly reached into her pocket for the coins she'd found. She ran up the garage stairs to Paul's studio. "Uncle Paul! You'll never guess what I found!"

Madeline followed up the stairs. Her hands, dirtied by the soil, only made her pink shirt grimier as she tried to brush the rain off.

Paul stopped painting. "What going on?"

Out of breath, Jane explained, "We were digging up the wildflower plants next door, and I uncovered these." She opened her hand to show the smudged gold coins.

"You're kidding!" He spread a few paper towels on his drawing table. "Put them here. Let's take a closer look." He gave me a quick glance and smiled at the original treasure hunter.

Madeline leaned against the table. "Do you think they're real?"

I examined the coins. "They sure look real."

"Am I rich?" Jane beamed. "Do I get to keep them?"

Madeline was wide-eyed.

I chose my reply carefully. "Well... they really don't belong to you, only to whoever owns the property."

The girls looked as if they had lost their best friend.

"Don't feel bad. Maybe, if and when we figure out who owns the land, they might give you a finder's fee."

I could see that my words did little to soothe the two hunters' feelings about being suddenly rich.

"Why don't you go upstairs, pull off your dirty clothes, and take a shower, and we'll talk more about our options over that snack I mentioned before."

The two sisters stood with solemn expressions on their faces.

"Get going. Do a tick check. Hurry up."

13

Tuesday Evening, June 1908
BREWSTER

IT WAS CLOSE TO 9:00 P.M., and Ellsbeth was upstairs in her bedroom. She could hear her parents talking downstairs. They both sounded sad but determined in their words. There was no staying in Brewster for Ellsbeth and her mother. They would be leaving in two days.

She changed into her night clothes, moved her almost-packed suitcase onto the wooden floor, and settled in under the sheets.

Her father came in to say goodnight. "Well, Ellsbeth, I'm sorry you got stuck in this mess between your mother and me."

"It's all right, Father."

"I've asked your mother if you can come visit me sometime in the future."

Ellsbeth smiled.

"I want you to know that your room will always be waiting here for you. I guarantee that."

"Thank you, Father."

He kissed her on the forehead. "Good night, daughter."

It was nearing midnight, and the young girl was still awake, thinking about poor Anna's father. How lucky she was. Even though they were leaving without her father, at least he was not sick.

She smelled smoke and quickly sat up in bed. The night was quiet, except for the sound of bullfrogs croaking from the pond across the road. Ellsbeth looked out the window toward Mr. Wilkins's house. She couldn't see any flames but remained troubled about where the smoke was coming from. She worried the old man had fallen asleep again in his chair.

She crept down the steps to the kitchen. Her parents were asleep in their bedroom on the other side of the house. She found no immediate sign of anything wrong in the house. Ellsbeth slipped on her boots, wondering if Mr. Wilkins's pipe had fallen and was smoldering in the ashes.

The grass was wet with dew, and from a distance, the old brick house appeared in good shape from the outside. As she rounded the oak tree, however, she heard glass breaking. Ellsbeth ran through the brush to the front porch.

She found Mr. Wilkins sitting on the brick steps, leaning against the porch post. "Mr. Wilkins! Are you all right?"

He opened his eyes. "Ellsbeth! Go for help. The flames were too much for me." He was clutching his heart.

"I don't want to leave you." She sat beside him.

"You must!"

Ellsbeth stood to leave.

Mr. Wilkins spoke in breathless tones. "Wait."

Ellsbeth stopped and turned back to her friend. She watched him struggle to pull something from his left shirt pocket. He handed her a piece of rolled paper that looked just like her treasure hunt map.

"Tell Anna to do the hunt… Like you did."

"When I dug up the pouch?"

"Yes."

He reached inside his right vest pocket and pulled out two larger rolled parchments. "Take these. One is for you and one for Anna. Hide yours… for the future. Give the other map to Anna. Tell her to hide it, too."

"I don't understand."

"Please, Ellsbeth, do this for me." He shoved the maps closer to her. "Now go, my little friend. I'll be fine."

"Yes, Mr. Wilkins. I will." She clutched the three maps close to her chest as she ran to wake her parents.

When her father smelled smoke and saw flames, he jumped into his truck to get help.

Ellsbeth quickly ran upstairs to tuck the maps under her bed pillow. She then ran downstairs to join her mother out on the road in front of the house, to helplessly watch and pray for Mr. Wilkins, only to find that the fire had fully engulfed the brick building.

"Mother, I don't see Mr. Wilkins on the porch." Tears filled the young girl's eyes.

Her mother held her daughter close. "I don't see him, either. He must have gone back into the house."

Ellsbeth turned away from the tragic scene. "Why did he go back in?" She buried her face into her mother's soft nightgown.

"He should have stayed outside." Her mother stroked her daughter's hair.

They stood there, helpless, until the sounds of other wagons, trucks, and loud voices of men filled the smoky night air.

Her mother shook her head and whispered, "That land is cursed."

The young girl glanced once more toward the fire and knew it was too late to save the brick house. It would surely be the last time she would ever see her friend. Poor Mr. Wilkins.

When nothing more could be done, Ellsbeth's parents walked their daughter back into their home. Through the rest of the night, they tried to console her, but nothing seemed to work. She wouldn't stop crying. They encouraged her to return to her room and try to sleep.

Ellsbeth dragged herself up the stairs and collapsed onto the bed.

Wednesday, June, 1908

As the sun rose on a new day, the blackened shell of Mr. Wilkins's house was a frightful vision below Ellsbeth's window. She couldn't bear to see such destruction. She closed her eyes and returned to her bed but couldn't sleep. Finally, it was close to midmorning before she rose and dressed.

Ellsbeth took the parchment rolls out from under her pillow, intending to hide hers and give the other to Anna, along with her treasure hunt map. She had made a promise.

She knelt on the floor next to her bed and unrolled one of the larger parchments. It had more Xs marking Mr. Wilkins's property, and her name was at the top.

She unrolled the second map. It was the same, but with Anna's name on it.

Still not understanding her role in this secret request, Ellsbeth rolled the bigger map back up, then wiggled a piece of the baseboard trim behind her bed loose. She reached into the hole in the wall and took out a small metal box. Inside it were a few of her favorite things: a medal she had won in a school contest, several blue-colored clam shells, some silk ribbons, a few pearl buttons, and the pouch that held her four gold coins. She remembered her father had said he would leave her room as is.

She took the pouch, coins, and the smaller map that she had found earlier out of the metal box and hid them deep inside her travel bag. Then, she folded the large, rolled map in half and laid it inside the box, next to her saved mementos. She pushed the box into the dark hole behind the wall and replaced the piece of wood within the baseboard trim. She promised herself she would return, but until then, Mr. Wilkins's map would be safe.

Later that morning, she ran to Anna's house. Ellsbeth found her friend hanging sheets on the line in the back yard. "Anna, I have something for you."

Anna stopped to see what was in her friend's hand.

"I can't stay long. I'm leaving for New Hampshire sooner than I thought. Did you hear about the fire? And Mr. Wilkins?"

"Yes. I don't think I can stand much more sadness."

"How's your father?"

"The same. Not so good."

Ellsbeth placed the two parchments into Anna's hand and explained what Mr. Wilkins had told her to do.

"I have to hide the bigger one?"

"Yes, and when things calm down, go and follow the smaller map for your treasure."

"Why?"

"Not sure. Just do it." She turned to leave. "Do your treasure hunt exactly like I did mine."

Anna was confused.

"Promise me you'll do what Mr. Wilkins wanted?"

"I promise." Anna watched her friend disappear around the bend.

Her mother's voice came from inside the house. "Anna!"

"Coming, Mother." She divided the parchments into her apron pockets and then ran into the house.

Later that day, Ellsbeth and her mother left Brewster, a day earlier than scheduled. Her mother wanted to get far away from Cape Cod, especially after the tragedy of the fire.

14

Present Day
BREWSTER

UPSTAIRS, MADELINE plopped on the bedroom floor.

Jane sat down on the carpet near her bed, dejected and angry at the same time.

Madeline took off one sneaker and flipped it over onto the carpet next to her. She looked at her sister and said, "Boy, you must be mad. It's not fair that you can't keep those coins." She quickly loosened the back of her other shoe, kicked her foot up, and sent the second sneaker high into the air and across the room, just missing Jane's head. It crashed against the baseboard.

Jane ducked. "Hey…! Watch it!"

Madeline covered her mouth. "Oops! Sorry." She ran toward the bathroom. "I'm first in the shower."

Jane reached for the misguided shoe behind her, hoping to throw it back to the other side and onto Madeline's bed, but she stopped. She noticed that the force of Madeline's playful weapon had done some damage to the wall. "Oh, that's not good."

A piece of the baseboard had moved and separated from the length of wood trim. She tried to push it back in, but it wouldn't budge. With a tap of her fist a few inches from the split, Jane hoped to jar it loose, so she could straighten the board. The length of wood fell away from the wall, exposing a long, narrow, black hole.

Jane bent closer to the opening and saw a shadow of something inside it. Always up for a challenge, she reached in and pulled out a metal box. After she swiped her hand across the top of the dusty black box, she shook it up and down. Something rattled inside.

She heard the water from Madeline's shower stop. Quickly, Jane hid the secret find under her bed. The sound of a hair dryer came from the bathroom. Determined to hide the discovery from Madeline, who had a tendency to tattle, Jane moved with record speed to replace the dislodged wood back into place within the baseboard trim. All looked normal. She hoped that whatever was inside the box would remain safe a little while longer and no one would take it from her.

15

July, 1908
BRIER LANE, BREWSTER

ANNA'S FATHER LAY ILL for another week. His fever never relented. His nightly coughing kept everyone awake in the small house. Anna cancelled all her extra work to stay home with her mother.

Rosalia struggled to nurse Michael back to normal, but to no avail. It only took three weeks for the sickness to take her husband. The night he died, Rosalia never left his side. She wasn't hungry. She couldn't sleep. She heard the children and Anna's voices, but the only thoughts on her mind were what was going to happen to her and her children, now that Michael was gone.

The funeral came and went. Neighbors delivered food for the widow and her four children. Mr. Freeman, out of the generosity of his heart, paid Rosalia for a month's work, so she could grieve and be with her children before she returned to her laundry duties.

Anna resumed her cleaning and errand jobs. The little family slowly began to reclaim their routine.

16

OUTSIDE, ON THE BACK PORCH, deli sandwiches, potato chips, and ice cream bars for dessert were served to my two tick-free nieces for a quick lunch.

Jane, showered, dressed, and hungry, looked out to the back woods. "Aunt Nancy, how did you find so many neat things on your property?"

"Probably just lucky. Besides, I'm always looking down, hoping to find something interesting."

Jane finished her ice cream. "My mom says I'm just like you. Always asking questions."

"She may be right. I remember, growing up, she thought I was weird. I liked Nancy Drew and Hardy Boys mysteries, and she preferred all the teen magazines."

"How are you going to find out who owns the property next door, so we can return the coins?"

"Let's clean up, and I'll show you." I led the girls into my office.

A tall, wooden file cabinet stood next to a large rolltop desk. Jane picked up a cracked blue-and-white teapot from a bookshelf. She heard a few clinks.

I noticed her curiosity. "You can look inside."

Jane lifted the porcelain lid to find several gold and silver coins. With eyes wide open, she looked toward me.

"From one of my adventures."

Jane replaced the china lid and returned it next to several books about pirates. "Some of them look just like the ones I found next door."

I opened one of the file drawers and pulled out a manila file. "Here's what I wanted you to look at."

The paperwork was spread across the desktop. "This is called a plot plan. It shows an 1880 street survey of Brewster. When I researched our house, I found it in the records of Barnstable County deeds." I pointed to a crudely drawn rectangle set amidst other squares on the drawing. "That's our house. The Doanne family owned this piece of land in 1880, when our house was built."

The girls leaned closer over the papers.

Jane put her finger on two long lines drawn across the page. "It says Old King's Highway. Is that the road out front?"

"Yes. It's just called Route 6A now." I pointed to a larger piece of land. "This property was owned by the Wilkins family, right next door to the Doanne family."

Jane studied the lines and words. "That's so cool."

Madeline straightened up. "Can I go and watch a movie?"

"Of course, honey. See what's on the Disney Channel."

Jane stayed put. "How will you locate the Wilkins family? What will you do next?" Jane still looked disappointed but also seemed interested. I knew she had always liked puzzles and usually won the game of Jeopardy at school.

"I would have to search the county records again, find Wilkins from 1880, and then go forward through the years, looking for the names of who owned the land, all the way to today."

"When are you going to do that?"

"That could be a problem. I'm going to be busy over the next few days with my museum presentations." I closed the folder and then hesitated. "You know, I do remember something I found, when sifting through all the information of who owned this property."

Jane perked up.

"This whole area where our house is situated was originally owned by a Samuel Smith. Then, he deeded it to his daughter, Bessie, in 1870. She married Roger Doanne in 1879, and in 1880, he built this house. But in 1908, something happened to the Doanne family. In a court document, I found evidence that Bessie Smith and Roger Doanne filed for divorce. She went to New Hampshire, and he stayed with the house in Brewster."

"Did people get divorced back then?" Jane hoped her parents would never do that. She'd be devastated.

"Yes, they did. I also found records of Roger going up to New Hampshire to get his ex-wife to sign over the land to him. I guess Bessie still owned the land that was gifted from her father, and since Roger built the house, he wanted to make sure everything belonged to him."

Jane remained seated in front of the open folder. "Can I stay a little longer in your office?"

"Of course. Just leave everything on the desk. I want to finish planting those wildflower plants. I'll be outside. Find me if you need anything."

17

Present Day
BREWSTER

AFTER A BEAUTIFUL SUNSET, once again, at Crosby Landing Beach, Jane was eager to return to the house to look inside the old metal box. By 9:30 p.m., she and her sister were upstairs and ready for bed.

Jane lay quiet, waiting until Madeline was asleep and wishing the owners of the coins she'd found next door would never be located. She wanted to keep the treasure for herself.

She reached for one of the emergency flashlights that Aunt Nancy had given to each of the girls. Carefully, she wedged one end of her summer quilt into the top of the open window behind her bed, closed it tight, and made a tent over herself. She then leaned over and pulled the metal box out from under her bed. She placed the lit flashlight next to her, so both hands were free to explore inside the box.

After one more quick peek from under the quilt to check if her sister was still sleeping, Jane focused on the box and anxiously wondered what was inside.

The dusty lid opened with only a slight push up, but it was too shadowy for her to see clearly. She tucked the light under her chin for a better view of the secret items.

The opened box revealed a few pretty ribbons, pieces of blue quahog shells, a school badge award, some pearl buttons, and a folded paper.

No gold, she thought.

The sunburst-shaped badge had faded ribbons at its bottom edge. Across the center of its circle was: *Spelling Bee Winner – 1906*. On the backside was the name *Ellsbeth Doanne*.

She whispered, "Doanne," as she nodded her head. Doanne was the name on the deeds and papers that Aunt Nancy had found. This girl, Ellsbeth, must have lived here a long time ago, and this had to be her bedroom. Jane wondered if the girl had other brothers or sisters. Why did she hide the box? Jane felt a kinship with her, because she also hid things from her sister in their shared bedroom at home, mostly buried in her drawers or high on the top shelf of their closet.

The items in the box didn't look very important. Jane picked up the folded paper. It was heavier than regular computer paper. She remembered, in school, they had talked about old maps, and she'd been given a chance to touch some of them. This paper felt just like those old maps. It crinkled in the night as she started to unfold it.

Jane stopped and listened for Madeline. Nothing. Then, she continued to slowly lay the paper flat in front of her. It definitely looked like a map. Her heart beat faster. The only problem was she didn't understand what she was looking at. There were some lines with Xs spread across the page, along with two names, Wilkins and Ellsbeth.

On the first floor below her, she heard the dining room clock chime 10:00 p.m. She tried to fight back a yawn, but it was no use. She was tired.

After everything was safely replaced back into the box, she pulled the quilt out of the window, leaned over, and pushed the metal strongbox deep under the bed. She quickly fell asleep, dreaming of the girl Ellsbeth, treasure, Xs, and pirates.

18

August, 1908
BREWSTER

FOUR MONTHS AFTER the death of her father, Anna was as nervous as her mother was about their money. They had been able to pay the mortgage for the first month with the help of Mr. Freeman's generous gift and had saved enough for the second month that was past due, but it just wasn't enough to make the mortgage current.

One morning, as Anna was about to leave for her cleaning job, Mr. MacGregor, the representative from the bank that held the mortgage, knocked on the door.

Anna smiled through her nervousness as she opened the door. "Good morning, Mr. MacGregor."

"Would your mother be at home?" He took off his hat.

"Yes. Please come in."

The banker entered, holding his hat and a brown leather briefcase.

Anna disappeared into the kitchen to find her mother.

Rosalia calmly removed her apron, pulled a few gray, wispy hairs behind her ears, smoothed her hair around the tiny bun on top of her head, and entered the front parlor.

"Hello, Mrs. Horvath. I hope you are faring well after the unfortunate event that took your husband?"

Rosalia summoned her daughter. "Anna."

Anna quickly returned and stood by her mother, ready to interpret.

Mr. MacGregor shook his head, visibly upset. "Your mother still does not speak English?"

"No, sir."

He opened his briefcase and laid papers out across the leather case. "You are two months behind on your payments. Do you have a plan to go forward?"

Anna repeated to her mother in Hungarian.

Rosalia stayed quiet.

Mr. MacGregor waited for a reply then replaced the papers into his case. "I see. My recommendation would be for your mother to sell one of her children. It may ease her burden."

Anna looked shocked. Unsure of what to say to her mother, she chose her words carefully.

Upon hearing the translated banker's words, Rosalia straightened her back and knew what to say this time. "Get out!" She extended her arm, pointed to the door, and repeated, "Get out!"

19

August, 1908
BREWSTER

THAT NIGHT, ANNA lay in her bed. She couldn't sleep. In her heart, she knew the lack of money would always be a problem, maybe too big of an obstacle for them to continue living in the house. All her extra cleaning jobs were never enough.

She turned away from seven-year-old Frank and five-year-old Thomas, not wanting them to see her sniffling. Baby Louis was downstairs with her mother. Anna's eyes closed, but her mind kept racing. If only Mr. Wilkins were still alive. Maybe he could have helped. He was such a good friend of hers. She missed him.

Suddenly, she opened her eyes. Where did she hide the treasure hunt map from Mr. Wilkins? The death of her father had given her no time for anything except helping her mother and doing extra cleaning jobs.

She sat up and checked on the boys. They were quiet. Anna lit a small candle and went straight to the bottom drawer of her dresser. She turned around toward her brothers in the dimly lit room. They were sound asleep.

As she pulled the bottom drawer out, she caught sight of a piece of parchment sticking out from beneath her sweaters. It was the smaller map. She reached farther in and could feel the other rolled map near the back. One map at a time, she thought, and lifted the small paper out, then closed the drawer as quietly as she could.

The parchment was stashed under her pillow, and the candle extinguished. With closed eyes, a smile on her face, and hope in her heart, she quickly fell asleep.

The Following Morning

After breakfast, Anna hurried out the door earlier than usual to her first cleaning job of the day. She called over her shoulder. "Viszzontlátásra, Mother."

The early-morning dew wet her leather shoes as she walked alongside the narrow Main Street. She had about an hour before Mrs. Powell expected her. Mr. Wilkins's burned house was on the way.

She turned onto the charred and deserted property. As she walked toward what was left of the foundation, she tripped on the top of the exposed basement steps that led to below the burned-out house. She caught herself just in time. Her heart raced as she thought of what might have happened, if she had fallen in.

Anna took a deep breath to calm down and unfolded the small map. Her name was written on the top, and Mr. Wilkins's name was upside down at the bottom. She smiled, thinking of her friend and his jokes. Her finger touched the oak-tree symbol near the property line of where her friend, Ellsbeth, had once lived. She traced the outline of Mr. Wilkins's house on the map. She could see a large X on the right side of the foundation, near the corner. She looked up and moved toward the old brick foundation, guessing at the X's location.

Her shoes grew wetter and blacker with soot. She grabbed a stick and began to pick at the dirt. After a few seconds, the wooden branch proved fruitless. She crouched down to brush the debris away. She looked at the map again, now smudged from her dirty fingers; it showed the X's location to be correct, when compared to where she was kneeling.

Anna continued sifting through the soil, turning her upper body from side to side, trying to find anything important. With no luck, she stood up, brushed her hands together, and looked for a stronger stick or flat stone, so she could dig deeper. A white object a few feet away caught her attention. The large clam shell was perfect! She snatched it up and returned to her digging.

Another two minutes passed before she uncovered the top of a leather pouch. Her fingers raked the shell harder across the ground. Her nose began to drip in the cool morning, her fingers smearing her upper lip and cheek with black streaks.

Finally, the pouch came loose from the dirt. Anna sat back on her heels, untied the leather strings, and then opened the pouch. Four gold coins spilled out across her lap.

20

Present Day
BREWSTER

THE SUN ALWAYS makes an early rise on Cape Cod, a spit of land nestled on the edge of North America. It's one of the first places to see the sunrise in the United States. The smell of bacon drifted up the stairs. Madeline was up and dressed by 7:30. Jane was still sleeping.

Downstairs, Madeline slowly nibbled on a crispy strip. She took a deep whiff. "That will get Jane out of bed. She loves bacon."

I filled my travel cup with coffee. "I hope she gets down here before I leave. I'd like to say goodbye to her."

"Oh, she'll be here any minute now. Watch." Madeline reached for another salty piece of meat.

As if on cue, Jane appeared at the kitchen door, stretching her long arms up into the air.

I greeted my niece with a smile. "Well, you seem to be getting comfortable here on Cape Cod."

"I guess I slept pretty good." Jane looked happy. "Are you leaving soon?"

"In a few minutes." I started to fill an extra water bottle for my day. "I'm going to ask both of you to behave and not get into trouble while I'm gone. Your Uncle Paul will be busy in his studio, so make good choices. You can watch movies or maybe go for a bike ride on the trail in the afternoon. Don't go anywhere without telling your uncle where you're going. Understood?"

Both girls nodded.

"Great. Be mindful of the weather—it might rain. I'll see you for dinner tonight. Maybe we can go to this neat fish shack in Dennis. It's right on the water."

"Fish shack?" Madeline looked disgusted.

"Don't worry. They have great fries and chowder."

21

June, Present Day
SEA PINES INN, BREWSTER

MAX STOOD BY the open window of his room, staring out at the cars driving by on Main Street. He grew more impatient by the minute. It was pouring, and he'd had no word from Tommy or the lawyer about when he could sign the paperwork to his cousin's house on Brier Lane. Even though his Cousin Marty had left no will, Max was sure he was the only living relative who would inherit the old house. Grandma's other brother, Thomas, had died of a heart attack back in 1950. Louis and his son, Marty, were the last of the Horvaths.

He retrieved a glass of water from the bubbler in the hallway and returned to gaze out the window. He was eager to officially get back into the family house, so he could continue his search. There had to be something more in the old house that connected Grandma Anna's pouch and its coin to the abandoned property on the other side of town, supposedly owned by a Mr. Wilkins. He'd prefer to tear the Brier Lane house down; the property was worth more money empty. By the time he's done with his search, he may have to demolish the house anyway.

The rain had slowed by 10:00 a.m., so Max decided to take a ride toward the empty lot. It might be a chance to clear his head about all that had been going on.

Traffic was lighter than before. He stopped on the side of the road opposite the lot. He could see the Caldwell Gallery on the right and an old rundown house on the left of the empty property. It would be great if he could park off the road to explore without being noticed.

He backed up and pulled onto the dirt-and-gravel driveway of the seemingly abandoned house, turned the engine off, and considered the weathered tiny house, with its porch cluttered with plastic containers and junk, as a possible parking space.

This might work, he thought. The rain had finally stopped. The sun came out, and a rainbow appeared in the Eastern sky. With a smile on his face, he exited the SUV.

Not wanting to take any chances, Max knocked on the weather-beaten door, secretly hoping no one was home. Another knock with no answer left him confident that he was clear to leave his car parked in the driveway and explore next door.

His deck shoes were not meant for the wet leaves, sticks, and tangled ivy that littered the ground. After about twenty steps in, he decided it was not a good idea to be in the woods dressed as he was today.

His cell pinged with a text, which helped him make the decision to leave. It was the lawyer. The papers for Brier Lane were ready to be signed. As he turned to go, his foot slipped. He was thrown off balance, sending him down into a hole.

22

Present Day
BREWSTER

AFTER AUNT NANCY left, the heavens opened up for a quick shower. Madeline dove right for the TV remote and settled in on the couch.

Jane grabbed another salty piece of bacon and hurried upstairs. After closing the bedroom door, she pulled out the old box from under her bed. Her greasy fingerprints marked the metal lid. She wiped her hands clean on her shorts. The room was bright, except for Madeline's side of the room, which still had shadows from a big tree just outside her window.

Jane sat down on the carpet and carefully unfolded the mysterious map in front of her. She turned the map upside down, then right side up. Which side was up or down? she wondered.

She recognized the name Wilkins as the Caldwells' neighbor back in the 1900s, and then at the bottom was Ellsbeth's name, written upside down. An outline of a house came clearer to her. She looked closer. Yes, it was the foundation of a house! She traced two lines and decided it was a road, like the lines on the survey map from Aunt Nancy's papers.

She studied it more. On one side of the house was a large, bumpy circle. The letters *OT* were faded but visible within the little, round drawing. She stared at the wall and wondered what they stood for…

"Oak tree!" She smiled in satisfaction.

Jane started to count the Xs that dotted across the paper. There were three inside the house's foundation, with the others spaced around the foundation and the outer edges of the map. She counted ten Xs. What did they stand for? She cocked her head again in thought. Maybe it was like in pirate stories, where X marks the spot to where treasure is buried. Jane could feel her heart beat a little faster as she recalled the pouch that she had already found next door containing the four gold coins.

She stood up near her window to look outside. The rain was almost over. The lot below showed a vibrant green. Turning around to find her sneakers, she caught sight of the leaves from the tree that was blocking all the light on Madeline's side of the room. She returned to the window. Under some of the leaves closest to her view were green clusters of baby acorns.

She spoke in an excited whisper, "That's an oak tree!"

She quickly went downstairs. As she reached the bottom step in the dining room, the rain finally stopped. Not caring if the woods were wet, she quietly slipped out the side porch door of the laundry room, with the old map tucked under her arm.

Jane stopped at what she believed to be the end of the Caldwells' property. Her hand rested on the old oak tree before she went deeper onto the ivy-covered, wooded property. After several feet, she stopped and unfolded the map to see if she could connect anything in the dense green with the written markings.

Puzzled, she could see the darker dirt to her right, where she had uncovered the leather pouch, then slowly walked closer in. Jane stuffed the map into the waistband of her jeans, hoping to give herself full use of both hands to search deeper and wider.

But disappointment quickly spread across her face at not finding anything new. She sat on a nearby boulder, facing the woods and away from the road. With hands brushed clean, she studied the map again.

Jane remained still, flipping the map around and around, looking for any other clues. From behind her, she heard someone shout and then a thud. She quickly turned but couldn't see anyone. Her heart skipped as her thoughts ramped up in an adrenaline rush.

She grabbed the parchment tight and giant-stepped across the green earth to safety. Long strands of ivy caught her ankles, but she managed to stay upright. She kept up her fast pace to reach the Caldwell house. Once inside the laundry room, she turned the lights out, so she could look back to see what was going on without being noticed.

As she scanned the woods, she spotted a man's head in the distance, moving close to the forest floor. He looked like he was crawling out of a hole. She could hear him cursing. That must be the basement opening that Aunt Nancy told them to be careful of.

Jane also caught sight of a big, black SUV parked in the driveway of the old house next door to the property.

Later, after dinner in Dennis, the girls had no complaints with the "fish shack" food. Madeline talked all the way home in the car, but Jane stayed quiet.

As everyone walked up the deck toward the front door, Aunt Nancy put her arm around Jane's shoulder and asked, "Everything okay?"

Jane nodded.

Madeline went upstairs for her shower.

Aunt Nancy asked again, "Jane, you know you can tell me anything, right?"

She smiled.

"You were awfully quiet driving home."

"I'm just a little tired. That's all."

"All right. Just wondering. Sleep well."

23

THE SMELL OF WET dirt irritated Max's nose as he brushed off his damp clothes. He glanced up in time to see a girl scrambling across the dense lot, heading straight for the Caldwell Gallery next door.

"Crap," he mumbled to himself. Who is that kid? And what's she doing on the property?

He was not the outdoor type and looked forward to getting to the safety of his car and then a hot shower at the Sea Pines. He'd be back. He smirked at the thought that the old house's driveway would be a good cover for his snooping around in the woods.

As he drove West on old Route 6A, his phone pinged several times, signaling new messages. If they were from his business partners, he was going to ignore them. They'd get their money soon enough. He hoped they wouldn't come after him. Besides, he had turned off his location data, so no one actually knew where he was.

Max snuck up to his room. He preferred not to talk to anyone and didn't want to explain his muddy clothes and dirty shoes.

Once out of the shower, his head cleared, Max had a lightbulb thought. If he found clues about more treasure at the Brier Lane house, maybe he wouldn't have to bother with the abandoned lot on the other side of town after all. Why should he spend the money to buy it?

Investing in that stupid restaurant for a friend, to whom he had owed a big favor, and then convincing the Mica brothers to lend him the money to back the restaurant had been a big mistake. No one in their right mind could have seen a pandemic coming or know that it would wreak havoc on everyone, especially restauranteurs.

He texted his employee, Tommy. *Stop looking for who owns that property. I'll call you later.*

As he closed his phone, Max felt an itch on his wrist. He scratched it, then noticed it had become puffy and red. Now it was really itching. He grabbed his keys and headed for the drug store in Orleans. Some bug spray and cortisone cream would be needed, if he intended to return to the woods.

As he drove along Main Street, toward the pharmacy, Max noticed a car parked in the driveway of the neglected house. Perhaps it wasn't abandoned. He wondered if he should stop and ask the owner if he could park there the next time he went into the neighboring woods, just to be safe. The last thing he wanted was to get noticed by the authorities.

He pulled up behind an old Volvo then made his way up the debris-filled stone steps and knocked on the door. After a few seconds, an older woman opened the door a crack. She had a ruddy complexion, and her curly gray hair was pulled into a bun.

"What do you want?" Her tone was sharp.

"I was wondering if I could—"

"Don't want any. Go away." She started to close the door.

Max shoved his foot between the door and the frame. "I just want to ask you a question. I'll make it worth your while."

The woman stopped to listen.

Max fumbled with his wallet and pulled out a fifty-dollar bill. "I was wondering if I could park in your driveway."

The money got her attention. She opened the door a little wider, revealing a shotgun just inside the doorway, a clear signal to strangers that this woman was no one to mess with. "What for?" She stared at him, slowly moving her hand toward the gun.

"I might be interested in purchasing the lot next door and wanted to look over the property." Max held on to the fifty in his hand.

"Why don't you get yourself a real estate agent?"

"I'm a private person. Don't want anyone to know my business."

The woman relaxed her hand. "I get that." She stepped back and opened the door wider.

After Max handed her the money, the two strangers exchanged cell numbers and a promise from Max that he would pay for any information she might have about the property. "If you see anything suspicious or out of the ordinary, give me a call."

"Got it."

"I'll be back tomorrow." Max returned to his car, confident that the old woman would be an asset to his search. Right now, he was going to the pharmacy and then to the lawyer's office.

24

1908
BREWSTER

ANNA'S SMUDGED HANDS trembled as she held the four coins. The realization of what she had discovered, and the possibilities of what she could do with these newfound riches, began to pulse through her body.

What are they worth? Would I be accused of stealing?

By the time she reached Mrs. Powell's house, her heart was still racing. Her voice cracked. "Good morning, Mrs. Powell."

Her employer noticed the young girl's nervous demeanor. "Anna, is there something wrong?"

"No, Mrs. Powell." Anna gathered her polishing rags.

"Well, see to it that you stay focused on your work."

"Yes, ma'am."

After a few hours, Anna grew exhausted from all the morning's excitement and couldn't keep going. "Mrs. Powell?"

Her employer looked up from her cross-stitch.

"I'm not feeling well. May I go home early?"

Mrs. Powell shook her head in exasperation. "Mind you now, you need to promptly return in a few days to finish the cleaning."

"Yes, ma'am."

Upon escaping from her work, Anna decided to pay a visit to the family friend, Catherine. *She'll help me,* she thought. *I know she will.*

Catherine had known Anna since she was five years old. She was her mother's first friend after arriving from Hungary and also her supervisor at the Freeman house. Anna's plan was to ask Catherine how much one gold coin was worth. No need to say she had found four of them.

On her way home, Anna stopped at the Freeman house. Catherine told her that Mr. Freeman was away to New York and wouldn't be home on Cape Cod for several weeks.

Anna stood quietly, lost in thought. Finally, she spoke up. "I was wondering if you could help me." She removed only one coin from her apron pocket to show Catherine.

"Oh, my goodness! Where on Earth did you ever get something like this?" Catherine leaned in closer to view the gold coin.

Hesitant to say too much that might arouse suspicion, Anna decided to take a chance and tell Catherine how she'd found the coin. After all, her family needed money, wherever it might come from.

Catherine sat quietly as Anna explained about Mr. Wilkins's gift and that Ellsbeth, too, had been given a chance to find treasure. Anna pleaded. "Do you know how much it's worth?"

"I'm not sure." Catherine took the coin in her hand to examine it up close. "Last week, I was visiting my friend Mary Stanton, the Paines' housekeeper," she said, returning the coin to the palm of Anna's hand. "Mary said she heard Captain Paine and another gentleman friend talking about money and profits and such. She overheard them say that over twenty dollars could be had for one gold coin."

Anna was dumbfounded. The family mortgage was $3.50 a month. It would be more than enough to catch up. "The coin looks different. Is it still worth money?"

Catherine caught Anna's eyes. "If Mr. Wilkins left this for you, I don't think he would trick you with a coin that wasn't worth anything." Catherine shook her head in astonishment and examined the coin once more. "The old man was a real character. Many people thought he had hidden riches somewhere on his property. This looks like a Spanish coin. I bet it's still worth something. It sure looks like real gold."

"What should I do? I'm frightened someone might think I stole from one of my cleaning posts."

"Anna, you know I'm very fond of you and want to help you."

Anna looked down at the floor.

"I believe your story."

The young girl relaxed her shoulders in relief.

"I would think it terrible if the gossips in town questioned your reputation. You're a very nice young lady who comes from a hard-working family. Give me until tomorrow. I'll have some guidance for you."

Anna took a deep breath and then gave her friend a hug.

Catherine held the girl's hand, then with the other hand gently folded Anna's fingers over the coin. "Make sure you keep it safe and don't tell anyone, so there'll be no suspicion."

"Yes, ma'am."

"You know, Anna, a bank is the last place I would ever take my money. I don't trust those flim-flam tricksters."

"Thank you so much." Anna ran home as fast as she could to hide her treasure.

As soon as the young girl disappeared from view, Catherine hurried toward her private quarters. She opened the bottom drawer and pulled out a small strong box. It was filled with a stash of various denominations.

Catherine untied one bundle, slowly counted out $20, then set the money to the side. "Gold is gold," she whispered to herself.

After closing the box, a smile grew across her face as she stuffed Anna's money into her bodice and patted it with confidence.

The Following Morning

Anna pulled the wooden wagon along the edge of the road as the morning sky grew redder by the minute. She repeated in a sing-song whisper as she struggled to deliver the Freeman house's clean laundry over the bumpy road, "Red skies in the morning, sailors take warning."

The sunrise before her was a beautiful crimson but signaled an ominous forecast. She had heard a few tragic stories about fishermen who had ignored the old adage, then found themselves in a terrible storm on the water.

She switched the wooden handle of the wagon from one hand to the other every hundred yards. Her thoughts jumped between possible good news from Catherine in exchanging the gold coin for dollars and what she was going to tell her mother concerning the source of the windfall.

She found Catherine in the kitchen, tending to breakfast. "Good morning, Catherine." The wagon was pulled to the side of the large room.

"Anna, I have something for you." Catherine wiped her hands on her cotton apron and gestured for the young girl to follow her.

"Yes, ma'am." Anna carefully unfolded her mother's invoice on the table and joined Catherine in the housekeeper's living quarters.

"I told you I would be able to help you."

Anna withdrew the gold coin from her dress pocket, stared at it for a few seconds, and then handed it over to her friend.

Catherine gave Anna the twenty dollars. "Now, you take this and give it to your mother for the mortgage."

"Thank you." Her heart picked up speed as she fingered the money.

"Make sure you don't lose it."

"Yes, ma'am. I won't."

"Don't give it to the bank. Just pay your bills and keep the rest at home."

"Yes, ma'am."

The clock chimed on the hour.

"I need to hurry. Mrs. Powell is always anxious if I'm even a few minutes late." Anna turned to empty the wagon of the clean laundry so she could be on her way.

"I'll get the payment for your mother's work. Today's a good day for you and your family. Enjoy your newfound wealth. Hurry up, then."

Anna smiled at her friend. Yes, she thought, it was a happy day. With the money wrapped in her handkerchief and stuffed in her bodice, plus payment for the laundry separate in a small pouch, Anna began the now easier task of pulling an empty wagon to her weekly cleaning job.

Halfway there, she decided to keep the other three coins secret and hidden, even from her mother. She would only tell the truth about the one coin and explain that Mr. Wilkins had made a simple treasure hunt for her and Ellsbeth.

25

Spring, 1916
BREWSTER

ANNA WAS GETTING restless. She longed to be on her own and free of all responsibilities but to herself. The household expenses had been current over the past years, thanks to her contributions and her brothers', who had picked cranberries in the fall and strawberries in the spring. Often, as the Horvath family walked home from the fields, the boys dragged their empty lunch buckets across the dirt road and dreamed of doing nothing at home. All Anna could think of was the extra work in getting rid of the purple stains in their clothes, especially on the knees and sewing patches, where holes seemed to grow bigger every day.

Finally, it was time for Anna to leave home. Now approaching her twenty-second birthday, she was confident her family would be able to succeed without her. She realized there were few opportunities in the small town of Brewster for her, economically and romantically. She wanted to see what was available if she traveled west.

Over the years, Anna was able to conceal the remaining three gold coins from her family. She hoped that her mother would never need them, and then she could use the coins she'd hidden away to start her new life. In the back of her mind, she would always be ready to hand them over, if needed.

Catherine had suggested that Anna move to Millbury, in western Massachusetts, known as the "mill town." There would be plenty of work, with prospects for advancement. She knew of the Gilbert family and had written a letter to ask if Anna could stay with them until she found her own lodging.

Armed with a letter of recommendation from Mr. Freeman, Anna set her course for the "mill town." Of course, she would continue to send some of her earnings home as soon as she found work.

On the last night before she was scheduled to leave, Catherine had agreed to exchange the second gold coin for Anna to pay travel expenses and buy extra items. This dear family friend knew Anna would always take care of her mother, if needed. Pleased that Catherine understood her hesitancy to tell of a second coin, she whispered a quiet prayer of gratitude.

Upstairs, Anna peeked around the divided panels that separated her from her brothers, to see if they were asleep. They were silent. Picking strawberries and cranberries was back-breaking work, even for the young. She was happy to be leaving.

Louis lay in his bed across the room, his eyes half open. He had stayed home that day to help with the delivery of the weekly laundry, an easier job than picking in the hot fields.

Anna sat on the edge of her bed behind the curtained panel. She thought no one could see her, but thanks to the gaps between the material and the wooden frame, it left a small view for Louis.

She lifted her bed frame and cocked it on an angle, away from the wall. On her hands and knees, she picked up a small section of the floor to reveal her secret hiding place. She smiled at how she had hidden so many things from her brothers' prying eyes. She lifted the white rolled map out of the hole, then looked once more behind her, to see if either of the boys was stirring.

All was quiet. Next, out came the leather pouch. She opened it and fingered the two remaining gold coins inside. They glimmered in the lit candle's flame. Anna quickly returned the money to the leather pouch, then everything went into the bottom of her travel purse.

Louis quickly closed his eyes and rolled over.

Confident her secret would be safe, Anna returned the larger map to the hole then replaced the section of floorboard nearest to the wall, within the exposed flooring. The faint line that marked the spot among the boards was barely visible to someone who wasn't looking for a secret place. Mr. Wilkins's map would be safe, hidden under her bed, until she returned to possibly find more treasure.

Two new outfits lay on her bed, ready to be packed, and one new pair of low Oxford shoes. Both midcalf, tea-length skirts were versatile and easily switched with white blouses for different social occasions. Her favorite was a Middy blouse, made of cotton duck that hung loose below the waist, just in case she had the opportunity to attend a baseball game or engage in outdoor sports with, perhaps, a newfound male friend.

Her new clothes were carefully folded on top of two house aprons, bloomers, and several older, less fashionable blouses. Anna disliked the large, unflattering aprons, made of dark-green chambray, but knew she would need the smock-like dresses whenever she found work in the "mill town." Feelings of dread and excitement rippled throughout her body as she imagined what might happen as she made a new life for herself and, possibly, found someone to love. She was ready.

Anna said her goodbyes to her mother and siblings before she set off for the early-morning train that would take her to Union Station in Worcester, Massachusetts. Her brothers stood on the front steps, watching their older sister begin her adventure.

Louis, at eleven years old, fidgeted and looked anxious to do something. Thomas, at thirteen, held his stomach and looked hungry. Frank, almost sixteen years, stood leaning against the porch's post with hands in his pockets, trying to look very mature. Rosalia took her place in front of the screen door, hands folded across her waist, and smiled with tears in her eyes.

By afternoon, Anna had arrived in Worcester. She walked a short distance to the Worcester Consolidated Street Railway and bought her tokens for the final ride by trolley to Armory Village and Burbank Street. She hoped the Gilbert family would be welcoming to her.

At the corner of West Main and Burbank was Burbank Hill. Anna struggled with her heavy suitcase as she passed the red-brick factories on both sides of the uphill climb.

At the top, rock walls lined the road as she passed a dozen or so large houses where many mill workers lived. The sight of several stately homes and farms gave her some comfort in what might lie ahead of her.

26

1916
BREWSTER

LOUIS RAN INTO the house and up the stairs as soon as Anna was out of sight. His mother called out, "Emlékezik! Deliver laundry after lunch."

"Yes, Mother." Louis closed the door to his shared bedroom. His brothers had each gone to their jobs, leaving him alone. He took a deep breath then slowly pulled his sister's bed to the side. His brow furrowed in curiosity. "Where is that hole?" he hissed to himself.

He knelt down, his eyes scanning the floorboards for any bumps, rough edges, or loose planks. With no luck, he sat back. He whispered again, "Where is it?"

A beam of sunlight shone through the one window behind him. It lingered long enough for him to notice the edge of the corner on one plank that rose slightly above the others. He moved closer and bent over. His finger felt a few scratch marks. Struggling with reddened fingertips, the board broke loose and lifted up.

At first sight of the rolled paper beneath the floor, a drop of saliva fell from his open mouth. He swiped it dry and then reached in for the mysterious document.

It was quickly laid flat. Louis recognized it as a map but wondered what it was for.

From downstairs, he heard his mother call his name.

"Coming." He rolled the map up, set it aside, replaced the loose board, and returned the bed to its original spot. The map was hidden under his pillow for now.

He raced down the stairs for lunch.

Rosalia gave her youngest son a quick, stern stare.

After shoveling his food down, he hurried back up the stairs to take another look. Sitting on the edge of his bed, Louis studied the markings. Nothing made sense to him. He traced the long lines in front of the drawing of the house and then smiled, nodding in recognition that it was the Old King's Highway.

His finger settled on letters at the top of the map. He scratched his head then read them out loud, "W - I - L - K - I - N - S." He relaxed as he heard himself sound the letters together and finally said, "Wilkins," and then, "Mr. Wilkins!"

Anna's name was also on the map but at the bottom and upside down.

His mother called again from downstairs, "Louis!"

He folded the map in half and stuffed the paper into his pants pocket.

The spring air felt damp as Louis pulled his laundry-filled wagon down Main Street toward the Freeman house. As he briskly walked along the road ahead, any passersby could see there was no dawdling coming from this young man. He parked the wagon outside of the mansion and found Catherine in the kitchen.

The old woman, now in her seventies, was soon to retire. "Mister Louis. How are you today?"

"Fine, ma'am."

"I'll meet you by the backdoor."

Louis retrieved the wagon outside and pulled it a few feet away from the kitchen. He took the canvas cover off the clean clothes and waited for Catherine to open the door.

"You look a little warm today. Did you run here?" She laughed and grabbed the first pile of folded clothes from the perspiring boy.

Louis smiled. His hand brushed against his bulging pocket that hid the map. He pretended to clean dirt off his pants and casually tried to flatten the bulge.

"Wait here. I'll get your payment." Catherine disappeared behind the open door.

He knew the housekeeper would be a while. She had been feeling her age, according to his mother. He sat on the threshold, opened the map and stared at the word, *WILKINS*. He turned the map around and around, trying to see any other clues or directions. It didn't make sense with both names, one right side up and the other upside down. He scratched his head.

Catherine appeared at the door. "What you got there?"

Startled, Louis jumped up and shoved the map back into his pants pocket. "*Uhhh...*, just an old piece of paper I found." He shuffled his feet.

A bell rang to signal that someone needed Catherine's attention. "Well, mind you don't get into any trouble. Your mother doesn't need that."

"Yes, ma'am." Louis headed down the lane and onto the road. Out of sight from Catherine and the eyes of Main Street, he led the wagon to a spot behind a large boulder. Once there, he took the map from his pocket and sat down into the wagon to study it again.

Louis had heard the scary stories from neighbors about old man Wilkins, and the tales had grown even more frightening as the years passed. He knew all about the fire, the ghost of strange Mr. Wilkins, and the cursed land. He knew better than to venture onto the property, but all the Xs across the map piqued his curiosity.

Louis recalled the latest adventure of pirates he had read about in the popular boy's pictorial magazine, *Fame & Fortune*, after his best friend, Johnny Davis, swiped it from his big brother. It was still early in the day. He decided to take his chances.

The wagon was strategically placed so no one could see it from the road. The Wilkins house was less than a mile away, going east, and he could pick up the wagon on his way back home. He returned to his fast pace instead of running, which might bring attention to his quest for answers. Halfway there, clouds began to form in the west, and the sun disappeared.

The air smelled salty, signaling to Louis that a storm was coming. As he approached old man Wilkins's property, he pulled the map from his pocket. Dense ivy covered the ground, and he looked around for anyone nearby.

Confident he was alone, he hid behind a large oak tree to unfold the paper once more. His eyes darted back and forth from the map to the blackened foundation, along with its center chimney that rose out of the ashes.

Louis walked toward the first location of where an X might be. He stuffed the map back into his pocket, knelt on the dirt, and began pushing away leaves, acorns, and black soil. From behind him, he heard rustling. Turning his head toward the sound, his heart raced. He wondered if it was a ghost, just like his friends had warned him about. He stayed quiet.

The same sound came, only louder than before. This time, he stood to get a better view. Out of the thick woods, he saw a rifle's muzzle aimed directly at him.

Louis froze.

Someone shouted, "Get away from here!"

Louis didn't move.

"Listen, boy. Get out of here!" An older man dressed in ragged clothes with a full, bushy beard appeared in the thicket. He flicked the rifle's end into the air then aimed it back on the frightened boy a short distance in front of him. "You get on, boy! I'll shoot you if I have to!"

"Yes, sir!" Louis turned and ran toward the road. By the time he retrieved his wagon, he was still shaking.

When he arrived home, he parked the wagon on the side of the house and ran upstairs to his bedroom. Within seconds, he had replaced the map in its original location under the floorboard.

He leaned back against his sister's bed and promised himself that he would never return to that scary place again.

27

Spring, 1916
BREWSTER

EZRA P. SMITH WATCHED the young boy run toward the road. He lowered his rifle then turned his back to the outside world once again.

His crudely built shack, hidden in the dense woods, was barely visible to a wandering eye. He walked toward his camouflaged shelter, which was covered with pine boughs and fallen branches. Thanks to the habitual dumping of construction leftovers from his easterly neighbor, Roger Doanne, Ezra always had an abundant source of raw materials, including a small iron bed frame.

This had been home for the old hermit since 1909 and every year after, during the three mild seasons of Cape Cod weather. Thanks to his old friend Wilkins, several unexpected but fortunate treasure caches had been found by Ezra around the abandoned property. They had provided him the opportunity to travel to a Boston rooming house in the deep winter, when the air turned frigid. Once there, he would also replenish his foodstuffs.

Ezra chuckled to himself, thinking of his old seafaring buddy, not one to spread his money around. Wilkins had always kept a close eye on his things. Not anymore.

He took a sense of pride in his no-nonsense hovel on the Brewster property. When word had come to him back in 1908 that Wilkins had died in a house fire and that the property was still empty, Ezra had decided to hide himself in the Wilkins's back woods. The burned-out property was practical, served him well, and was free. A well-placed rumor, courtesy of himself, about sacred ground and curses had long served to keep people away. No one was interested in buying the land.

Ezra Phillip Smith was hungry that morning. He had arrived late last night from his winter sojourn at the rooming house back in Boston, on Beacon Hill. His large leather suitcase, with his initials E. P. S. engraved above the lock, lay unopened on the blanketed bed.

With no more interruptions, he thought it was a good time to take stock of the new dry goods. Cold food from here on in would be his menu until late fall, fearing the savory smells of anything hot would bring unwelcome visitors. Not much bothered the quiet man, except for people. King Phillip, as he preferred to be called as a signal to his Indian heritage, favored not being told what to do or say. The few winter months away were all he could stand, as far as contact with humans.

After storing cans of corned beef, pork-and-beans, milk, olives, and peaches, he carefully wrapped twelve Clark bars in brown paper and then stuffed them into a metal box, closing the lid with a clang. His razor, shaving soap, travel suit, boots, and his most favorite tool, a brass compass from the old pirate, Bully Hayes, were stored in the suitcase until next winter. In a secret compartment sewn into the lining of the case lay one gold coin wrapped in linen cloth. After checking the rare coin was securely hidden, he proceeded to conceal the suitcase in a dark corner, on top of a wooden platform, and covered it with sheet metal and pine boughs.

Last November, before he left for Boston, he had found the legendary golden Brasher Doubloon near the burnt foundation, on the chimney side of the Wilkins's brick house. Curious about its value, he had taken it to a coinage expert in Boston, who had offered to buy it for $1,000 or fifty gold coins. King Phillip had decided to wait for a higher offer. Tomorrow would be a fine day to rebury the doubloon for its own safety.

Within the hour, Ezra set out to see what had been discarded by his neighbor, Roger Doanne. The first item that caught his eye was a copper bucket with a dent in its side. He picked it up. Then, his foot stepped on a narrow object. Upon pulling it away from the dirt, he discovered it was an awl with a cracked handle. It would make a good carving tool. Ezra threw it into the bucket. A piece of copper flashing, found in a pile of leaves, made its way next to the broken awl. It was a good haul today, he thought.

Much to his pleasure, the rain that had started with a few big drops moments earlier, had turned into a torrent, hopefully making more gold pieces easier to find as they shone against the black dirt. To his annoyance, nothing was found.

Sleep came quickly to the old man. Even the few leaks in the roof, dripping rhythmically into his newfound copper bucket, couldn't keep him awake.

Morning came with sunshine and warmer temperatures. After a refreshing drink of stored rainwater, King Phillip fetched the special coin and retrieved his compass from the suitcase, then set out to hide his treasure.

Once the coin, nestled in a leather pouch, was buried in the dirt, he returned to the shack to do some carving. He sat on the edge of his iron bed frame and slowly turned the finial from the end of a side bar. The hollow tube revealed a deep opening. Next, he cut a narrow piece of copper from yesterday's find and began to slowly carve the doubloon's map coordinates onto the flat copper: N41° 46' 33.8466" W70° 1' 2.3524.

Once finished, the carved piece was slid into the side of the iron frame and the finial replaced. Perfect, he thought.

Feeling a little luckier than others, he still wished he had been as frugal as old man Wilkins.

28

Present Day
SEA PINES INN, BREWSTER

A WEEK HAD PASSED since Max arrived on Cape Cod. He only needed to stay a while longer.

The morning coffee smelled good as he stepped into the hallway on the second floor. Downstairs, the dining area was empty except for a young family out on the screened porch. Perfect, he thought. He wanted to be alone with his thoughts. His phone became his only companion for breakfast.

Later, upstairs, white documents and yellow papers were spread across the small table, waiting to be checked and rechecked.

Max pulled up his bank accounts online. Most of his money, plus the cash from his partners, had been sent to his friend's bank account. The restaurant, in turn, had spent most of it on startup costs and trying to stay afloat during the pandemic, while most customers were staying home. He had a little more than $10,000 left in his own personal accounts.

He took a deep breath and wished he would find something of value in the Brier Lane house, or at least on the Wilkins property. His Grandma Anna was not crazy, just forgetful.

29

1916
MILLBURY, MASSACHUSETTS

THE GILBERT FAMILY welcomed Anna into their home, much to the relief of the young woman. Her room was upstairs on the third floor. The shared bathroom was down a flight of stairs, but it had a lock on the door. Finally, Anna was all by herself.

That night, Anna couldn't sleep. Worried about what kind of job she would find and if she even would find one, she finally fell asleep after midnight.

Mrs. Gilbert had breakfast ready at 7:30 a.m. Before Mr. Gilbert left for his supervisor job at the Mayo Woolen Mill No.1, he'd suggested Anna try the Mayo Mill for employment.

Anna remembered seeing the large brick building that housed the Mayo Woolen factory as she'd stepped off the trolley, when she first arrived. It was on the corner of West Main and Burbank Street. If she did get hired, it was within walking distance from the Gilbert house.

As Anna sipped her coffee, young John Gilbert came rushing into the kitchen.

"Mother, can I play baseball after school today?" He began to gulp down his breakfast.

"After you finish your homework." Mrs. Gilbert flipped a pancake in the large black skillet on the stove.

Anna smiled at John and asked him, "Where do you go to school?"

"Down the hill."

"I think I passed it when I was walking to the house. The Burbank School?" She poured a drizzle of syrup over her pancake. "Is your teacher nice?"

"Oh yes, and she's real pretty."

After he left for school, Anna lingered at the table with her coffee.

Mrs. Gilbert sat down next to her. "Now, don't you worry. If you don't find something, I'm sure Mr. Gilbert will help you."

"Thank you. That's nice to know."

Later, Anna, dressed in one of her newer blouses and skirts, walked down the hill toward the mill. The sun was shining, and the air was crisp. The closer she got to the mill, the more concerned she became about what was ahead of her. She calmed herself with the fact that she was not afraid of hard work.

She opened the entrance door just as a well-dressed man with glasses and a small mustache came rushing out. "Excuse me, young lady."

Anna stepped back to let the man pass. "Sorry."

The man turned around and said, "If I were you, I wouldn't do business with those people."

Anna stood puzzled. "Oh. I was just looking for work."

The man took a few steps and then turned around. "Well, I am in need of some help."

"Really?"

"Yes. Do you have any experience with children?"

"Why yes, I do. I have three small brothers at home."

"Well, I have a rather obstinate thirteen-year-old daughter who needs tending to." The man stood tall. He had a soft appearance about him, unlike his original comments upon first meeting. "Are you interested?"

Anna was dumbfounded. "I think so, sir."

"Here's my card." He handed a business card to Anna. "The name's Deering. Come by tomorrow at around 2:00 in the afternoon, and we'll discuss your position."

Anna's hand trembled as she read his card.

She turned around and, with card in her pocket, walked as fast as she could up the hill toward the Gilbert home.

Mrs. Gilbert was shaking a rug out on the side porch.

Anna ran down the driveway, waving the business card in the air, and called out, "Guess what?"

"Slow down, young lady." Mrs. Gilbert held the screen door open to an enclosed porch. "What's happened?"

Anna could hardly catch her breath, but after a few moments to calm herself, she told her landlady the good news about Mr. Deering and his offer of a job.

They sat down on the porch swing. Mrs. Gilbert read the card. "Oh, I've heard of this man. He's a salesman at the Corset H. Company."

"So, you know of him?" Anna took the card back into her hand to study it further.

"Only from talk around the area. I heard he does pretty well."

"Do you think it would be a good idea to go and talk with him, to see what the job entails?"

"Absolutely. Not sure how you're going to get back and forth. The factory is a bit too far to walk. You may need to take the trolley down on West Main Street."

"The only address on the card is for the factory. I don't know where he lives, and I think that's where he wants me to work."

Mrs. Gilbert stood up. "Let's wait until Mr. Gilbert gets home and see what he says."

"Certainly. That's a wonderful idea." She followed Mrs. Gilbert into the house. "Do you need me for anything, or may I go up to my room?"

With a nod and an approving smile, her landlady, now becoming a fast friend, disappeared into the kitchen.

Anna ran up the stairs.

30

THE FOLLOWING MORNING, outside on the back porch, I lingered with my coffee for a bit.

Jane joined me. "Aunt Nancy, there's something I need to tell you."

I nonchalantly stirred my coffee, trying not to be too concerned about what she might tell me. "What's going on?"

"You know, when I found those gold coins, I was really disappointed that I might not be able to keep them. Actually, I was mad."

"I know, honey." I placed my hand on top of hers.

"A few days ago, I found something upstairs in the bedroom." Jane started to fiddle with her fingers.

"Really?"

"Yeah. Madeline flipped her shoe at me, and it hit the baseboard, knocking it away from the wall. I waited to put it back until Madeline was in the bathroom. I didn't want her to think she'd get into trouble. That's when I saw something inside an opening in the wall."

My heart skipped a beat.

"It was a small metal box."

I knew our house had a lot of secrets, but this was a new one. I was curious but remained calm, waiting to hear the whole story.

"Inside the box were some things from a girl who lived in the house, in that bedroom."

"What was her name?"

"Ellsbeth Doanne. I remembered the name Doanne from those papers you showed us in your office."

"You're right. The Doanne family lived here in the early 1900s. I'd love to see the box."

"There was something else."

"Go on."

"There was a map with a lot of Xs all over it and a drawing of a house's foundation, right on the road in the front of your house… Rt. 6A. When I studied the map some more, I realized it could be the burned house next door."

"Wow. Why didn't you tell me about it?'

"Because of the Xs, I thought there might be more coins, like in pirate maps. I knew I couldn't keep the coins from before, so I thought I could find others by myself, when you're not home, and maybe not tell you."

I was quiet for a few seconds.

"I'm really sorry. I should have told you. I know it was wrong."

"That's okay, Jane. Can I see the box now?"

"Well, I have something else to tell you."

I sipped my coffee, trying to remain calm. "Go ahead. I'm listening."

"Yesterday, when you were gone to Boston, I went next door and tried to follow the map to find more coins."

"And…?"

"I didn't find anything, but I kind of had a scare."

"What do you mean?" Now, I was concerned.

"You know that hole in the ground near the road? The basement steps you warned us about?"

"Yes."

"I heard something, and then I saw a man climbing out of the hole. He was swearing, so I ran back into the house."

"That was the right thing to do."

"I turned off the lights in the laundry room and looked outside. All I saw was the back of his head as he headed toward a big, black car parked on the other side of the property."

"Do you think he noticed you?"

"No. When I saw his head pop up from the ground, I turned and ran."

I mulled her words over, but not for long. "Shall we go look at that box together?"

Jane smiled. She seemed relieved the truth was out.

31

1916
MILLBURY

MR. GILBERT WEIGHED IN over dinner on whether Anna should follow up with Mr. Deering. "Haven't heard anything negative about the man. It might be a better job than at the mill. Some factory work is not for the faint of heart and can be downright dangerous."

Anna lost some of her appetite when, to the displeasure of Mrs. Gilbert, her husband proceeded to tell the story of poor Foster Gordon.

"Back on December 4, 1914, Foster, our overseer for the vats of dye, somehow tumbled into the boiling mass. The man died on the way to the hospital. Filled the mill with an awful stench of burnt flesh—"

"Mr. Gilbert! Enough, please." She gave him a stern look. "We have young children present."

"Sorry, dear. I just wanted Anna to know what she might be getting herself into, if she worked at the Mayo factory. Of course, the Corset factory is probably nicer. I heard it has over 50,000 feet of office and factory space, including places for the workers to rest."

Anna went to bed with an uneasy stomach, not only from her queasiness about Foster Gordon but her anxiety concerning the following day and her coming meeting with Mr. Deering.

The next morning, the sun broke through the upstairs windows of the Gilbert house. Anna waited for her turn in the bathroom. By 8:30 a.m., she entered the kitchen to see young John rush out the door for school.

Mrs. Gilbert stood near the stove with her back to Anna. "Sit down and have some coffee."

Anna slid the chair away from the table and took her seat. "Thank you."

"How about a piece of toast with some delicious peach jam? I made it myself last fall." Mrs. Gilbert joined Anna at the table. "Today's a big day."

"Yes, it is. I'm hopeful."

"Good. Stay positive. You have some time before your appointment. Why don't you go down to Horne's, across from the mill, and find something nice for yourself?"

"I better not. I don't have the job yet, but I was thinking of going early to explore Worcester's Main Street."

"That's a fine idea. I'll make you a sandwich, in case you're hungry when you get there."

"Thank you, again. You have been so kind to me. I don't know what to say."

"You just be yourself. I'm sure you'll find success."

Anna confidently walked down the hill to Burbank and West Main, buoyed on by the spring air and the thought that she had the courage to leave family and home and find a new life for herself. Not many young women her age could do that.

Within a short time, the big city of Worcester lay before her. As she walked along Main Street, she passed bakeries, drug stores, the MacInnes Department Store, and several lovely hotels. By the time she reached Jackson Street, it was almost 12:30 p.m. She pulled out the sandwich from Mrs. Gilbert and nibbled on the bread until she came to the Corset H. Company. With its three stories and towering presence of red bricks, it dominated the corner of Jackson and Beacon Street. It took Anna's breath away, she quickly rewrapped her lunch and stored it in her purse for later.

As Anna entered the red-brick building and its reception area, she could see several desks in front of large wooden file cabinets and lots of windows. It was tidy, pleasant, and didn't smell like a factory. She walked over to the first desk.

"Excuse me, I was wondering if a..." She looked at the business card and read, "A Mr. Charles Deering was in?"

The woman behind the desk looked her over and said, "If you would please wait here, I'll see if he's available. What is your name, and what is your business with Mr. Deering?"

With that, Anna froze in her tracks. She never gave him her name. "My name is Anna Horvath. I think he was considering me for a position that involves taking care of his daughter."

The woman showed no expression or interest in Anna. Her voice was stern. "Please wait here."

Anna watched the dour receptionist walk away from her and turn left into another office. The few minutes that she was gone out of sight seemed like forever to Anna. She held onto the small, white card in her damp fingertips and waited. She could see her chest rising and falling. She took a few deep breaths to calm herself.

Finally, the woman returned. "Mr. Deering will see you in a few minutes. Take a seat over there."

Anna followed orders and quietly sat down.

She picked up a copy of *Worcester Magazine* from a small table next to her chair and began flipping through its pages.

"Miss Horvath, please follow me."

Anna obediently trailed the woman toward the small office. She could see Mr. Deering behind the desk. He was staring at some papers.

Without looking up, he ordered, "Please take a seat. Your name again?"

Anna sat down and introduced herself. "Miss Anna Horvath."

He repeated, "Miss Anna Horvath." He wrote it down, then finally looked up at her. "May I call you Anna?"

"Of course, sir." She wiped her hands on her dress.

"I remember you saying that you have little brothers."

"Yes, I do."

"Well, my daughter Martha is turning thirteen, and I believe she needs someone to be with besides her mother. For instance, when she leaves the house for school or shopping."

"I understand, sir."

"Do you have any references I might see?"

Anna pulled out Mr. Freeman's letter of recommendation and handed it to him.

Mr. Deering read the letter and, after several seconds, looked over to Anna. "Everything seems to be in order. Will you come by the house to meet Martha and see if you're interested in being a companion for her? You'll find her mother is quite busy."

"Of course, sir.

"I'll send a car for you around 8:00 a.m. tomorrow."

"Yes, sir."

"Leave your address with the receptionist. I'll see you tomorrow."

"Thank you very much, sir."

Anna tossed and turned all night, anxious about how she would fare with young Martha and what her duties would be.

At 7:00 a.m. Anna heard Mrs. Gilbert making breakfast in the kitchen. She listened for the bathroom door to open then ran down the hallway to take her turn. A short time later, she was dressed and downstairs, seated at the table.

Mrs. Gilbert poured Anna some coffee. "Did you get some sleep?"

"No, not much. I'm sure I'll sleep better tonight. It's always the unknown that keeps one awake."

"Very wise thinking on your part. I'm sure you'll do fine. You appear to have a good head on your shoulders."

"Thank you for your confidence in me."

Mr. Gilbert entered the warm kitchen. "Good morning, my dear. Your coffee will get me out of bed every time." He sat next to Anna. "Who's coming to pick you up?"

"I actually don't know. All I know is, I should be ready to leave by 8:00 a.m."

Mr. Gilbert looked at the clock. It read 7:45. "I'll wait until the car comes to make sure everything is okay."

"Thank you so much. I'd appreciate that." Anna twisted her fingers together.

Five minutes later, John came bounding into the kitchen to join the others. "I saw a car outside. It's a beauty." He thrust a spoon into his cereal bowl. "Is it for you, Anna?"

Mr. Gilbert got up to look outside. "It sure is a nice-looking car. I think it's one of those new Dodge cars."

Anna ran upstairs to collect her purse and jacket.

At the bottom of the stairs, she called out, "Bye, Mrs. Gilbert!"

As she approached the car, Mr. Gilbert was standing outside the driver's door, talking to the young man inside the car. "How's your father doing, Eddie?"

Anna stood back, listening.

"Doing well. He has a new job at the Corset H. Company. That's how I got this."

Mr. Gilbert stood back. "Anna, this is Eddie Wallace. I guess he'll be your driver for today."

Anna lowered her eyes.

Eddie jumped out of the car to open the rear door for Anna. He greeted her with, "Miss Horvath."

Anna climbed into the back of the car and settled herself onto the cushioned black-leather seat.

Eddie closed the door, tipped his hat to Mr. Gilbert, and then popped back behind the steering wheel. He adjusted the rearview mirror to catch a glimpse of the pretty young girl he was going to be chauffeuring around in the future.

Anna noticed how handsome the driver was when he turned his head around to back out of the Gilbert's driveway. As the Gilbert residence disappeared in the background, Anna couldn't help thinking of how exciting her life was becoming.

32

1916
MILLBURY

WITH FURTIVE GLANCES at Eddie's strong-looking hands as they maneuvered the car, Anna wanted to talk but wasn't sure what to say to this handsome young man. She tried to remain calm and ladylike as factories, a few shops, and small- to medium-sized houses flew past her window view.

Within the hour, the car slowed to turn onto Hillside Avenue in West Newton, near Worcester. Anna sat taller for a better view of her new employer's house. Near the driveway entrance, a large oak tree had nestled itself atop a long rock wall that edged the property.

Eddie stopped halfway along the side of the house. He got out of the car and quickly opened the door for Anna. "Miss Horvath, you have arrived at your destination." He tipped his hat as she exited the auto. "Good luck, Miss."

With a cautious stride, Anna walked toward the front door. After she straightened her skirt and checked her hair reflected in the side windows of the wooden entrance door, she quietly knocked to announce her presence.

The door opened, and a young black woman with a pleasant appearance greeted Anna, "May I help you?"

"Yes, I'm here to see Mr. Deering."

"Oh, you must be Anna. My name is Ella. Won't you come in?"

"Thank you." Anna stepped over the threshold into a beautiful foyer with a lovely wooden staircase that ascended to the second floor.

She watched Ella disappear down a hallway, and within seconds, she reappeared. "Follow me, Anna."

The young woman did as she was told. She clutched her handbag against her chest; it was the closest tangible item she could grasp to steady herself as she followed Ella to a paneled study serving as Mr. Deering's work office.

Mr. Deering sat behind his desk. He looked up. "Anna. Thank you for coming. Please be seated."

Anna relaxed as she sank into a tufted chair.

"I trust you had an uneventful car ride in my new Dodge Brothers auto?"

"Oh, yes. It was wonderful." She pulled her skirt lower and caught glimpses of the wooden beams that decorated the ceiling and corners of the walls.

"Are you ready to meet Martha?"

Anna nodded.

"I'll get her."

She could hear him call up the stairs, "Martha. Please come down. I'd like you to meet someone."

Soon after he returned to his desk, Martha strode into the room looking a little smug, as if she felt bothered by this interruption.

Anna assumed thirteen-year-old girls would be pretentious, but she was willing to give this position a try.

33

Present Day
BREWSTER

MADELINE WAS IN the art studio with Paul while Jane and I went upstairs, so I could examine the contents of the old box she had found.

"I'm really sorry, Aunt Nancy. I just wanted to keep it a secret for a while."

I watched Jane pry the baseboard away and pull out the metal container. As she handed it over to me, she pointed to its front. "See? There's no lock or anything."

I lifted the rusty lid. "Oh, Jane, I can understand your hesitation." I started to look through the relics of the past and picked up the orange-and-red badge. "I had one like this when I was in school." I turned it over and read, "Ellsbeth Doanne. You're right, this girl must have lived here. The last name is correct, one of the owners, and the date coincides with my research of when they would have lived here." I admired the collection of old pearl buttons and blue clam shells.

Jane leaned closer to me and then touched the folded parchment. "That's the map I was telling you about."

I laid it flat on the bed. "It is the Old King's Highway," I said, as I traced the long lines in front of the house's foundation.

"Look how many Xs there are," said Jane with eyes wide open.

"Yes. I'd have to assume they stood for something important. Someone wanted to not forget where certain items were buried."

"What should we do?" Jane looked out the window to where the leaves of the oak tree fluttered in the morning sun. She turned around to face me. "That *OT* in the circle on the map has got to stand for an oak tree, like this one." She tapped on the window to get my attention to look outside.

I stood next to her. "You're quite the detective." Inside, I was beaming at the thought that my niece was just like me. "Let's go show Uncle Paul and Madeline."

Again, Jane looked relieved. She didn't have to hide anymore.

"You replace the baseboard and meet me downstairs."

Jane quickly did as she was told and then followed me down into the dining room.

We gathered the family and sat outside on the back porch to explain everything that happened to Jane, including the fact that the man in the black SUV had scared her. Paul was a little upset, but he joined in on the speculation about what might be buried next door. Surprisingly, Madeline stayed with us and actually seemed interested.

After much discussion, and by the time I'd finished making lunch, we still hadn't decided exactly what we should do. Go and dig where the Xs might be, and see if we could find more gold coins? Or stop and gather additional information about who else had lived on the deserted property, before we start digging?

I remembered I had some library books to return, which brought us all back to reality. "Anyone want to go for a ride to the other end of Brewster?"

Madeline and Jane both agreed to join me.

"I always make a game of driving in the tourist season. I carefully plan my route, so I never have to make a left turn."

The girls chuckled at their crazy aunt but joined me, anyway. As we pulled out of the driveway, we turned right. "The library is going to be our last stop, because it's on our left side. So… let's go see the beach first."

Our next right turn was Crosby Landing. After a quick stretch on the beach, we jumped back into the car.

Madeline piped up from the back seat. "Are we close to the library, yet?"

"Yes. I've got another beach to show you before we make our one left turn for the day." We drove down Brier Lane to get to Mants Beach, where we used to stay before we moved to Cape Cod from Ohio.

I saw Jane, from the front seat, looking at the old houses. She quickly called out, "Hey, that looks like the black SUV that was parked near the empty property the day I was trying to find where the Xs were on the map."

I turned my head and noticed the black SUV that Jane had pointed out was parked in the driveway of the house where Smitty had asked me to search for her missing ring. And yes, it could be the same SUV that had blocked her car.

I turned around three houses away and drove slowly back. "Jane, how do you know it's the same car that you saw?"

"Because, when we got our SUV, we wanted Dad to get the darkest tint on the windows. We thought it was so cool. Like movie stars and all."

Madeline gave a thumbs-up in the back seat with a big smile.

"But Dad said no, so we got the regular tint from the factory." Jane took another look back toward the SUV. "That one has the dark windows, almost black."

Hmmm. That's an interesting turn of events, I thought, and then wondered why the man who had shooed me off the Brier Lane property last week was snooping around next door to us. "You could be mistaken, Jane."

"I'm pretty sure that's the same vehicle, Aunt Nancy. I notice these things."

That night, I called Smitty to ask if she had some time to stop over the house for a minute. I wanted to ask her a few questions. She answered with a quick yes.

34

THE NEXT DAY, PAUL took the girls to Plymouth Plantation, while I stayed home to meet with Smitty. I wanted some questions answered regarding the SUV, and I had more research to do on Ancestry.com, using the archives of old newspapers.

With coffee in hand, I busied myself in the office on the computer. I started in 1900, scanning all articles from the *Barnstable Patriot* that mentioned anything about fires or accidental deaths in Brewster. Within the hour, I'd found an article dated June 10, 1908. It stated,

> *On the evening of Tuesday, June 9, 1908, there was a fire at the house of John Wilkins, residing on Main Street in East Brewster. All was lost, including Mr. Wilkins. No cause of fire was determined.*

Smitty's familiar sedan drove into the driveway at around noon. Pleased she was prompt, I invited her into the kitchen.

"So, what's up?" she asked as she sat down at the table.

"Did you ever see or meet anyone at Marty's house when you were cleaning?" Smitty looked quizzical. I gave her a few seconds of silence to gather her thoughts.

"Yes. I remember one man in particular."

"Really? Did you see what he was driving?"

"A black SUV."

"Who was he?"

"Not sure. It was a few months before Marty died."

"Did you talk with him?"

"No. Marty never introduced me to him. I don't think the two were very close."

"Why do you say that?"

"They didn't talk much to each other. One time, when the guy went into the bathroom, I asked Marty who he was. He said, 'Nobody important.'"

"Anything else?"

"Yes, there was one thing. The guy stayed in the bathroom a long time. I wanted to get in to clean it, so either he was snooping around, or he really had to go and wanted privacy, and then he disappeared downstairs. You know, into one of those Cape Cod basements, real small and round. Just big enough to hold a boiler, water heater, and electric panel."

I explained to Smitty the importance of the black SUV and how it might have a connection to the Brier Lane house and the empty property next door to us. I was grateful she could tell me a few things.

Then I asked her, "Want to come with me to Brier Lane? If no one is there, I could make one more search for your ring."

"Sure, I'll go with you." Smitty had a twinkle in her eye.

It was nice to have my old friend back in my life. "It looks like you're feeling better about your experience from last year."

"Much better. Time does heal. Maybe I could be your partner in crime for the day. I'll be the lookout. Hopefully, that black SUV will be nowhere in sight."

I grabbed my metal detector after we decided to drive together to Brier Lane.

Heading west down Main Street, Smitty added, "If the black car is there, we could go back another day."

"Sounds like a plan. The guy who caught me wasn't very friendly."

Luck was with us. No black SUV in sight. Smitty stayed in the car while I started to search for her ring beside the garden shed. It took about five minutes before I heard a binging. As I bent over to dig it out, I heard a car door slam and a man's voice. I stood up and turned around to see the SUV and the same man from before, talking to Smitty outside of my car. I laid the detector down and quickly joined the two.

Smitty was trying to explain why we were on the property. "I lost a ring the day I found Mr. Horvath. I just want it back."

I added to the conversation. "Yes, that's true. When I was here last, I was also looking for the ring, but you never gave me a chance to explain."

"I see," said the man. "Sorry about that. I was in a rush that day."

He was calmer today.

"I think I just found the ring. May I go and retrieve it?"

"Why not?" He walked toward the house as if nothing bothered him.

"Thank you." I hurried back to the shed, dug a little deeper, and there it was… Smitty's antique ring. As I brushed the dirt off my hands, I had a thought. Maybe he'd let me go in the house on the pretense that I needed to use the bathroom or wash my hands? I'd really like to see inside.

I handed the ring to Smitty and then knocked on the screen door of the house.

The man appeared behind the screen. "What do you want now?"

"I was wondering if I could use your bathroom to wash my hands?" I started to brush the dirt off. "I'm on my way to do some errands."

He just stared at me. I felt awkward, but I was determined to get a peek inside, so I stared back at him.

He opened the door for me, pointed to a room off the kitchen, and then left me alone. In the small bathroom, the medicine cabinet was wide open, and small orange bottles lay in the sink. The linen cabinet was also open, revealing a few towels on the shelf and several rolls of toilet paper.

I didn't see anyone when I left the bathroom. I remembered Smitty had said there was a basement. This was my chance to take a look upstairs. I glanced into the living area and saw the same disarray that the bathroom held, hinting at someone possibly looking for something. I nonchalantly walked up the stairs. As I ascended, I saw outlines of where pictures had once hung.

There was one large room with three beds in it and a smaller bathroom off to the side. The pictures had all been turned over and lay on top of the beds with their dust covers ripped open. The drawers on two dressers were open, with clothes and bedding hanging over the edges. Other items were strewn on the floor.

A black trunk near the back wall appeared untouched. If I didn't know better, I would have assumed it was a robbery. The trunk looked interesting to me, and as I got closer, it resembled a pirate's strong box, with two locks on the outside. Whoever was here didn't know what it was and couldn't get the trunk open.

I heard a door shut below me. I hurried down the stairs. Just as I reached the bottom step, the man appeared in the living room. He didn't look happy.

"What were you doing upstairs?"

"Sorry. I couldn't find you... To thank you. I'll be leaving now."

"Excuse the mess." The man softened his tone. "I'm in the middle of remodeling. Hopefully, this old dump will be sold soon."

"Well, thank you very much." I left to join Smitty.

Once in the car, Smitty spoke up. "Nancy, I'm positive that he's the same man who was here, visiting Marty Horvath, a few months before he died."

"Yes, I figured that. The house is a mess. It looks like he was searching for something."

"What a horrid man." She glanced out the car window.

THE OLD CAPE MAP

"Now, I need to figure out how he's connected to the property next door to us."

35

Summer, 1916
MILLBURY

EVEN THOUGH MARTHA gave Anna a smile, she could tell the girl wasn't going to have any part of this new arrangement.

The young girl stood next to her father's desk. "Why do I need a babysitter?" She side-glanced over to Anna. "No offense to you, Miss Horvath."

"None taken, Martha."

Mr. Deering looked up at his daughter. "I'm afraid you do not have a say in this matter. Your mother is very busy, and I'm usually gone for work."

"Oh, Father, Mother doesn't do anything important. She's always at the tennis club or on one of her social outings." She sat down in a chair near the windows with folded arms. "It's not fair. I'm a grown woman."

Anna stood between Mr. Deering and the impudent Martha. She looked at her new charge, and with all the courage she could muster, she said, "I'll make a deal with you. If we don't get along with each other after two weeks, I'll leave."

Martha looked agreeable.

Anna held her hand out. "Deal?"

Mr. Deering watched.

Martha stood, held her hand out, and said, "Deal."

After shaking hands, Anna turned to her employer. "Shall I start tomorrow morning?"

"That would be fine." He grabbed his sport coat and headed for the door. "I'll send the car for you at 8:00 a.m."

On the ride home, Anna looked lost in her thoughts.

Eddie said, "It looks like we'll be seeing more of each other."

Anna kept quiet.

"Still scared?"

"Oh, I'm sorry. I'm just thinking."

Eddie could see a smile growing across her face in the rearview mirror. "You'll do fine. Miss Martha is a typical teenager. My sister was just like that when she was growing up."

"The problem is that I only have experience taking care of my brothers," Anna replied. "I don't have sisters."

"You can talk with me about it. I'll be here for you. You can always find me, either in the garage or in the kitchen."

"Thank you, Eddie. You're very kind. I just may take you up on that offer." Anna's shoulders relaxed, and she began to look out the window at the lovely trees that dotted the suburban streets.

"What do you think of my little town of Millbury?"

"Very nice. Of course, I do miss the sea breezes back home on Cape Cod. Never had much time to walk the sand, but when I did, the rhythmic tidal flow of the sea against the shoreline was always so calming."

"Sounds nice, but you can't beat these mountains and farmlands. My favorite hike is up Mount Wachusett. When the weather is nice and we both have some days off, I could take you there."

"I'd like that. We could picnic. I'll probably need some distractions."

Eddie turned onto Burbank Street, adjusted the throttle, and said, "Looking forward to it."

36

Spring, 1917
BOSTON

PRIOR TO EZRA LEAVING Boston for Cape Cod in the warmer months, he had planned to visit a doctor for some chest pains he'd been having. All of their fancy mumble jumbo never impressed Ezra, and his opinion about doctors usually proved true. He was not confident as he left the office with unanswered questions, along with a small, amber-colored bottle of chocolate-coated nitroglycerin pills.

The night before, a well-dressed gentleman staying at the same rooming house as him had recommended he visit a Mrs. Stella Marini, a well-known herbalist, for smart advice. She had helped his wife with her malaise. He said he would return to her for help, if he ever needed it.

After several wrong turns, Ezra found her address on Massachusetts Avenue. He walked down a steep stairway below street level, assured that this woman knew what she was doing. Ezra reached for the wrought-iron handle on the door. After a quick turn, a bell rang, announcing his presence.

A turbaned woman of about forty years of age opened the glass and curtained door.

She greeted Ezra with, "Come inside." She then turned her back to Ezra and called over her shoulder, "Shut the door."

Ezra did as he was told and followed her to a small, round table with two chairs. A crystal ball sat on top of a red tasseled cloth, flanked by lit candles. A strong smell of incense permeated the darkened room.

He was not fearful. Many times, he had sought the wisdom of fortune tellers in his travels around the world.

The dark-complexioned woman settled into one chair. "Why are you here?"

Ezra sat opposite her. "It's my heart. I need something to settle it down."

"Do you have money?" She folded her hands together, her long nails glowing red.

"Yes."

"Then we may do business." She stood and disappeared behind a beaded curtain.

He remained seated, noticing the strange items that decorated the little room. A large stuffed owl peered down at him from the top of a tall, glass cabinet. On one of its shelves were several plaster hands displayed with palms exposed; lines were drawn on them and labeled with numbers. Three of the shelves held an assortment of brown bottles with white labels. Ezra wondered what was in them and whether she was going to give him a treatment from one of them.

Mrs. Marini reappeared, sat down, and slid a pouch across the table. Before Ezra could grab it, she stopped his hand. "The money?"

"How much?"

"Two dollars." She kept her hand on the pouch.

Ezra withdrew the correct coinage and placed it on the table.

Mrs. Marini picked up the coins, held one coin close to the candlelight for inspection, and released the medicine. "We are done here."

"What is it?

"Herbal tea. You must boil… two cup… water, add pinch of tea, simmer. No more, no less." She stood up. "You may leave me now."

Ezra headed for the door. "But what is it?"

She whispered, "Foxglove."

As Ezra walked to his hotel, thoughts of confidence made him feel calmer than when he'd left the so-called doctor's office. He knew of the plant that slows the heart. Old Bully Hayes talked of it, when he sailed with him and Wilkins.

He'd do just fine for a while, until he returned to Boston for more of Mrs. Marini's herbals next fall.

Ezra returned to the Cape by late afternoon. The spring trees were just beginning to flower. He did not look forward to the yellow pollen from all the pine trees, but he'd get through it. First thing in the morning, he would brew some of the tea from Mrs. Marini. It would take most of the day to steep, if the sun wasn't hot enough. Stored in a mason jar, the potion would be safe and ready for whenever he needed it.

The sun shone bright all the next day. By evening, the tea was prepared. As he settled in his bed for the night, Ezra wondered if he should have sipped the brew instead of drinking it. He felt his chest; no pain or quickness. That was a good sign.

He finally closed his eyes as the night air began to chill his tired body. Ezra nestled himself under a blanket on top of his sturdy iron bed frame.

At midnight, a sharp pain woke him from a deep sleep. By the time he sat up, his heart was beating so fast, he couldn't move to get the potion of tea. Within seconds, he couldn't breathe.

He stopped struggling and closed his eyes, hoping it would pass. Deep in the woods, Ezra P. Smith wasn't expecting death to come so quick and violent. He had thought he was invincible.

By the end of July, Ezra's neighbor, Mr. Doanne, decided to stay inside with his windows closed and curtains drawn, to keep the heat and rotten smell out. The stench of something dead in the woods was enough to make him gag.

The recent heat wave had affected the Brewster townspeople for many reasons, and Doanne was no exception. The windy shoreline gave some respite but not enough. He even considered leaving for Boston but thought better of it when, by mid-September, the smell had begun to subside.

37

Present Day
BREWSTER

AFTER WE RETURNED home, Smitty left for her afternoon cleaning job. I couldn't stop thinking about the guy from Brier Lane and what he was looking for.

I made a cup of coffee and put in a call to my favorite Brewster detective, Tony Gomes. He was out of the office, so I left a message for him.

"Hi, Tony. This is Nancy C. Sorry to bother you, but I'm calling with a question. About a year ago, there was an elderly man, Marty Horvath, found dead in his house over on Brier Lane. Our housekeeper, Martha Smith, was his regular cleaning lady and the person who found him. She said it looked like he had been dead for several days, if not longer. I promised her that I would try to find out what he died from — natural causes or something else? Can you give me any answers? She seemed to be the only one who cared about him. Thanks in advance.

Well, it's now a wait-and-hear operation for me.

I looked out the window of my office only to see Paul and the girls pull into the driveway. Looking forward to spending the rest of the day with my three favorite people, I went to greet them.

The following morning, the girls were rested and ready for another adventure. I proposed a hike in the woods next door, not for wildflowers, just a look around.

"What do you think? Who wants to explore with me?"

Madeline didn't seem interested and decided to stay back with Paul in his studio, but Jane presented a different face and a big smile.

"Sure. Let's go." Jane stood up, waiting for my instructions.

"Change into some long pants and socks, for ticks. I have an extra set of clippers for the thorny wild roses. Meet you here on the porch in five."

I had never gone deep into the woods next door before, always staying near the old foundation of the burned-out brick house. Today would be different. I also knew, in a few weeks, the woods would be too dense to get through, but right now, in late spring, the ground cover and scrub would be manageable. It was go now or wait until fall.

I would usually clear my paths alone, sort of treating my outdoor work as a form of therapy; taking me into solitude and a world of my own. Today, I didn't mind Jane's company. As we stepped into the thick greenness, she seemed as eager as I was and hopeful of finding something noteworthy.

I let her go ahead of me and noticed her stop occasionally to spot the deer paths, just like I would do. The property encompassed almost five acres, larger than our property. Halfway in, I heard Jane's foot make a crunch on the forest floor. We both stopped and looked at each other.

"What was that?" I asked.

She shrugged her shoulders then slowly lifted her foot away.

I walked closer to examine the dirt. "It looks like a rectangular object of some sort."

We both began brushing debris away with our feet.

Jane knelt on the forest floor and pushed away more dirt with her gloved hands.

I crouched down and saw a piece of metal. "This could be a lock of some sort."

Jane added, "Maybe it's treasure."

"Let's see." I knelt next to her, scraped away more black soil, and exposed the top of an old suitcase. The lock broke away as I tried to lift the top.

We both stared at the contents.

After a few moments of silence, Jane looked to me. "What's a suitcase filled with clothes doing in the middle of the woods?"

"These aren't clothes from today. They're from a long time ago." I picked up the dirty, faded pieces of material. "This is a linen collar that men wore from the early 1900s."

"No kidding?"

"Yes. Look at this." I held up a ragged black suit jacket.

"That's so cool, Aunt Nancy." Jane reached in to touch a faded shirt with a few insect holes in it.

There were other unrecognizable pieces of clothing, a pair of men's leather shoes, a small amber glass bottle with a label that read *chocolate-coated nitroglycerin*, and even a small ceramic bowl with a moldy shaving brush inside.

"Whoever this suitcase belonged to had a heart problem." While I was eying the rest of the contents, I saw Jane start to rub more soil away from the front of the case. She quickly uncovered someone's initials.

She read aloud, "E. P. S." Then, her eye caught a circular object at the bottom of the case. She picked it up and handed it over to me. "Look! A watch."

I turned it over in my hands, opened it up, and saw that it was actually a compass.

Jane touched the circular instrument. "It's really neat, Aunt Nancy."

I brushed some more of the dirt away. "It's funny how time and weather can hide things from a wandering eye. Just like on the beach, you never know what's buried beneath the sand as you walk the coastline."

"Should we take it all back and show Uncle Paul?"

"I guess there wouldn't be any harm if we did. Maybe preserve it for historical purposes." We replaced the found items back into the suitcase and closed the lid.

I stood straighter and glanced around the property, a habit I'd developed over the years. Always wondering if anyone was watching. Sure enough, there was Mrs. McPhee, standing on the edge of her property. Our eyes met in an awkward glimpse. I quickly looked away.

Jane stood up with the suitcase in her arms. "Who's that?"

"Someone you don't want to mess with. We've had a few run-ins with her over the years. She always yelled at the kids, because they were making too much noise or were too close to her property line, whenever they wandered over to get a ball or something."

"She looks creepy."

"She's actually harmless, just harbors a very intimidating presence. Let's go."

As we walked back toward the house, I explained to Jane what I knew about Mary McPhee. "Rumors around Brewster were that she had no children with her husband, Patrick or 'Patty.'" I stopped and pointed to the house across the street from us. "When we first moved in, I met a Mrs. Bangs, who used to live in that old house. She told me Mary had too many miscarriages. Then, I guess her husband died sometime in the late sixties. After his death, Mrs. Bangs said Mary blamed the Boston doctors who had botched his gall bladder surgery."

Jane twisted around to view the old McPhee house. "Mrs. McPhee has such a sad story."

"Yes, she does. Mrs. Bangs died a few years after we talked."

I kept turning around to see if Mary McPhee was still there. I thought to myself, there have been too many past events that keep me on guard for people who want something from me, either information or a treasure that I have, and they want it for themselves. Mrs. McPhee was no exception.

38

Spring, 1917
MILLBURY

A LETTER FROM ANNA'S mother, written in Hungarian, had arrived back in December with the news that her older brother, Frank, before his sixteenth birthday, had joined the army. Anna thought he'd always looked and behaved older than he actually was, so the army must have allowed him to join as an ambulance driver. She had heard stories around town of other young boys signing up at even younger ages, sometimes with a parent's permission, or possibly lying about their age. After over five months with no word about how he was doing, she was worried.

By early spring, Anna and Eddie had truly fallen in love. Their friendship had blossomed, and it was natural for deeper feelings to develop. They were together at their work most of the week and after hours, with the approval and watchful eyes of Mr. and Mrs. Gilbert. The older couple treated Anna as the daughter they'd never had and also became fond of Eddie.

Anna's job as chaperone for the Deering's daughter was progressing. Martha and Anna were getting along, even though they had, on occasion, agreed to disagree.

On one Friday, they were in Martha's bedroom, and Anna was helping her put away her clothes. She held up a cute tweed skirt. "This is very stylish."

Martha lay on the bed. "I don't like it."

"Really? I would love to wear this."

"You can have it." Martha reached for one of her expensive fashion magazines from a stack that included the latest *Vogue*, *Cosmopolitan*, and *Sears*.

Anna leaned in to look at one of the pages. "Look at those prices. You certainly have expensive taste."

Martha flung the Sears catalogue to the edge of the bed. "These are already out of date."

Anna hung a blouse in the closet. "I suppose you want me to get you the latest magazines from the drug store?"

Martha sat up and quickly answered, "Oh, would you please? Pretty please?"

"Yes. I will stop on my way home and deliver them to you on Monday."

"Have you spoken with my parents about Saturday evening? I really want to go over Marjorie's house."

"I mentioned it this morning to your father."

"What did he say?"

"I think he was expecting someone important within the hour, and he told me he'd think about it."

The young girl lay back down on the bed. "Oh, I know Mother will probably say no. She's so strict."

"She's only looking out for you."

"Anna, they always listen to you about what you think I should do or not do."

Anna smiled at her charge. They had developed a cordial give-and-take, and Martha had trusted her to intervene with her parents on several other social matters.

"I'm sure they'll let you go."

"Thanks." Martha walked over to a small jewelry box on her vanity table and withdrew a few coins for Anna to buy the latest magazines.

"So, you've met some nice friends, now that you're almost finished with your first year in high school?"

"Pretty nice. They certainly like my clothes."

"What do you mean?"

"I can trust you Anna, can't I?"

"Of course." Anna sat next to her on the edge of the bed.

"Well, I've found that some of the other girls like my style so much, they're eager to buy some of my outfits."

"Buy them?"

She opened the Sears catalogue. "You know Mother and Father really don't notice my clothes, except for school clothes. They trust me on those matters."

"That's true, but...?"

"I order things and then turn them around and sell them to some of the girls at school."

"Is that where you get your extra money for things they always say no to?"

Martha beamed. "Pretty smart, huh?"

Anna chose her words carefully. "I guess it doesn't hurt anyone. I'll keep your secret." She picked up a *Vogue* magazine. "I do enjoy the fashion, too."

Ella stopped Anna in the upstairs hallway at the end of the day as she was preparing to go home. "Anna, Mr. Deering would like to see you in his office before you leave."

"Thank you, Ella." Anna worried as she went downstairs to his office. She was eager to go home today. All she could think about was Eddie, her mother, and her brother Frank away at war. "Mr. Deering. You wanted to see me?"

"Yes. Please sit down."

She wondered if he knew about Martha's business deals. Was she going to get fired? She quickly sat down in front of the desk.

"Anna, I wanted to let you know that, as soon as Martha has her last day of school, she will be traveling to Bermuda for a few months with her mother."

Anna relaxed. "Do you have any dates for their departure?"

"Not yet. But I'll keep you informed. You certainly have been good for Martha. You deserve some time off."

"Thank you, Mr. Deering."

She stood to leave.

"Oh, Anna, one more thing. I know you may be worried about receiving no pay during the summer. So, I have decided to pay you one half of your wages while my wife and daughter are away. I wouldn't want you to leave us for other employment. Would that be agreeable to you?"

Anna was dumbfounded. "Mr. Deering! Yes. Thank you so much." She stopped before her exit. "Oh, I forgot to ask something. Shall I tell Martha she can spend the evening at her friend's house?"

"Who?"

"Marjorie Stanton."

Without looking up from his desk, which was filled with papers, Mr. Deering replied, "Sure. She can go."

Anna hurried upstairs to tell Martha and then gathered her things. She met Eddie in the back driveway to tell him the good news.

Eddie was waxing his new Ford Brothers auto. Not as expensive as Mr. Deering's, but it was a nice little beauty in Eddie's eyes.

Anna ran up to her new love. "Guess what?"

"Slow down. Anything wrong?"

"Oh, no. Mr. Deering just gave me some time off, and I'll still get paid. Don't know when, but soon this summer." She gave Eddie a peck on his cheek and explained about the Bermuda trip. "It's only half of my wages, but I've been saving, so I'll be all right."

"I wonder if I will get some time off. Is the Mister going too?"

"I don't think so. Just the ladies."

"If Mr. Deering gives me time off, maybe we could take my new car and visit your family on Cape Cod?"

"Oh, that would be wonderful. I haven't seen them in over a year."

Anna scooted close to Eddie in the front seat of his new car as they drove to the Gilbert house on Burbank Street. "All day long, I've had a notion that something bad was going to happen. I don't know what I was worried about. I've had nothing but good news today."

"I know. And if Mr. Deering gives me a week off also, we can go to the Cape."

When Eddie dropped Anna at the Gilbert house, he called out to her as she stood outside the car door, "I have to do an errand for my father, but I'll be over right after."

"Okay. See you later."

As soon as Anna entered the Gilbert house, her smile faded and the foreboding feeling returned. Something was wrong. Mrs. Gilbert sat on the tufted chair in the front parlor with a somber look on her face. She was holding a telegram addressed to Anna Horvath. Telegrams were always bad news, especially with the war going on.

Anna wished Eddie was with her as she slowly opened the yellow envelope with Western Union Telegraph across the top. It read:

Your brother Frank has been killed in action. Please come home.

Anna's hands shook as she read the words over and over, then spoke them out loud, between her tears. She needed Eddie right now.

39

1917
MILLBURY

CHARLES DEERING BEGAN to clean his desk for the evening, marking his calendar to remind himself to pay Anna her summer wages.

His wife, Georgia, entered the paneled office. "Charles, dear, has Anna left for the day?"

"Yes. I've informed her she will have an extended vacation while you and Martha enjoy the sunshine in Bermuda."

"I wanted to say a few words to her. It's such a bonus to have her help me with Martha."

"I know, dear." He leaned back in his chair and stared outside, suddenly lost in his thoughts.

Georgia leaned over the front of his desk. "Is everything going well at the company?"

"Well, there have been some stirrings about the future of the Corset H. Company. Have you spoken to your sister, Mary, as of late?"

"Not recently. She's been so busy with the incorporation of the company's name change from Corset H. Company to the Ivy Corset Company, plus her terrible divorce and, of course, the upcoming wedding of her and William." Georgia slid her fingers along the edge of the desk, walking closer to her seated husband.

Charles stood up. "I'm not sure what will happen. I'm feeling a little insecure in my position." He moved toward the window.

Georgia moved to put her hand on his shoulder from behind. "Oh, Charles, I'm sure everything will turn out fine."

"I can't help wondering why Mary would pass me over when considering the company's representative to the annual meetings of the Empire Corset Club."

"I don't think it was intentional."

"I just don't understand." He shook his head. "I'm the company's top salesman."

Georgia rubbed his back. "I know, dear."

He turned around to face her. "Someday, I'll be able to buy a house for you and Martha on my own, instead of always renting."

"Charles, you know you don't ever have to worry about that. My sister Mary and Father have always provided well for me."

"I'm aware of that." Charles looked pensive.

"You have been the top salesman for over twelve years. If we happen to part ways with the family company and decide to start our own corset company, then I have enough to help you with that."

"You are a dear, Georgia." With a slight smile, he kissed her on the cheek "When you return in August, we'll talk more. Until then, I want you and Martha to enjoy yourselves and not to worry."

"Sounds wonderful." Georgia hurried to grab her purse. "I'm off to the tennis club. Joan is picking me up. Don't wait up for me. Ella has a nice dinner waiting for you and Martha."

Georgia disappeared into the foyer before Charles had a chance to tell her that Martha was going over a friend's house. He picked up a few contracts to look over, hoping to catch up on some items that needed his attention. With no schedule for the evening and dining by himself, he could do whatever he wanted.

40

Late May, 1917
CAPE COD

AFTER HEARING ABOUT Frank from a teary-eyed Anna an hour later, Eddie returned to the Deering house and got permission to take the coming week off.

He arrived early the following day to pick up Anna at the Gilbert house. Few words were spoken as they drove through the countryside on their way to Cape Cod. Eddie wasn't sure what to say to Anna. He thought of his younger sister and how he would feel if she died, but words would not come to him. He decided he would just quietly be there for her.

Anna stared out the window, thinking of Frank and how much he would be missed. Always the sensible one, she knew he had dutifully passed some of his earned money on to his mother for the family household, keeping only a little for himself. What would become of her mother and younger brothers? Would one of the boys need to quit their schooling to work longer hours? She fingered one of the gold coins in her pocket and planned to give it to her mother.

Anna looked over to Eddie. How handsome he was! She smiled, reaching for his free hand. He quickly looked toward her then wrapped his hand around hers. Hesitant to tell Eddie about the treasure she'd found back on Cape Cod, she remained silent as she looked out the front windshield. The decision to give her mother only one of the two remaining coins was settled in her head. It was the least she could do for her mother in her time of grief. Eddie would be a good provider, if and when they married. She and Eddie would be just fine together.

By late afternoon, the two quiet travelers pulled onto the grassy driveway of the Brier Lane house in Brewster. Anna stared at the tiny house. "I don't remember it being so small."

Eddie turned the auto off. "Oh, it looks nice. Cozy, and well kept."

"Yes, I guess the boys have been taking good care of it." She slowly exited the car.

Eddie joined her. They walked toward her childhood home, hand in hand.

Louis appeared behind the screen door. "Anna! I'm so glad you came home. Mother is beside herself." He glanced over to Eddie and then back to his older sister.

"This is Eddie Wallace, a very dear friend of mine. Eddie, this is my younger brother, Louis."

Louis shook Eddie's hand and then turned back to Anna. "People have been bringing food to us all week. I don't know where to put it." He placed Anna's bags on the stairway. He looked to Eddie. "Are you staying?"

Anna answered, "Of course. He'll sleep on the couch in the parlor. Where's Mother?"

"In her bedroom. Doesn't come out much. Thomas and I are worried about her."

Without hesitation, Anna headed for her mother's bedroom, located off the kitchen. Eddie went outside to check on the car. Louis followed behind his sister.

"Mother." Anna reached down to hug the teary-eyed woman dressed in black.

Rosalia started to whimper, clutching her handkerchief with one hand and wrinkling a photo of Frank in his uniform in the other. "Miért?"

"I don't know why, Mother."

"Miért?" Rosalia kept shaking her head in denial.

Louis stood by the door not knowing what to say. He went outside to join Eddie.

"Hey, Louis." Eddie was crouched down, checking on the tires.

Louis ran his hand over the black fenders. "Very nice."

Eddie stood up and wiped his hands on a rag. "Yeah, I'm proud of it. Where's your brother…, Thomas?"

"He had to go to the bank. Should be back soon." He walked closer and peered inside the car.

Eddie grinned. "Want to sit behind the wheel?"

"Really?" Louis's eyes went wide.

"Sure. Get in, but don't touch anything."

Anna appeared at the front door. Eddie looked toward her. Their two eyes met in a comfortable glance. He asked Louis to get out of the car and then made his way over to Anna.

"Eddie, can we sit here on the steps to talk?"

"Of course."

"My mother is distraught. I'm not sure how long I'm going to have to stay with her before I'm comfortable enough to leave her."

"I understand. I can stay around at least a week." He held her hand.

"Oh, thank you, Eddie. You're so supportive of me." She laid her head on his shoulder.

Louis passed his sister and her new boyfriend on the steps and went into the house. "I'll check on Mother."

"Thank you, Louis." Then, Anna explained, "My mother informed me there will be no funeral mass, because there is no body. But there will be a memorial mass in a few days. Would you mind coming with me?"

"Of course."

They sat there for several minutes until they spotted Thomas walking toward them on the road. As he turned onto the driveway, Anna stood to give her other brother a hug. They both cried in each other's arms.

Thomas pulled away. "The bank is questioning how Mother will be able to support herself without Frank's contributions. I said very little. Just listened and told them we'd be all right." He pushed his hands into his pockets with eyes downward. "What should we do, Anna?"

His sister put one arm around her brother and said, "Don't worry. I have a plan. Everything will be fine." The two siblings walked slowly toward the house.

Eddie watched them pass him.

As they reached the door, Anna stopped and turned around. "Thomas, I almost forgot. This is Eddie Wallace from Millbury, and Eddie, this is Thomas." With one arm around her brother, she patted his heart with the other. "He's a good boy."

The two men shook hands.

Anna seemed to have a calming effect on the Horvath household, as if everything would be well. Rosalia finally felt like eating something, even if it was only a bowl of chicken soup and a piece of bread.

Anna readied the table with a roast chicken and potatoes, a gift from a neighbor. Bedtime came early; all were exhausted. Rosalia retired after kisses all around. Even Eddie got one.

Anna made sure Eddie had a pillow and blanket for the parlor couch. His feet hung over the edge, but he kept a smile on his face the whole time, until Anna went upstairs to her old bed for the night.

He tossed and turned. It was too quiet for him. Eddie missed the sounds of his neighbors back home. Upstairs, the Horvath family went right to sleep.

41

THE MCPHEE HOUSE on Main Street has always been a sore spot in the town. Mary McPhee kept to herself and never cared what other people thought of her. Town officials tried to get her to clean off some of the boxes and debris from her front porch. She tricked them by only removing a few items, to pacify the higher-ups, but within a week, she'd put them all back.

Mary McPhee stroked her friend, Penelope, cat number three in a long line of furry companions. As the TV blared out the lives of her favorite soap operas, she rocked near the side window of her Brewster home. At the commercial break, she stood to get a closer look at a flicker of movement on the property next door.

"What's that?" she whispered to herself. "Penelope, you stay here. I'm going to get me a look-see." She grabbed her binoculars from under a small table that held a picture of her and her husband on their wedding day.

Once outside, near the edge of her property and behind a large pine tree, she peered through the old magnifiers. Under her breath, she mumbled, "What's she doing over there?" She lowered the binoculars, squinted, took a few steps closer, and then looked again through the glass. When satisfied, she quickly returned to her house.

"Penelope, it's time we give that Mr. Appleton a call."

Within the next few minutes, Max answered.

Mary was terse. "I've got some information for you."

Max was quiet.

Mary continued, "The Caldwell lady and some girl seem to have dug up something next door. A box of some sort."

Max quickly answered, "I'll be right over."

Mary yelled into the phone, "Don't forget my money! You promised..." The line went dead before she could finish her sentence. "Well, he must be in a real hurry."

She leaned down to pick up Penelope. "Maybe tonight we could order a fancy takeout for dinner." Penelope purred and rubbed Mary's arm. "Don't worry, I'll share."

42

1917
BREWSTER

EDDIE WAS UNCOMFORTABLE. The air was still and steamy. The couch was lumpy. He stood up, stretched, and then went outside to the porch. He walked over to his car to get some fresh clothes from his suitcase in the trunk.

Anna appeared on the porch. "Good morning."

Eddie walked closer. "Were you able to sleep last night?"

Anna pecked him on the cheek. "Yes. Actually, I was."

He wiped his brow with the back of his hand. "It's really warm today."

"Why don't you take the boys to the beach? There's a nice one less than a mile… Breakwater."

"I might just do that." He reached for the screened door. "Not much of a swimmer, but I like the ocean breezes."

"You go on in. Mother has already made some coffee for us."

Since word had arrived in Brewster about Frank's death, the Horvath family had experienced a full week filled with tears. By the time Anna came home, their grief became bearable and not as visible. Anna's mother looked better this morning. Stronger. Everyone seemed to be in a better mood.

Eddie had a broad smile on his face. "Who wants to show me the Brewster beaches this morning? It's been a long time since I was last at the ocean."

Thomas agreed to be the tour guide for Eddie. Louis decided to stay home.

Within the hour, Anna sat at the kitchen table next to her mother. She asked in Hungarian about the family finances.

Rosalia put her hand up to stop Anna from speaking. "I am learning English."

Anna was taken aback. Her mouth opened, and then it turned into a smile. She hugged her mother. "I can't believe it. When? Who?"

"Frank." And then Rosalia reached for her kerchief to dab a tear forming in her eye. After a deep sigh, she said, "Please, Anna... Speak slower."

Anna discovered that her mother had been frugal, and Frank had given his whole pay, not part of it, over to her in the months before he left for the war. The family was going to be fine after all. They only had a few more years to pay off the mortgage.

Rosalia held Anna's hand. "I never forget what you did. The coin you found... saved us. You are good daughter."

Rosalia's words made Anna confident enough to leave and excited to drive back with Eddie in a few days. The gold coin would go back home to Millbury and be put aside for happy times, maybe a wedding.

Louis listened from the back steps, hoping to catch anything more about where his sister had found the gold coin that had helped the family, years ago. Was it because of that map upstairs? He hadn't thought about it since the old hermit threatened him. He was still frightened whenever he passed that property. Maybe he should think about going back again.

Before the young couple left, Anna went upstairs to retrieve the map from beneath the floorboard. No need to keep it here in Brewster. One day, she'd tell Eddie about it.

As soon as Anna and Eddie pulled away and drove down the street, Louis ran upstairs, moved the bed away, and lifted the floorboard. He shoved his hand into the hole only to find it empty. The map was gone.

He sat on the floor, berating himself for not hiding it somewhere else until he had enough courage to revisit the cursed property again. He blamed himself. After a while, he soothed his bruised ego by assuring himself it wasn't all his fault. Anna should have shared the secret with the family. That would have been fair.

43

Present Day
BREWSTER

JANE CARRIED THE OLD suitcase into the garage and laid it on the workbench.

Paul emerged from his studio and joined us, followed by Madeline. "What'd you find?" he asked.

"Come and take a look." I gestured to come closer. Then, I slowly opened the case. Dirt fell away from the sides and crumbled onto the table.

Jane wiped her fingers across the nameplate where the initials were engraved.

Paul whistled in disbelief. "You found that on the property next door?"

"Can you believe it?" I held the jacket up into the light. "It's got to be from the early 1900s."

Paul leaned in to take a closer look.

Madeline watched as I searched deeper into the suitcase.

I held up the medicine bottle to the light. "Look at this. Nitroglycerin. I remember my mom had to take these, back in the early seventies, for her heart."

Jane reached for the compass. "Isn't this cool, Uncle Paul?" She brushed away some of the dirt then opened the small brass case. "Look. There's something written on the inside." She handed it over to me.

"You're right." I took an old rag from under the bench to clean it more. "It says, *Bully, 1860*." I looked away for a second in thought. "The Internet is our next step. Let's see what comes up when we input the name and date." I looked at Jane. "Want to help me?"

"Sure!"

"Paul, is it okay if we leave this here for a short time?"

"No problem." He returned to his studio.

Madeline picked up the edge of a cotton shirt with her fingertips. "This stuff really smells."

I looked at my nieces. "Wash up, and let's go searching." I watched them race up the steps of the studio toward the main house. I followed with the same excitement.

We settled in my office with Jane and Madeline next to me at my desk. I entered, *Bully 1860*.

We waited a few seconds in silence until a whole page about a pirate, William Henry Hayes, appeared. The *Wikipedia* entry was the most informative.

I read aloud, "*James A. Michner and A. Grove Day warn that it is almost impossible to separate fact from legend regarding Hayes. They described him as 'a cheap swindler, a bully, a minor confidence man, a thief, a ready bigamist—'*"

Jane leaned closer. "What's a bigamist?"

"Someone who marries several times but never gets divorced from any of them."

"Oh. Do you think he's the same man as the Bully on the compass?"

"Look at this entry. *Was a notorious American ship's captain who engaged in blackbirding in the 1860s and 1870.*"

Jane cocked her head. "What's blackbirding?"

"I've heard of it before. It means kidnapping or forcing people to work as slaves in places distant from their native countries."

"How sad."

"It also said that Bully Hayes was murdered after a mutiny on his ship in 1877. The suitcase is from early 1900. It's not the right time frame."

Madeline stepped back to leave. "You guys keep searching. Keep me posted."

Jane looked at some of the mementos displayed around the room from all my pirate research. "So, whoever owned the suitcase might be connected to Bully Hayes."

I leaned back in my chair. "You're probably right. But the question remains, how?"

44

THE MESSAGE FROM Mrs. McPhee was a pleasant surprise for Max. He called Tommy, his connection on the Cape, to meet him at Sea Pines Inn.

Max was waiting in his car in the parking lot. Tommy pulled next to the SUV. Max opened the window and signaled him to get inside.

"What's up?"

"I need your help. We only need one car." He started the engine and pulled out onto Rt. 6A.

Tommy clicked in his seat belt. "Are you still thinking about that empty lot?"

"You might say I am. But not for buying. Just looking around on it."

On the way, Max explained his plan further.

Tommy sat straighter in his seat. "So, you think there might be treasure on that property?"

"I'm positive it's connected, somehow, to the Brier Lane house. I want to know for sure."

"When we arrive at the house next door to the land, there's an old lady who is letting me park in her driveway, so we can stay off the main road. She's a tough old broad. Keep your mouth shut. I'll do the talking."

"Yeah, boss."

Tommy thought about finding treasure and how much he could get. His old man told him never to trust anyone and always make sure you get your fair share, no matter what.

45

1918-1920
BREWSTER

IT HAD BEEN OVER a year since Anna's brother died in the war to end all wars. Anna and Eddie anticipated their marriage would happen very soon, but another tragic event gave them a pause in their plans.

The Spanish Flu pandemic reared its ugly head in the spring of 1918. It reoccurred in the fall and winter of the same year, becoming more deadly with each wave of sickness. Then, as quickly as it had appeared, it stopped its deadly scourge in the spring of 1919. Through people's own immunity and the tragic statistic of 50-100 million people dying worldwide, it mutated into a less deadly seasonal virus.

Anna and Eddie thought it better to wait to get married. Asking her mother and brothers to travel to the city could possibly expose them to the consequences of catching the flu, or maybe even death. It wasn't worth the risk.

Finally, the wedding date was settled. The joyous event was to take place on June 10, 1920, at Our Lady of the Assumption Catholic Church in Millbury. Anna had previously registered at St. Brigid's on the other side of town, but because Eddie had been baptized at Assumption, it was decided to have the ceremony at his church.

The Gilberts volunteered their family homestead for the reception. It was going to be a small but very romantic wedding. According to Anna, even Prohibition couldn't damper the festivities. She usually bubbled over, explaining it to anyone who'd listen, including Martha.

The teenager was giddy. She had never been involved in a wedding of someone she was close to. "Tell me about your dress."

Anna sat next to her charge in Martha's bedroom one afternoon before summer vacation. "Mrs. Gilbert is making my dress. She said she would give me the latest tea-length, hanky-hem skirt. It's going to be like a dream."

"What about your hair?"

"I'm getting it bobbed. I found the most darling cloche hat."

"Will you have a long veil?"

"I hope so. Lace is very expensive. I've been looking around but can't find anything in my price range."

Martha grew silent. "I wonder if my mother has anything up in the attic."

"Would you ask her for me?"

"I'll ask her tonight."

"Oh, thank you, Martha."

By the end of that day, Mrs. Deering presented Anna with a beautiful piece of lace, imported from Vienna and perfect for a long veil that would trail on the floor. As Anna exited the door to the back yard, she carried the lace wrapped in a white sheet. She saw Eddie standing by his car, patiently waiting to take his beloved home.

With a broad smile, he opened the front passenger door. "You are glowing."

"I am." Anna kissed her fiancé and jumped onto the car seat.

Eddie climbed in next to her. He kept smiling as Anna explained where she had gotten the beautiful lace for her veil.

"Have you decided what you're going to wear as the groom-to-be?"

"Yes, I have."

"Well, tell me."

Eddie took a deep breath. "I'm having my best three-piece suit cleaned and pressed. My mother found a white wing-tip collar shirt with matching bow tie. And... my father has given me his pearl-studded cufflinks that he wore on his wedding day."

Anna sat back, relieved in his choices. "Thank you, Eddie. It will certainly be a fairy-tale wedding with you as my prince."

The Gilbert household was all abuzz on June 10. The Horvaths arrived from Brewster the day before in Thomas's old Chevy one-ton truck, paid for with a lot of extra savings on his part and a buddy who needed to sell it... quickly. Mother Horvath sat inside the cab with Thomas. Louis braved the weather outside, on the truck's back bed, next to the family's wedding gift, a lovely maple rocker that Louis had made in school.

Rosalia stayed with the Gilberts, and the boys went to Eddie's parents. It was a packed house for both families. No one minded. It was what you did for family.

The wedding ceremony was quick but made longer because of the traditional Holy Mass. Our Lady of the Assumption was large and built in the style of most Catholic churches, resembling a cross. There was a large central aisle, or nave, that led to the altar, with rows of pews on either side. Two small side altars honoring Joseph, the father of Jesus, and Mary, the mother of Jesus, flanked the ornate center altar, which was built in the Baroque style.

Anna imagined herself a princess walking through a castle with Eddie as her prince. That night, he carried her over the threshold of their honeymoon suite at the St. Charles Hotel in Millbury.

46

Present Day
BREWSTER

AFTER LUNCH, THE SKIES grew cloudy. The girls looked bored. I went up to the hayloft above Paul's studio and found Danny's old Nintendo 64. It was kept in a big, plastic storage container along with several game cartridges. I grabbed Donkey Kong 64.

Once downstairs in the living room, I called out to the girls, "Who wants to go back in time?"

They both looked at their crazy aunt.

"What do you mean?" asked Madeline.

Jane looked closer. "Is that an old Nintendo?"

I started to hook it up to the television. "It sure is."

The girls looked curious.

"Just be careful. Your Cousin Danny would be upset if you broke it."

Jane stood up. "Don't worry. I'll take care of it."

I left them to start the laundry, listening to the familiar gaming sounds from when Danny was small chiming in the background. I put the sheets in the washer and went outside to see if the clouds might pass over us or bring some rain. I've always loved the smell of fresh sheets from a clothesline. I decided to take a chance and hooked the clothes poles onto the rope.

As I turned to go back inside, I thought I heard some activity next door on the empty property. It sounded like someone was talking and branches cracking underfoot. I listened again. There was definitely someone walking around.

I returned inside to check on the girls. They were still glued to the screen, enjoying the old game.

I wanted to see what was going on next door, so after a quick spritz of bug spray, I wandered into the woods and headed toward the spot where we'd found the old suitcase.

The sounds got louder but were still garbled. Concerned that they were coming from a place I didn't want anyone to know about, like the suitcase area, I kept walking but a little slower, as I wanted to see who was there but not get myself noticed.

After a few minutes, I could see two men. One was blond and short, the other looked like the man from the Brier Lane house. What are they doing here? Most importantly, they were standing near the area where we found the suitcase. I wondered how they knew where it was. Or had they just stumbled upon the location through dumb luck?

I started to approach them but stopped to hide behind the stump of a large fallen tree and watch. As they were looking down, I heard a cell phone ring. Some more unintelligible conversation transpired, and then they turned around and hurried back toward Mrs. McPhee's property line.

I walked back to my house. Something was up, and I wanted to know what those men knew that I didn't.

47

Present Day
BREWSTER

MRS. MCPHEE LEANED against two stacked plastic storage tubs to get a better view of the two men traipsing across the next-door property. One hand patted the second fifty-dollar bill stored in her blue-flowered polyester blouse pocket, while the other reached for binoculars that were perched on top of the dark-green lid of the highest tub.

Penelope circled her pants leg. "Such excitement, sweetie. Almost better than my soaps."

She bent over to scratch Penelope's head. When she resumed her position, the two men had turned around and were heading back toward her. "That's interesting. What'd I miss?"

Mrs. McPhee waited until they reached their car, then she descended down the top steps of the porch. Penelope followed her and went to greet the strangers. She rubbed against Tommy's calf.

"*A-chew!*" The blond guy sneezed. He threw a kick, sending Penelope into the air.

"Hey! Cut that out." Mrs. McPhee hurried to scoop up her cat.

Tommy held his hand over his nose. "Get it out of here." He rushed to open the car door.

Max stood by the driver's side.

Cradling Penelope, Mrs. McPhee narrowed her eyes at both men and then announced, "I'll call you if I see anything else important, but you'd better leave him behind." She gestured to the blond guy.

Max shouted back, "Okay! I'll be waiting." He turned to Tommy and said, "Get inside, and shut the door."

The old woman stroked Penelope's head as she watched the SUV pull out onto the road. "Don't worry, my sweet. That Tommy person will never try to hurt you again." She headed for the porch. "I'll make sure of that."

As Max and Tommy drove back to the Sea Pines Inn, Tommy kept sneezing.

"What's the matter with you?"

"I'm allergic to cats." Tommy wiped his nose with the back of his hand. "Can I turn on the radio?" Tommy reached for the dial.

"No." Max gripped the steering wheel.

Tommy occupied himself with checking emails on his phone.

By the time they pulled onto the inn's driveway, Tommy was eager to get out of the car and find his nose spray.

Max stared out over the steering wheel. With no eye contact, he quietly said, "I'll call you when I need you."

"Yeah." Tommy hurried to his car then grabbed his inhaler from the glove box. The presence of a cat and his allergic reactions always made him feel vulnerable. His father made fun of him and said he was pathetic. Annoyed, he peeled out of the Sea Pines parking lot.

Max held his phone a few seconds, as if trying to decide if he should return a call to his ex-wife, Roberta. It had been a bitter divorce. He shifted his weight in the driver's seat, hit her number, and then waited for her to pick up.

Her voice was angry. "Max?"

"Yeah. What's up?"

"Where are you?" She gave him no time to answer, her questions coming in rapid-fire. "What are you up to? Are you aware that some people are looking for you? I don't want anything to do with you and your hairbrained schemes." She stopped to take a breath.

"Slow down, Roberta. Let me answer." He remembered how she'd always questioned his whereabouts and hated his gambling. Her quick words raised the hairs on his neck, just like before.

"I'm waiting. So, answer me."

"Who are the people you're talking about?"

"They came to the house. You know I don't like that."

"Who came to the house?"

"Two men. They said something about the restaurant that closed. If I recall, you said it was a great investment. Typical of you. Never thinking things through. Taking chances."

"What did they say, and what did you tell them?" Max's leg started to bounce in a nervous tic he'd always had.

Her voice suddenly changed. "Not much, until they mentioned one thing."

"What?"

"After I said I rarely talk to you, since the divorce, I told them you were on Cape Cod."

Peeved that she had told them anything, he held back his anger.

"Then, one of the two men turned and asked me if Stevie was having fun at UMass Amherst. Said he remembered that the Central dorms were kind of wild and that your son should be careful." There was silence on Roberta's end.

Max was at a loss for words when he heard that the guys knew about Stevie. Was his son in danger? Another few seconds dragged on with no one talking. "Don't worry, Roberta, I'll never let anything happen to Stevie. I promise you. I'll take care of it."

"He'll be home next week for summer vacation."

"Good," said Max. "He's safer with you."

"You better take care of this whole mess and quick."

Max agreed, saying with determination in his voice, "I promise."

The last thing Roberta said before she hung up was, "You owe me for all the crap and heartache you've put me through. Stevie was the only good thing you've ever given me."

48

Present Day
BREWSTER

THE SUN PEEKED from behind some clouds as I finished hanging the sheets on the clothesline. Inside, I found the girls still enthused with Nintendo. As I walked past them toward Paul's studio, the phone rang. It was Molly.

"Hi, Mom."

"Hi, honey. How's everything going? Got your classroom set up yet?"

"No, just starting. I have plenty of time before school starts. I have some really cool ideas to decorate the room for the kids."

"That's wonderful. How is Peter?"

"Great. He found a job in Milford. Here's the best news yet. You know we've been looking for a house to lease close to the Millbury schools. And a few weeks ago, remember I mentioned to you and Dad that we went to see an interesting old house that used to be a barn?"

"Yes, I recall."

"But we couldn't move in until the fall? Well, there's been a change in plans. I'm standing in the old house's kitchen."

"What? Why didn't you call us? We could have helped you move."

"I've been so busy since graduation, and I knew the girls were coming, plus all your remodeling… All I can say is, surprise!"

"Oh, my goodness. I can't believe it." I sat down at the small desk by the door that leads into the old barn, now an art gallery for Paul's art.

"Mom, it's so exciting. Peter and I have made a lot of friends here, mostly through the other teachers. It's been wonderful. We had been staying with friends, and then we got the call from the rental agency that we could get into the house right away."

"When can we come and visit?"

"How about tomorrow?"

"That sounds good. I'm sure the girls would love to come. They still have a week left of their time with us. Let me go ask your father if he can get away. My schedule is clear."

"Okay. Call me back."

I hurried out the door to find Paul. "Guess what?"

"I can't guess. Tell me." Paul never liked guessing games; he preferred teasing.

I told him everything, beginning with the two men I had tried to follow in the woods and ending with Molly's surprise. "Can you get away tomorrow?"

"First, will you please be careful. Second, I think I can get away. Let me make a phone call to a client who was coming over tomorrow. They said they were not in a hurry for the painting."

"Okay, let me know ASAP. Love you." I went to find the girls.

Paul echoed back plus one extra word, as he always does. "Love you more."

The next morning, the drive to Millbury was fairly easy. We first stopped at Dunkin' for coffee before crossing the Bourne bridge and then drove 495 to the turnpike, finally connecting with Route 146 and landing on Main Street, in Millbury.

As we turned down Burbank Street, we passed old rock walls and white clapboard houses. The road was uphill and twisty, but

Molly's directions were easy to follow. Before we knew it, we had turned down their driveway, and I could see Molly waving at us.

It was a shared driveway, with the original small house to the property to our left and Molly's leased house on the right. I got out to give her a hug.

Molly broke away, bubbling with excitement. "I talked with the woman who lives in the main house. She said the property dates back to 1890, and our house was originally the old barn. It was converted into a house sometime at the turn of the century."

"Well, let's go in. I can hardly wait to see it." I let Molly lead the way, while the girls trailed behind us and Paul walked around to inspect the outside of the house.

Once inside, Molly became the perfect tour guide. "Pretty soon, I bet I'll know all the nooks, crannies, and secrets of this house. Peter's excited, too."

With three bedrooms upstairs and one down, there was plenty of room, if or when Peter and Molly got married. They might even buy the house. I liked Peter and had high hopes for the two of them.

As we went upstairs, I noticed the bathroom was odd. I had to step up to get into the tiny narrow room, which contained only a toilet and a sink. The downstairs bathroom had a tub and shower; a little inconvenient, being so far away from the upstairs bedrooms, but adequate for two young people.

Peter came in. He was trim and athletic, with a full black beard. Molly gave him a hug, and so did I.

"Mrs. Caldwell, good to see you." Peter went to wash his hands in the kitchen and then joined us in the living room. "What do you think of the place?"

"It's very cozy and interesting." I walked toward the front windows. When I turned around to catch the view to the back of the house, I felt a little dizzy. "Oh, oh." I looked away. "The archway looks a bit off. I think it's making me dizzy."

"Oh, Mom, it's an old house, so all the floors are crooked, and the walls are not straight."

"Well, the best way to fix this problem is to hang a planter on each side of the room opening. That way, it distracts your eye away from wanting to see something perfectly straight. It's an old trick."

Peter spoke up. "Mrs. C., I'll get right on that and hang a planter on each side of the doorway."

Molly added, "That's a great idea. It was bothering me, too."

My stomach seemed to settle, and I grew curious about what was under us. "Can we go down into the basement?"

"Absolutely." Molly looked toward the door, only to see her Dad come in. "Just in time, Dad. We're going down into the dungeon."

I saw Paul smile. "I wouldn't miss the most important part of this old house."

Molly opened the door. "Follow me."

All of us went single-file down the narrow steps. After a quick turn to our right, the basement opened before us. The foundation was made of field stone, just like a lot of old Cape Cod houses. I noticed a few sections were recently mudded with cement. Toward the rear of the basement, older cement was crumbling between the stones. Peter began to show Paul the furnace and wiring. I thought it looked up to code, but it was old and in need of repair.

I wandered over to the other end, by the steps, to go upstairs. I was fascinated with an old door that had two small glass windows across the top. "Where does this lead to?"

Molly came near me. "I think it goes to the outside. We haven't opened it yet."

Peter joined us, reached for the doorknob, and pulled. It didn't budge.

Paul tried to open it with no luck.

Peter tried once more. Nothing. "I guess it's just as well. I'm not worried about anyone getting in. I'll take a look at it later."

I moved closer and tried to see through the darkened windows at the top of the door. It was totally black.

Molly started for the steps. "Who wants some lemonade?"

I was thirsty. "Sounds good to me."

49

June 11, 1920
BREWSTER

AFTER THE WEDDING, Louis was anxious to search Anna's room before the Horvaths left for Cape Cod. His fifteen-year-old brain was impulsive in his search for the elusive treasure map from the Wilkins's property.

Thomas called up the stairs, "Louis! Come on. We're leaving in a few minutes."

"I'll be right there." He hesitated until he came up with an excuse. "I want to leave a note for Anna."

"Okay. Hurry up. Mom wants to get home before dark."

He had searched every drawer in the dresser, under the bed, and under her pillow. Finally, he centered his attention on the closet. Nothing in the shoe boxes up on the shelf or in the pockets of her clothes. Discouraged, he thought it might be in her shoes. Nothing.

In the back corner, stored in a cotton bag, were Anna's boots for winter. He turned them upside down, gave one a shake, and out dropped the map. Elated, he quickly pocketed the find then looked around and straightened anything that looked out of place.

Then, he found a pad of paper and scribbled a note to Anna, like he had said he would do.

Happy wedding to you and Eddie.
See you around.
   Louis

The Horvaths arrived home just before sunset, exhausted. Thomas cleaned the car out while their mother made herself a cup of tea. The Gilberts had packed a picnic supper for them on the ride home. She nibbled on a leftover sugar cookie with her tea.

"Louis, where are you?"

"Upstairs, Mother. I'm going to bed."

"Sleep good. Don't forget you're going to clean out the Adams's barn tomorrow."

"Yes, Mother."

Louis had forgotten. He was hoping to go back to the Wilkins property, instead. That would have to wait, he thought. He fell asleep with the map under his pillow, trying to figure out where to hide it. It would be his secret now.

The Following Day
EAST BREWSTER

Mr. Adams couldn't stand his wife's constant complaining about the barn being too cluttered and a fire hazard. He was grateful he had some help today.

"Good morning, Mr. Adams," Louis greeted the stout and graying man who was going to be his boss for the day.

"Ahhh, my good friend Louis. How's your mother?"

"Just fine. A little tired today after the trip to Millbury."

"And how was the wedding?" Mr. Adams opened the two massive doors of the red building.

"Very nice, but it's good to be home." Louis followed him into the barn. He looked around at what he thought was just junk. "Where do you want me to start?"

"In the back. I'll be over there." He pointed to the back, in the middle of the wall. "If anything looks broken, put it in this box. I'll look at it later."

Louis filled the box in less than a half hour and carried it out to the driveway. He grabbed another, bigger box and then continued his cleaning and sorting.

Mr. Adams moved closer to Louis and inspected the few salvageable things left intact against the wall. "We're making some progress."

By lunchtime, Louis had filled ten boxes with old car parts, wires, broken glass, and things he didn't know what they were. He was getting hungry.

His boss stopped looking through the boxes for anything to save and said, "Let's break for some lunch." Mr. Adams rubbed his back from all the leaning over and sat next to Louis on the edge of a picnic bench near a tall, black walnut tree.

"You're turning out to be a big help for me. Thank you."

"Mr. Adams, there's a small trunk in there, but I couldn't open it to see if there's anything in it."

His employer looked up to the sky in thought. "My boy, you've asked me about a very interesting piece." He took a sip of his coffee. "Can you keep a secret?"

"Sure." He thought of the old map and how he would never tell anyone about it.

"Come on. Let's go take a look-see."

The small trunk was about fourteen by eighteen and sixteen inches high. At first glance, it looked like it was made of iron. "Want to help me pick it up and take it outside?"

"Okay." Louis leaned down to lift but struggled, as did Mr. Adams.

"It's real heavy. One reason I never paid much attention to it as the years went by and I got older."

The two managed to lift it and slowly walked it out into the sunshine. Louis noticed a big key sticking out of the lock on the front.

Mr. Adams pulled a stool close.

Louis knelt down to open it. He turned the key and heard a few clicks and thuds. He tried to lift the lid, but it wouldn't budge. "It must be stuck." The young man looked frustrated. He kept turning the key back and forth and pushing up on the top. Finally, he threw the key on the ground. "It won't open. I give up."

"Take it easy, fella. This is a Pirate Strong Box. I got it when I sailed with Josiah Hardy out of Chatham, on the clipper ship, *Ocean Pearl*."

Louis eased up on his frustration. "You went to sea?"

"I sure did. We were coming from Spain, loaded with goods and headed for Boston, back in 1871. No one wanted the dang thing, cuz no one could open it. And as you can see, it was downright heavy, made out of wrought iron."

Louis ran his hands over the sides and top, looking for a way to open it.

"Do you want it?" Mr. Adams cocked his head and waited for an answer. "I bet you could figure it out."

Louis stayed quiet. He thought it would be a great place to hide the map. "Okay. I'll take it." Then he wondered how he was going to get it home.

"Here's the deal." Mr. Adams lit up his pipe. "I'll pay you for today, and maybe you could give me an extra half day tomorrow, in payment for me telling you the trunk's secret."

"It's a deal." The two men shook hands.

The next morning, Louis appeared on the Adams property, eager to get his half day of work done. The trunk sat inside the barn door. Thomas said he would come and retrieve the trunk on his lunch hour and bring it home for his brother.

The hour struck 11:00 a.m. Mr. Adams signaled to Louis that he was done for the day. Louis joined him near the open barn door.

"Are you ready?" The older man had a twinkle in his eye.

Louis nodded his head.

"Okay. Run your hands on the right side of the chest near the top. Push anything you see that sticks out."

The young man did as he was told. There were three buttons that looked like a decoration near the top. He pushed and tried to slide two of them with no luck. The last one seemed to move a little. Louis tried again. He took both hands and pushed to the side. He pushed again, and a small rectangular shape slid sideways to reveal another button underneath. He looked up at Mr. Adams.

"Go on, push that one."

Louis shoved his finger into the hole and pushed as hard as he could. He heard a loud clank. Then, he moved to the front and lifted. The lid opened. He sat back on his thighs and wiped perspiration from his forehead. He had done it.

"Good job, Louis!" Mr. Adams pointed to two long bars that ran from one side of the lid to the other and connected to the hidden button with a spring action. Louis looked inside. It was empty, but he didn't care. It was a secret hiding place for his map.

He ran his finger over the fake keyhole that locked the trunk when the key was turned. He smiled in satisfaction. "Pretty clever."

"Ain't it? When I figured it out, I was so proud of myself. That fake keyhole is an escutcheon." Mr. Adams patted Louis on the back. "It's called an Armada chest. I was told it came from the Spanish Armada fleet of 1588."

Just then, Thomas pulled onto the driveway.

"Thanks, Mr. Adams. This trunk is a real gift." Louis locked the trunk. He made sure the secret button was concealed and hid the trick key in his pocket before Thomas came near.

When the boys lifted the trunk, Thomas yelled out, "What the heck do you got in this thing?"

Louis smiled. "That's for me to know and you to never find out."

50

1920
MILLBURY

THE NEWLY MARRIED couple had planned to live with Eddie Wallace's parents until they found something of their own. His sister had moved out, so the whole upstairs was empty.

This was moving day. After Anna finished packing her suitcases at the Gilberts' house, she threw her shoes into a canvas bag for transporting to their new home, never bothering to inspect the cotton bag that held her boots. They were shoved into the canvas pouch next to the loose shoes. The map never crossed her mind, either. Her life was too exciting right now.

Eddie waited outside for Anna's signal that she was finished. She called out the upstairs window, "I'm ready."

He jumped into action. He flew up the stairs, gave his new wife a kiss, and scooped up everything at one time in both arms.

"My, you're strong." Anna was in love with this handsome man.

Across town they drove, anxious to set up housekeeping. The Wallaces were very gracious with letting the newlyweds arrange the furniture upstairs any way they wanted. The two bedrooms upstairs served as their home. The twin bed was taken apart and stored in the long closet under the eave to make room for a double bed. The smaller of the two rooms became a sitting room for them, to read, sew, or entertain friends. The new rocker, along with an older upholstered chair, a settee, a standing lamp, and a small table with two chairs from the Gilberts' barn, served as a cozy arrangement. The addition of a small bathroom between the rooms was a bonus.

The Deerings had given Eddie and Anna a two-day holiday after the one-night honeymoon. Wednesday morning came too soon for the couple to return to work; they wanted to stay as close to each other as possible.

Mrs. Wallace loved watching her son interact with his new bride as they ate breakfast. He was so caring and affectionate. She turned to her husband and whispered as they sipped their coffee, "They make my heart sing."

Mr. Wallace grinned and continued reading his daily paper.

Later, around 5:30 p.m., Anna and Eddie entered the kitchen after their first day of work as a married couple. Mrs. Wallace looked to her son first.

"How was your day?"

"Good. But something's different about Mr. Deering. I can't put my finger on it." Eddie pulled a chair out for Anna to sit next to him at the table. "Dad, have you heard anything over at Ivy Corset?"

"Nope."

Eddie helped himself to the beef stew. "Well, I know the new Deering Corset Company that Mr. Deering opened seems to be doing okay, but he's not his usual, talkative self."

Mr. Wallace lowered his paper. "I could never understand why, in all that's holy, Charles opened his own corset company." He returned to his daily news. "And only a few minutes from his competition, the Ivy Corset."

Anna waited for a chance to add to the conversation. "Young Martha is still her usual teenage self."

Mrs. Wallace placed the rolls on the table. "Anna, how old is Martha now?"

"She'll be turning eighteen soon."

"I wonder how long the Deerings will be needing you as a companion to their daughter."

The young bride wiped her mouth with a napkin. "I've thought about that. Maybe her mother will still want me there at the house in some capacity."

Eddie took a few more bites of his stew. "Maybe. I know I was surprised to see that Ella Jenkins, their housekeeper, left to go back with her family in New York."

Eddie's mother showed a wry smile on her face. "I hope they'll keep you on. Of course, maybe there'll be some extra work for you sooner than you think that involves a grandchild for us..."

Anna blushed.

Eddie spoke up. "Mother, don't embarrass my wife. If she wants to work for a while before we start a family, then so be it."

"I was only asking." Mrs. Wallace got up to refill her husband's coffee.

Later that night, Eddie cuddled with Anna before they fell asleep. "I meant what I said to my mother. You can decide what you want. I'm not going to tell you what to do."

Anna sat up in bed. "Oh, Eddie, I was thinking of working a while longer. I'd like to save as much money as we can, before we start our family." She leaned over to kiss him. "First, we need a house of our own. Don't you agree?"

Eddie gently rolled over onto his beloved. "Whatever you want, my love."

51

WE ARRIVED BACK HOME on the Cape from Millbury very late, so everyone slept in. In the morning, I found the girls in the kitchen, looking for something to eat. Jane had grabbed an apple as I entered the kitchen.

"You guys hungry?"

Jane nodded between bites.

"After breakfast, you want to come back outside with me? I'm curious to go and have another look at where we found the suitcase."

"I'm in." Jane looked enthused.

"Madeline, you want to join us?"

"No, thank you, I'll stay here. Uncle Paul said I could keep working on my watercolor."

Nothing appeared to be disturbed where Jane and I had found the case. That was lucky. But as Jane took a giant step over a large fallen branch, she slipped, lost her footing, and fell backward.

"Are you okay?"

"I think so." She started to push herself back upright when she stopped, turned around onto her knees, and started to brush some dirt away.

"What's the matter? Did you find something else?" As I reached for her arm to help her up, I looked on the ground and noticed the same things Jane did.

I eventually helped her up, but both of us couldn't take our eyes off what was exposed in the black soil.

"Aunt Nancy, what are those?"

"Honestly, they look like bones." I bent down to examine the cream-colored pieces. Without touching them, I grabbed a stick and pointed to the rounded piece. "This one could be part of a skull." I could see a few other bones to the side. "Maybe an arm, leg, or vertebrae. Possibly human."

Jane took a step backward.

I cautioned her. "It's okay, Jane. Just don't touch them."

"I won't. I've never seen human bones up close before. Only in science books and maybe the Natural History Museum."

"Sorry you had to see them this way." I took her hand. "Let's go back and call the police."

"The police?"

"Yes. This could be a crime scene."

As soon as we returned to the house, I called the Brewster Police and asked for Detective Gomes. Luckily, he was there.

"Tony, its Nancy Caldwell. I might be involved in another situation. I think we've found some human bones on the empty property next door to us. Can you come over?"

Without hesitation, he answered, "I'll be right there."

By the time I was finished explaining to Paul what we had found, Tony pulled into the driveway.

I met him at the side door on the deck. "Tony, glad you could come over so quickly. Come on in."

"What's going on?"

Jane appeared behind me. Madeline stood behind Jane.

"These are my nieces, visiting from Ohio." The girls gave a slight wave.

"Nice to meet you." He pulled out his notebook. "Do I need this?"

"Maybe. Come with me and I'll explain as we walk." I grabbed a hand brush.

Jane started to follow us. "Can I come too?"

"Of course. Madeline, you should probably stay inside."

"Okay, Aunt Nancy."

All three of us stood around the dug-up area. Tony crouched closer. "So, you first found a suitcase?"

"Yes. The same day Jane and I discovered the suitcase, I returned to the woods by myself and noticed some other people walking around in the area. I left. Got a call from Molly and planned to visit her the next day. Then today, Jane and I returned to the spot where we'd found the suitcase. That's when we discovered this." I waved my hand over the visible bones.

Jane tried to join the conversation. "I slipped on that." She pointed to the rounded piece in the dirt.

I spoke up. "I think they're human. What do you think, Tony?"

Tony put his notebook into his shirt pocket. "I see." We watched him take some photos with his phone. "Let me make a few calls first. I'll be right back. I'm going to get some yellow tape and cordon off the area, so we can find the location again." He left for his car. As he walked, I could see him talking on his cell.

Jane took the brush and started to sweep away some of the dirt.

I stopped her hand. "Maybe you should leave everything alone. Let the professionals do their job."

She kept staring down at the ground. "Okay. I don't want to get into trouble." She quickly called out, "Look!"

"What?"

"Over there." She pointed a short distance away from the piece that resembled the top of a skull. "See it?" She stepped closer and pointed again. "That's a metal bar or something."

I took another look then sidestepped around the bones, grabbed my stick, and lifted up some small, rusted chain links. "I think this is an old bed frame and springs, or what's left of it."

"Oh, Aunt Nancy. I can't believe it. You think this is all connected to the suitcase?"

"Pretty sure. I bet, whomever this was, he either died in his sleep or someone did him in while he was sleeping."

I could hear Tony coming back through the woods. "What did you find out from your superiors?"

"I explained the situation to them and sent the pictures. They'll get the state involved, and then the medical examiner will be called in, if needed." He took a few more photos with his phone. "We'll know more by tomorrow. Can we park in your driveway?"

"Absolutely. Whatever they need to do to find out what this is all about and who it might be is fine with me."

Tony turned back to me. "Oh, by the way, you know the man your friend found dead last year? The autopsy didn't show any evidence of foul play."

"Thanks for the info, Tony."

"No problem."

52

1924
MILLBURY

FIVE MONTHS AGO, Anna and Eddie celebrated their fourth year of married life, and Anna discovered the reason she hadn't been feeling well and was always tired. She was three months pregnant. They never expected their lives to be in so much flux.

Mr. Deering's new company was still in its growing stage, and Eddie hadn't been called into work as much as before. He decided to leave his job at the Deerings and apply at the post office. He received a job offer. With a secure government job and the possibility of advancement, they agreed that Anna, now pregnant, should also leave the Deering household.

Martha Deering, at twenty-two, had begun to travel more, especially taking long trips to Europe, funded with money from her wealthy Aunt Mary, which had resulted in Anna having her hours reduced. They both felt it was time to leave, and the Deerings agreed, giving them each a severance check for $50.

For the following months, they spent every minute of their busy day looking for the perfect house, thanks to money saved and hope in their hearts. It was Mrs. Gilbert who answered their prayers. At the other end of Burbank Street, a barn was being converted into a house and was available by September for a good price.

The future new parents jumped at the chance and made an offer, which was accepted.

On Friday the first of October, Eddie and his best friend, John Black, moved their minimal amount of furniture to the house, while Anna, pregnant seven months, mostly watched and directed the men as to where the boxes should go. With three bedrooms upstairs and one down, there was plenty of room for more furniture to fill a dining room, living room, and kitchen, if they had it, but that would be in the future.

Anna sat in the maple rocker by the front door, periodically adding to her journal. She had hoped a journal would keep her sane. She was not as fortunate as her husband, who had developed a good friendship with a co-worker at the post office. She needed a way to share her feelings and dreams, instead of keeping them bottled up inside of her. She massaged her belly as she gave directions.

"John, all the clothes go upstairs into the back bedroom."

John gave her a broad grin. "Yes, ma'am."

Mrs. Gilbert walked in behind him. "Good morning, Anna. How are you today?"

"Doing as well as expected. The doctor said things are moving along right on schedule."

"That's good to hear. I'm glad to see you sitting down." Mrs. Gilbert peered into the kitchen. "Can I make you some tea?" She withdrew a plate of cookies from a large satchel. "I made them fresh this morning." The gingerbread cookies gave a nice scent to the half-empty house.

Anna sat straighter. "They smell wonderful. I think there's a box marked pans by the stove." She started to get up.

"Stay right there, young lady. I know my way around a kitchen." Mrs. Gilbert disappeared from Anna's view as Eddie carried in a mattress.

Anna watched him struggle through the doorway. "I wish I could help you."

"Nope. The doctor said no lifting." He began to push the mattress up the stairs.

John appeared at the top of the stairway. "Hold on, Eddie. Let me give you a hand." He grabbed the other end of the bulky rectangle.

In a few minutes, the two men returned to Anna's view and laughed all the way outside to John's truck for the next load. It brought some calmness to Anna as she sat in the rocker, feeling frustrated and helpless that she couldn't contribute to the work.

By evening of the same day, the big move was complete. Mrs. Gilbert had generously brought over fried chicken, potato salad, and a chocolate cake. After she finished setting the table for Eddie, Anna, and John, she called out before she left for home, "Enjoy my friends."

Anna sat first, saying, "Everything looks delicious. What a treat."

The two men repeated in unison, "It looks delicious."

Anna took her time eating while she watched her husband and his best friend devour the satisfying food. She looked contented as she listened to the clink and clank of their knives and forks, plus their "oohs" and "ahhs." The fresh smells of fried food, the tangy vinegar aroma of German potato salad, and the anticipation of the sweetness of a piece of chocolate cake was pleasing.

By 6:30 p.m., John said his goodbyes. "Hope you two sleep well tonight in your new home."

Eddie grinned. "We will." He walked John out to his truck.

Anna took her time as she cleaned the dishes.

Eddie came from behind her and kissed her on the neck. He grabbed a dish cloth and began drying the plates. "I love you so much."

Anna smiled. "Love you, too." She placed the last glass on the drain board. "John is such a good friend. I'm pleased he asked you to join him in the Knights of Columbus at the church."

"Yeah. They seem to be a nice group. I'm looking forward to it."

53

October 19, 1924
MILLBURY

ANNE CALLED HER HUSBAND to come outside on the porch. "Eddie! Come quick."

He joined her outside.

She pointed to the dusky sky. "Look at that airplane."

"Yeah, I see it." He clenched his fist.

"It has red lights under it in the shape of a cross."

"And, if you look closer, you can see the letters, *KKK*."

"Oh, my goodness. Shame on them." She held her swollen belly.

"They've been holding meetings all over New England and gettin' beat back."

Anna turned to Eddie. "You need to promise me you'll never go to any of their meetings."

Eddie was quiet.

"Eddie, please. You're going to be a father soon. I need you to be safe."

"No need to worry about me."

Several hours later, Eddie blew a kiss to his wife as she lay sleeping. The clock ticked closer to 11:00 p.m. He crept down the stairs of their new home and into a shed in the back yard. He grabbed his baseball bat, looked around for anything else he might need, and decided the wooden bat was good enough.

Once in his car, he headed for the post office on Main and Southbridge Street in Worcester, for the night shift on the loading dock, and then drove right past it toward the fairgrounds by Elm Park. He didn't like lying to Anna about why he wasn't going to work tonight.

As he drove, he gripped the wheel and prayed that no harm would come to him or his fellow Knights of Columbus. He thought it was important that the Klan be put in its place. There was no room in America for hatred and prejudice against anyone, especially Catholics.

He pulled onto the grass next to John's truck and stood tall beside his friend. In the distance, they could see the glow of torches carried by over a thousand Klansmen. "What's the plan?"

"According to McBride, we wait until they get close to their cars, then it's free rein." John carried a two-by-four with a nail on the end.

Eddie could see some younger men holding lumpy burlap bags. They were ready and waiting to hurl stones at the cars of the men dressed in white robes. Before he knew it, the riot started.

The Klansmen's cars had their windows smashed or were lit on fire. Eddie threw a few swings at the headlights of two cars. He watched men jump onto the running boards and assault the drivers. He had never liked violence, but he couldn't stop thinking about how the KKK had already threatened many churches across the state and tried to burn them down. Some had been totally destroyed. The thought of his child growing up in an anti-Catholic and prejudiced society made him swing harder at the next cars he encountered.

By one in the morning, the Klansmen were gone. No police had come to break up the riot or protect the Klansmen.

The two men stood in the field, looking at the burned-out cars and the aftermath of a justified anger, at least in their eyes.

John wiped the sweat from his brow. "We showed them. Didn't we?"

"I guess so. I'm relieved it's over and they left."

"They won't be meeting around here for a long while."

Eddie walked toward his car. "Good riddance."

John walked next to him. "I still can't imagine these guys accusing good-standing citizens, like the Irish, Italians, those French Canadians, and us Catholics, of taking jobs away from them."

Eddie carried his bat low. "There's plenty enough work to go around. They were even preaching against the teachers."

John reached his truck first. "I'd never do anything to hurt this great country and our way of life."

"You're right, my friend." As Eddie settled behind the wheel, he noticed his hand was bleeding. He grabbed his handkerchief, wrapped it around the palm of his hand, and drove home.

Anna woke early the next morning, surprised that Eddie was already up. She quickly went into the bathroom to use the toilet. She found the sink spattered with blood and Eddie's bloody handkerchief in the waste basket. Her heart skipped a beat.

She called out, "Eddie! Where are you?" She held her puffy stomach as she moved as fast as she could down the stairs. "Eddie, where are you?"

She found him sitting at the kitchen table. His head drooped over his swollen hand. He looked up at her. "I'm sorry."

"What happened?"

"Oh, Anna, I'm so sorry. I never should have gone."

"Gone? Gone where? I thought you went to work." She sat opposite him, trying to get a look at his bandaged hand. "Tell me, what happened?"

He sat a little straighter. "We went to the fairgrounds."

"Who did you go with? And why?"

"John and I went, with some of the Knights and others who wanted to make things right. We went to where the Klansmen were holding a rally. Things got out of control."

"You promised you wouldn't do anything dangerous." She reached for his injured hand.

Eddie pulled his hand back but then slowly stretched it out for her to inspect. "I must have gotten a piece of glass or metal in it. I never even noticed until I got back into the car."

"Oh, Eddie." Anna gently unwrapped the bandages.

He winced in pain.

When she could see how badly the skin was swollen, she stopped touching it. "We need to get to the doctor. I'll drive."

"You can't, Anna. You don't have your license yet, and can you even fit behind the steering wheel?"

"I'm stronger than you think. Give me a minute to get dressed." Anna climbed the stairs as quickly as she could. Soon, she returned. "Get in the car."

Eddie obeyed his wife's command. The drive to Worcester seemed like an eternity, even though it was less than fifteen minutes.

Eddie reminded his wife, "It's right before the railroad bridge and on the right side of Green street."

Anna gripped the steering wheel. "I see it. I hope Dr. Halloran is there."

"I'm sure someone will be there to help us." Eddie took some deep breaths to calm himself. He told himself everything would be okay.

That night, at home in Millbury, Eddie lay on the bed upstairs. Anna sat by his side, watching him. The bleeding had stopped, the piece of metal removed, and a dose of iodine had been administered. Anna could hear the doctor's orders in her head.

"It's a wait-and-see process. Your husband is strong and healthy."

She distracted her scary thoughts about her husband by writing in her journal. She wrote about her childhood and how she had saved the family with Mr. Wilkins's gold pirate coins. Also, that the map was safe with her, for the future.

In the morning, Anna was set to wash the wound, apply a generous dose of honey, and wrap fresh bandages. Then, she would repeat this routine in the evening, unless Eddie needed his wound dressed more frequently. She was haunted by Eddie's cries as the doctor dressed the wound with stinging iodine.

54

AFTER TONY LEFT, I tried to start dinner but couldn't concentrate on what to make. No one seemed to be hungry. I settled on pizza and a salad. That would be easy.

As I retrieved the pizza from the chest freezer in the laundry room, I looked out to the wooded property next door and wondered if Mrs. McPhee would be interested in what we had found. Maybe she could contribute some information to the mystery.

Jane came into the kitchen and looked like she had a lot of questions. I secretly hoped I could answer them. "You like pizza, don't you?"

"Oh, yeah." She peaked at the pizza box to see what kind we were going to eat. "Aunt Nancy, I was wondering."

Here it comes, I thought. "What about?"

"How could a body just be there all these years, without anyone noticing?" She sat at the table with a glass of soda.

"Years ago, people did whatever they wanted to do. There were rules, but not many. People would just dump things that they couldn't repair."

"Like those antique cars I've seen in the back of your woods?"

"Yes." I turned on the oven for the pizza. "The woods would eventually swallow them up. You couldn't see anything, if they were buried far enough and deep enough."

"But what about the body?"

"It was common to bury someone on your property, if you had enough land. No one really cared."

"That's just creepy. I can't imagine having people buried in your yard."

"Thank goodness, times have changed." The stove chimed, signaling the temperature was hot enough. I slipped the pizza into the oven.

Plates and napkins were gathered on a tray. I handed it to Jane. "Would you mind taking this to the porch?

"No problem."

I followed behind her with a pitcher of iced water. "You know, I was thinking of going over to talk with Mrs. McPhee tomorrow."

"Can I come?"

"If you want to."

"She seems so lonely. Can I make her some cookies?"

"That would be very nice. I'll help you after dinner."

By 9:00 p.m., the chocolate chip cookies were cool enough to pack into a Tupperware container. Jane nestled the final treat in and closed the lid.

"Do you think she'll like them?"

"If she doesn't, that means more for us." I patted her on the back. "You did a nice thing."

"Thanks, Aunt Nancy."

After breakfast, Jane and I grabbed the cookies and headed into the woods. No word had come from the police as of 9:30 a.m. We slowly passed the yellow tape surrounding the supposed crime scene, stopping for another look before we headed toward Mrs. McPhee's.

Jane looked over to me. "I'm a little nervous. What if she gets really mad?"

"Don't worry. I'll be right with you. I have a hunch she'll like the cookies."

We approached the porch door. I rapped on the side of the wooden door frame. After about five seconds, I knocked a little louder. I could see Jane was uneasy, so I reassured her with a smile. After another few seconds of no response, we turned to step away to leave. From behind me, I heard the door open.

"What do you want?"

"Mrs. McPhee, I'm Nancy Caldwell from next door. Sorry to bother you, but my niece, Jane," the young girl stepped closer to show the Tupperware, "thought you might enjoy some of her fresh-baked cookies."

"Why do you think I would like that, young lady? You don't even know me." Her cat inched toward the opened door. "Get back here, Penelope." The gray-haired kitty circled Mrs. McPhee's ankle.

"I thought everyone liked fresh-baked cookies." Jane opened the lid for the woman to see what was inside.

"Huh, they do smell good. I guess I could try one, to see if they really are tasty."

My estranged neighbor stepped back to let us through her doorway. It was the first time since we'd moved in that I had ever seen the inside of her house. I felt honored. "Thank you, Mrs. McPhee."

"I'll make some tea." Mrs. McPhee left us alone in the living area. Penelope followed her into the kitchen.

Before we could sit down, we both stared at the scattered newspapers, *TV Guides*, and piles of old mail, trying to find a clean spot to sit. Jane settled into a small, tufted chair after moving a colorful Afghan to the side.

I moved some newspapers to the end of a loveseat in front of a low, wooden coffee table before sitting on the small couch. I motioned for Jane to put the cookies on the coffee table. I shifted some orange medicine bottles aside to make room for the

Tupperware. Then, we sat in silence. I tried to capture any details of this secretive woman from the few pictures, knick-knacks, and furniture displayed around the tiny room. I noticed Jane was staring at a shotgun leaning against the door jam. It took me by surprise, but before I could say anything to Jane, Mrs. McPhee returned with three cups of tea.

She placed them next to the cookies. "I hope you don't take sugar, cuz all I have is honey."

I spoke up. "Honey is just fine.'

Jane added, "Can I have some water?"

With a slight annoyance on her face, my neighbor replied, "No tea for you? *Hmph*. Go dump your tea and get yourself some water."

I opened the lid of the Tupperware; the cookies did smell delicious. "I'm glad you like my niece's gift. I've also come to tell you some news."

Jane rejoined us with water in hand.

"I figured there was something else. I'm not donating to charity, nor do I want to volunteer for anything." She reached for a cookie.

"No, it's nothing like that. It's about next door, the empty property."

"What's going on over there? I saw activity yesterday but couldn't get a good look-see."

"In the beginning of the week, Jane and I found an old suitcase in the woods next door."

"I saw you carry something out." She nibbled on her second treat.

"The next day, I noticed some men in the woods. That worried me."

"So what? That's private property. No business of yours, is it?"

"No, you're right. When they left, I returned with Jane to see if anyone had disturbed the location where the suitcase had been found. By accident, we uncovered human bones in the same area." I waited for that to sink in.

With her mouth full, Mrs. McPhee said, "That's odd."

I expected a bit more of a reaction. "Can you recall anything about the property? Who owns it now? I'm trying to figure out who the bones might belong to."

"Not really. I mind my own business. Keep to myself."

"Did you ever notice any activity next door, after you first moved in?"

"No. Brewster was very quiet then. Not like now."

"That old white house across the street from both of us, did you know Mrs. Bangs who lived there?"

"You mean Dottie?"

"Yes. When I researched our house, I took a peek at the town records, to see how old it was, and that name came up as an owner."

Another cookie seemed to soften her tone. "Well, back about forty years, I would sit with Dottie every other day of the week. Her son hired me to watch her." Mrs. McPhee sipped her tea. "She told me some crazy stories. Like when she was young, she'd be up in her bedroom and would see a man walk out of the woods, across the street from her house, and head toward Orleans. He'd be dressed in a black suit."

"You mean the woods between our houses?"

"Yup."

I looked at Jane to see if she'd caught that bit of information. Her eyes were wide open, so I knew she'd heard it.

Mrs. McPhee continued, "Mind you, there was no house there, because it had burned down. Crazy stories from a crazy lady."

The room fell silent for several awkward seconds.

"We called the police about the bones. We're waiting on them to call back."

Mrs. McPhee's demeanor quickly changed. Suddenly, the neighborly attitude was replaced with the sour Mrs. McPhee I remembered.

"You two should leave now. I don't have time to be talking with you anymore. I've got some business to take care of." She got up, opened the door wide, and waited for us to take the hint to leave. "Thanks for the cookies."

As we walked back home, Jane commented, "That was weird."

"Yes, that was a bit strange. I bet she's hiding some information. She stopped being friendly when I mentioned the police."

Jane spoke up. "What's with the gun by the door?"

I raised my eyebrows. "I saw it, too. You know, everyone's different. Some people feel safe when there's a gun in the house. Personally, that's not for me, even after all the things that have happened to me over the years."

We reached the old oak tree at the edge of our property.

Jane stopped for a second and asked, "What about the man Mrs. Bangs said she saw coming out of the woods? Do you think that could be the same man who owned the suitcase? Could the bones be his?"

55

Present Day
BREWSTER

THE COOKIES DID indeed taste good. Mrs. McPhee ate several more in front of the TV while she waited for Max to answer her call.

Max picked up. "What's up?"

"You should probably get over here. I've got news for you."

"What?"

"Make sure you bring my money." She hung up.

As Mrs. McPhee continued eating, she thought about that lady and her niece. Their visit was pleasant enough, but fifty dollars cash sure beats a few social niceties any day.

Max arrived within the hour. "What's so important? It'd better be worth fifty bucks."

"That Caldwell lady came over to tell me that, yesterday, she found an old suitcase and the remains of a body next door."

Max stared at her. "What did you say?"

Mrs. McPhee held out her hand for the money.

He struggled to pull his wallet out.

She kept her hand extended, palm up, and waited until Max filled it before continuing. "She called the police, so they'll be crawling all over the place, snooping around."

He was quiet, then asked, "What else?"

"Not much more. I'll let you know if the police come by and when they've left, so you can inspect that property in peace, or search for whatever it is you're looking for."

"I'm not looking for anything. Of course, if it becomes a crime scene, maybe I can get the land for a better price."

56

Present Day
BREWSTER

ON THE WAY BACK to Brier Lane, Max kept going over what he knew about the empty lot. It was once owned by a Mr. Wilkins. His Grandma Anna had said there was a treasure map, courtesy of Wilkins. So, it made sense that whatever he needed to succeed in his mission had to be stashed somewhere in the Brier Lane house, where she grew up.

The dead body probably wasn't connected to anything, or was it? He was also running out of time. He decided that a week was enough at the Sea Pines Inn. He checked out and then drove directly to Brier Lane. It wouldn't be long before the Mica brothers picked up his trail, and now that the police had their attention on the property, he had to find something sooner rather than later.

He stopped to pick up a deli sandwich from Brewster Market. While waiting for his order, he called Tommy. "Hey, can you meet me at the Brier Lane house?"

By the time Max arrived, Tommy was already there with a full car. Max got out of his SUV. "What's going on with all the stuff in your car?"

"I was going to talk to you about that." Tommy stuffed his hands into his pockets. "I got kicked out of my apartment. The landlord is selling, and they wanted me out."

Max headed for the porch. "Not my problem."

Tommy hurried to open the door of the house. "I was thinking maybe I could crash here for a while. You know, watch the property for you."

"Well, I'm living here now, and I don't need anyone else bothering me."

"You left Sea Pines?"

"Yeah." Max threw his sandwich on the cluttered kitchen table.

"Boss, I don't have any other place to go." Tommy stepped aside as Max passed him to get his suitcases from the SUV.

Max stopped short from lifting the heavy luggage himself and turned around. "Come to think of it, might be a good idea to have you here for the dirty work." He started for the house empty-handed. "Bring my suitcase inside. I'll let you stay for a while."

Tommy jumped down the porch steps and headed for the car. "You won't regret this. You'll see. I'll be a big help."

Max rolled his eyes then sat down at the table to eat his lunch. "Grab a few garbage bags and start tearing apart that bookcase over there. Look in every book and examine each one of those figurines. Look for anything loose inside the pages or maybe something written in a book that mentions the words map, treasure, gold coins, or the name Wilkins."

"You got it, boss." He whipped the plastic black bag open.

Within the second hour, Tommy had gone through all the books and piled them in boxes that lined one wall. He looked around for his next job. He called upstairs, "Didn't find anything. What else you want me to do?"

Max came to the top of the stairs. "Check in the bathroom next to the kitchen. Throw it all out."

"Okay." Tommy shook his head in disgust. What was he doing? He was too smart to be cleaning out someone's house.

He filled a garbage bag, added it to the boxes of books piled in the corner, and returned to the bathroom. He knew he didn't have any other choice right now. His old man had thrown him out a few years ago. It was for the best; Tommy couldn't take another punch from his father. He'd have to stay in this dump. Maybe he'd find some treasure for himself. Yeah, he thought, the boss said to look for anything that pointed to gold coins.

Upstairs, Max sat on the edge of a bed, his head hung low. He got up slowly and went downstairs in search of a beer.

He found Tommy scrolling through his phone.

"Hey, get back to work." He grabbed some pretzels from an open bag on the table.

"Sure. Almost done in the bathroom. Can I have a beer?"

"Yeah. Help yourself."

"Thanks."

"When you're done, go outside and clear out the old shed."

"Okay."

Max returned to the second floor. His mind couldn't fathom any other place to look, except that old trunk in the corner, which he couldn't open. And it was driving him crazy.

57

1924
MILLBURY

FROM THE UPSTAIRS bedroom, Anna noticed the morning sun was breaking through the clouds, revealing a rosy sky. She had fallen asleep in a chair beside Eddie. He was still sleeping. With a yawn and a stretch, she heard the downstairs clock ticking a familiar sound and wondered what hour it was.

She was wearing her nightgown and robe, yet she didn't remember changing her clothes. Anna rubbed her eyes. The urge to go to the bathroom crested within her body, forcing her to literally run down the hallway before it was too late.

Bloodied bandages remained in the wastebasket by the side of the sink, a reminder of the seriousness of her husband's accident. She drank a glass of water, which helped to clear her head a little. After a quick peek on Eddie, she dressed for the day, made some coffee downstairs, and then returned to the bedroom with clean bandages and more honey.

She sat in silence for a minute, just watching him. What was to become of her, if Eddie didn't survive or was maimed, hindering his work at the post office? Suddenly, the life inside of her moved, causing her to stop and switch her thoughts to positive feelings. No, she decided. Everything will work out.

Anna leaned back, only to see Eddie stir under the covers.

He opened his eyes. "Anna, I'm sorry." He tried to reach out to her but pulled back in pain. "Damn it."

His head fell back to the pillow as Anna tenderly helped his hand lay flat against the blanket. "You slept through the night."

"Thanks to the doctor giving me that stuff over there." He looked toward the dresser where a small bottle of Bayer & Co. Heroin stared back at him.

"The doctor warned me to use it only if you really need it." She stood and hid it in the top drawer, out of sight.

Eddie turned his head to the wall.

"How about you get up and use the bathroom?"

Eddie was quiet.

"Eddie, you must get up." She started to pull the covers down.

"Leave me alone. It hurts too much."

Anna stared at her husband. She had never seen this side of him. "I'll get you some hot tea and toast. You'll feel better soon."

Eddie rolled over and stared at the closed drawer. He didn't care what the doctor said. He needed what was in that bottle. It was his body, and he knew it better than anyone. But when Eddie tried to turn in the bed, the pain took his breath away. His eyes fell back to the drawer.

With a painful determination, he swung his legs over to the side of the bed. He could hear Anna in the kitchen. His breath labored, he slowly stood, took four steps to the bureau, pulled out the drawer, and grabbed the bottle. With an aching shove of his upper arm, the drawer closed. Anna's stirring in the kitchen stopped. Eddie moved back to his bed as quickly as he could and then placed the bottle under his pillow.

When Anna returned, she found Eddie sleeping, or at least she thought he was. The tray was still on the nightstand, toast and tea untouched. She quietly left the room.

Within seconds of her shoes hitting the first squeaky step of the stairway, Eddie sat up, struggled to unscrew the lid, and then swallowed one of the fifteen white tablets. Back under the pillow went the Bayer bottle, as Eddie wondered how long it would take for him to return to work. He needed to go to work. The baby was coming. They needed him. The heroin would help him heal faster; he knew it.

The following day, Eddie was feeling better. When Anna changed his daily bandages, there were no signs of fresh blood. Later, he surprised Anna in the kitchen as she folded some laundry. He quietly came from behind her.

"I love you."

She turned. "Oh, it's so good to see you up and smiling."

Eddie sat down at the table. The Bayer bottle was hidden in the pocket of his robe. "I think I'll be able to return to work in a few days."

"Let's see what the doctor says today. You have an appointment at three o'clock."

"Whatever you say. I'll go up and get dressed."

"Okay."

By two o'clock, Eddie returned downstairs. "I'm feeling pretty good. I think I can drive myself. You stay home and get dinner ready."

"Are you sure?"

"Yes." He really did feel better. The heroin tablets masked any pain that lingered.

Anna still didn't have her driver's license, so she agreed. It was best she stay home.

Eddie felt his head was clear enough to navigate the roads. "See you soon," he called over his shoulder as he left through the back door.

Sitting behind the wheel, he emptied ten of the heroin tablets into his handkerchief for later.

Dr. Halloran was not at the medical office. The nurse said he hadn't felt well enough to come into work today and asked if she could help him.

Eddie handed her the near-empty Bayer bottle and asked for more. It was easy enough to convince her that he was still in a lot of pain. With his wife about to deliver their first baby and Eddie not being sure of when he could return for more medicine, she agreed to his request.

On the ride home, he felt confident that the refilled bottle, plus what was left in his handkerchief, would be enough to get him through his coming workdays. He felt hopeful that, before he knew it, his hand would be completely functional again. After all, he knew himself better than the doctor, and he would be careful not to become addicted to the pain medication.

58

December 1924
MILLBURY

EDDIE HAD USED UP most of his sick days back in late October, so he had no choice but to go back to work. The little bottle of Bayer Heroin had helped him over the last months, especially on the days when his hand wouldn't work as fast as he was used to on the loading dock.

He had been careful not to use too much of the medicine, cutting the tablets in half. Each day, he'd wake up and want to take a bigger dose, to help himself get through the coming workday. By mid-November, he began to limit himself to every other day, persuading himself that this would be the last pill each time the potentially addictive medicine touched his tongue.

It was an unusually cold December day. Every bone in his body ached. Eddie needed another dose. He counted what was left in the bottle... Only five half tablets left. I'll be okay, he convinced himself. His hands shook as he closed the lid without taking one.

Anna watched Eddie from the front windows as he pulled out of the snow-covered driveway. She tugged her woolen sweater tighter around her distended belly. The baby was due any day, and she hoped she was prepared. The only thing that worried her was that Dr. Halloran had been absent more than usual, due to his illness. His office had recommended she use a midwife for the delivery or try to make the drive to St. Vincent Hospital.

Mrs. Gilbert recommended Mary Nolan as a good midwife. Anna hoped the storm swirling outside wouldn't last much longer, as she gathered up all the items from the midwife's list.

She wished her mother could be with her, but that was out of the question. Last fall, Anna had received word that her brother, Thomas, had left their home on Cape Cod for better prospects in Boston. He gave his truck to Louis, since he was the only one left home with their mother. This allowed Louis to find a good job with the state highway department. Besides, winter was never a good time for travelling.

Phones had been installed on Burbank Street. Louis agreed to get a phone installed at the Cape Cod house, so Anna could call her family. The expense of the new convenience needed to be kept low for both families, so they always made calls near bedtime, when the rates were cheaper.

It was still snowing. Anna's anxious mind raced with questions of the future. What if Eddie got into a car accident? She couldn't stand the idea of losing him and raising the baby on her own. Did they have enough money to support their first child?

A steamy cup of chamomile tea couldn't calm her inner ramblings. She even looked at their bank accounts and Eddie's life insurance policy. It wasn't enough. Where would she find extra money?

As snow frosted the windows, she thought she should find her older boots upstairs in the closet. The zipper was broken on her new ones. By the time she reached the hallway, she was out of breath. As she stepped toward the bedroom, a contraction startled her. She stopped and massaged the cramp away.

Anna made it to the edge of the bed and calmed herself until she could move again. At first, it was hard for her to bend over. She knelt down to pull out her shoes, slippers, and finally her old boots from the back of the closet. Satisfied that kneeling felt like a good position, she leaned back against her thighs, surrounded by all her footwear, and rested.

The sight of the winter galoshes reminded her of Mr. Wilkins's treasure map. She had forgotten all about it. The bulkiness of her large belly disappeared as she shook the boots, thinking of the possibility of extra money. She shook them again. Nothing. Her hand swirled around inside. Then, she shook all the shoes, one by one, only to be disappointed at not finding the map. She almost started to cry, but the realization that she couldn't get up off the floor frightened her more. After several attempts to lift herself up, she gave up and let out a scream of frustration. And where was that stupid map? Tears clouded her eyes.

Unwavering, she pulled herself closer to the bed. Finally, with an awkward push of her hands atop the edge of the bed, she was able to stand. Just when she felt safe, a rush of wetness exploded between her legs. Another scream.

She shouted to the ceiling, "I've got to call Mrs. Nolan!"

The phone was downstairs. Against what she knew was common sense in her condition, Anna felt she had no other choice. Slowly inching her body into a sitting position, she sat on the top step to begin her journey down to the telephone. With each jarring bounce from step to step, her body hardened with pain. Halfway down, a stronger contraction attacked her body.

It felt like an eternity before she could reach the phone. With trembling hands, Anna asked the operator to connect her to Mrs. Gilbert, who, in turn, called Mrs. Nolan. Then, Mrs. Gilbert left a message at the post office for Eddie that the baby was coming.

The two women found Anna sitting on the floor beneath the telephone. As they helped her into the bedroom off the kitchen, the lights flickered from the storm.

Anna pleaded, "Please, God, help me. Where is my Eddie?" Another contraction rippled through her. "Dear God, where's Eddie?"

Later that snowy December night, Kathleen Rosalia Wallace was born, healthy and beautiful. Eddie arrived late. He stood by the side of the bed and, with shaky hands, held little Kathleen, wrapped in a cream-colored cotton blanket.

He needed to sit down for fear he would drop her. As a new father, his face should have showed happiness, but it was masked with fear, instead.

59

Autumn, 1925
MILLBURY

AT TEN MONTHS OLD, Kathleen was an active baby and required constant feeding and attention. Anna loved her little one, but the new mother grew exhausted each evening.

Eddie began drinking whiskey that was brought into Millbury from a few close French-Canadian connections. It helped ease the constant ache in his hand and the anxiety about his future that plagued his inner thoughts. He usually fell asleep soon after dinner.

Anna was worried about her husband. She had hoped Prohibition would have stopped him from drinking so much, but he managed to somehow find what he needed each night. Several times, she was almost afraid to ask where he got the alcohol.

After Kathleen was finally asleep for the night, Anna found Eddie downstairs, fast asleep.

"Eddie, wake up."

He stirred in his favorite chair near the fireplace. "What's wrong?"

"Nothing. I was thinking maybe we could take a drive to see my mother."

"When?"

"Tomorrow. Don't you have the weekend off?"

"Yes, but I was planning on helping John fix his truck." He grabbed the empty glass that balanced on his lap.

"Oh, please, Eddie. I really miss Cape Cod. The leaves are falling, and it's so beautiful out. I'll pack a picnic lunch for us." Anna stood to give him a kiss on his cheek.

His face softened, but he remained quiet.

She stood in front of him, waiting for an answer. "Eddie?"

"I guess so. But let's leave before sunrise, so we don't get home too late."

"Thank you, dear. I'll make sure everything is ready to go." She busied herself in the kitchen, preparing the next day's picnic lunch and whatever else was needed for little Kathleen. One thing she wouldn't pack was his whiskey.

They left early in the morning. Kathleen was swaddled on Anna's lap as the little family drove to Cape Cod. Soon, the sun shone brightly through the falling leaves and autumn colors.

By noon, they pulled onto the driveway of the Horvath home on Brier Lane. Anna got out first and carried the baby to the porch door.

Her mother greeted her with a big smile. "Anna, I've missed you." Kathleen was quickly transferred to Rosalia's arms. "How was the drive?"

"It was lovely. We stopped a few hours ago for a midmorning sandwich and then drove right here."

Eddie came in, carrying the baby's bag. "How are you, Mother?"

"Just fine, now that I have Kathleen in my arms."

"I'm so happy Eddie agreed to take a drive to see you Mother."

Rosalia sat at the table, playing with her first grandchild. "How are you doing, Anna?"

"Doing as well as expected, as a new mother. Trying to get rest, but there's always so much to do." Anna made herself a cup of tea. "Where's Louis?"

"He should be home shortly. Been very busy with his new job at the highway department."

"Even on weekends?"

"He's making good money."

"Just like my Eddie."

Rosalia stood up, still holding Kathleen. "I think she needs a nap. She's already asleep."

"Of course, Mother. I'll stay here and get dinner started."

Within the hour, Louis finally arrived home. He made his way into the kitchen. "Anna." He placed his thermos into the sink.

"Louis, it's good to see you." She hugged her little brother.

Louis responded with a stiff embrace. "Good to see you, too. How's the baby?"

"She's doing fine. Eddie is, too."

"Speaking of your husband, where is he? I didn't see him out front."

"I think he's checking the tires for the ride home, out in the back."

Louis grabbed two bottles of a local brew and left out the rear door. "Hey, Eddie."

Eddie looked up, seeming relieved to see that Louis had some alcohol in his hands. "Thank the Lord you're home and have delivered some decent refreshment to your thirsty brother-in-law."

Louis opened his bottle. "How's your hand?"

Eddie lifted his injured hand and made an awkward fist. "Some days are good and other days are bad." He held his drink up in the air with his other hand. "That's why I need this, even if it tastes terrible."

They both laughed and continued sipping as they made their way around the house to the front porch.

Eddie leaned back into a wooden rocker. "Not sure what I'm going to do. Down at the loading dock, those mail bags are getting heavier every day." He closed his fist a few times to stretch his tendons. "Even if they transfer me up to sorting letters, the damn hand is still going to hurt."

Louis looked at his brother-in-law. "Rumors at the highway department seem to hint the post office might bring back that pneumatic tube system."

"You mean those big tubes that shoot letters through the pipes?"

"Yeah. They say those letters can fly at thirty miles an hour underground to other sub-stations." Louis finished his bottle.

"Sounds promising, but I don't know. I would still need to lift the bags into the tubes and then into the pipes."

"Hey. Listen to me. You'll be okay."

Anna called out, "Dinner's ready."

As the men reached the screen door, Eddie smiled. "They call the guys who work on the pneumatic the Rocketeers."

Louis closed the door. "Hey, maybe you'll be famous."

Rosalia had planned a lovely early dinner. Everything tasted delicious.

After dinner, Anna cleaned the dishes while Rosalia tended to Kathleen. The men returned to the porch. Anna thought there would be several minutes available for her to see if the map might still be in the house. So many things had happened to her since she'd left home. As she climbed the stairs, she doubted her own mind as to whether she did or did not take the map to Millbury with her.

With a quick slide of the bed, she zeroed in on the floorboard underneath. Memories of her hiding the map became clearer, but under the wooden plank, the cavity was empty. She leaned back with a quizzical look on her face then bent over to look again. Nothing.

Louis must have found it. After all, he slept up here. She decided he must have taken it. Now she was angry. How dare he take something of hers?

She ran downstairs and headed for the front porch. "Louis, could you help me upstairs for a minute?"

Eddie looked toward his wife with a question on his face.

Louis stood up and shrugged his shoulders. "I'll be right back."

Anna sat on the edge of her old bed, waiting to talk with her brother.

Louis was in no hurry as he walked up the stairway.

Anna waited to catch his eye and then asked, "Where is it?"

He faced her. "Where's what?"

She pointed to the floor. "You know what I'm talking about."

He confronted her, smelling of alcohol. "No. I really don't."

"I can't find something very special to me. I always kept it upstairs."

"I don't know what you're talking about." He shook his head as if his sister was crazy. "Are you feeling okay? Maybe you're tired from taking care of the baby."

Anna stood up. "I'm not tired. Just frustrated and confused."

Louis turned to leave. "I have to go. I don't have time for your games."

Anna grabbed his arm. "Louis, don't dismiss me so quickly. We have to leave soon, and I want you to tell me the truth."

Rosalia yelled from below, "*Louis*! I need you."

"I told you I can't do this right now. Besides, Mom needs me." He stopped and turned away from his sister. "She always needs me, now that I'm the one stuck here with her."

"Stuck?"

This time he stared at her. "Yes, stuck. I have to stay here while you and Thomas get to go off on your own, which means I'm the only one left to care for her."

Neither spoke for a few seconds. Finally, Louis descended the stairs in silence.

Louis's words hit Anna with the realization that he was right. Her little brother was the last one home. He had become responsible for their mother, whether he liked it or not.

The ride back to Millbury was quiet. Anna was lost in her thoughts as she held onto Kathleen. Besides feeling guilty and anxious about the family, she wished she had not been so careless with Mr. Wilkins's map. Few headlights passed them as they drove home.

Anna faced the blackish car window and whispered to herself, "Where could the map be?"

Eddie turned his head for a second and then asked, "Did you say something?"

"No, dear. It was nothing."

60

Summer, 1942, Seventeen years later
CAPE COD

LOUIS COULD HEAR his mother humming a Hungarian lullaby in the kitchen.

"Coffee's ready, Louis."

"Be right there, Mom." He grabbed his hard hat, work vest, and lunch from the counter beside the white enamel sink, along with a thermos of fresh-brewed coffee.

Rosalia smiled at her youngest. "You're such a good boy, Louis." She patted him on his shoulder as he left through the back door.

Louis was still a child in his mother's eyes. At thirty-six years old, he was indeed a good son and had assumed the loving role of caretaker for his mother. Thomas and Anna had visited as often as they could over the years, but the day to-day care of their mother still remained with him.

On the way to work, he picked up Jimmy Tate, who was waiting for him on Underpass Road.

Over the idling of the truck's engine, Jimmy jumped onto the passenger seat. "Hey, Louis."

"Jimmy." Louis pushed the gears into drive and headed toward Orleans and the state highway department office.

"How long you been working for the state?"

"Since before '25."

"Isn't that when they started building the two-lane Cape Highway?"

"Yup. I was part of the first group of workers."

"I heard they've got plans to make the road bigger and take it all the way to Hyannis."

"Yeah, but not for a few years."

They passed the empty property where old Mr. Wilkins once lived. Louis thought of the many times, over the years, he had returned to the empty property to try his luck with the map, but he always came up empty-handed. He shook his head, thinking of the possible lost treasure, but he was making good money and the need to find buried riches had slowly disappeared.

Jimmy looked over at Louis. "I really appreciate you getting me this job. As much as I love this country, I didn't want to go to war."

"No problem. The Horvath family owed you one. Your father, God rest his soul, was there for me and my mother when we needed help."

"Yeah. Back then, he was a big wig in the army. Sometimes, I thought he could do anything."

"When your father told my mother he would find Frank's remains, or at least where he was buried, and possibly bring him home, well, I don't know what to say... Except, thank you."

"I'm happy the old man wasn't around to see what the Japs did to Pearl Harbor."

Louis had no comment about that horrific day in December, 1941, except to change the subject. "Jimmy, save your money, like I'm doing. It's good work, and there'll be plenty."

"I guess we'll always need good roads."

Louis straightened his back behind the wheel and promised himself, when Mom went, with all of his saved money, he'd travel. The mortgage had been paid off years ago, and Mom didn't require much. For now, he would stay on Cape Cod.

Louis arrived home hot and tired after a long day of working outside. When he reached the porch door he called out, "Mom, I'm home."

There was no response. He went into the kitchen and found a half-empty pot of water boiling and pieces of cut cabbage piled on the sideboard. He turned the burner off and hurried toward his mother's bedroom. He found her sitting on the floor, her head leaning against the edge of the bed.

"Mom!" He rushed to help her up.

She opened her eyes. "Louis, I don't feel well."

"I'm calling the doctor."

By that evening, he was also on the phone with Anna. "Mom might have had a stroke. The doctor said they'll keep her overnight and do some tests. I think her right side is paralyzed." He reached for a drink. "Will you call Thomas for me?"

"Yes. Shall we drive down?"

"No. Let's wait for news from the doctor."

Anna hung up.

Eddie wasn't home. He had the night-shift duty tonight and also over the next few days. Kathleen stood at the sink, drying the dishes from dinner.

Anna explained to her daughter what had happened to her grandmother and then sat at the kitchen table with her thoughts. Finally, she stood and told Kathleen, "I've got to go down to the Cape. I want to see my mother. I don't care what Louis says." She ordered, "Run upstairs and pack a few things for an overnight stay on Cape Cod."

Kathleen did as she was told. "Will we only be gone a few days?" she called down the stairs.

"Yes, dear. And it will be just the two of us." Anna walked over to the bottom of the stairway. "Your father can't get time off work at such short notice."

"All right, Mother." Kathleen was intrigued about a road trip with her mother. At sixteen years old, her travels had been limited. And, yes, she felt concerned about her grandmother, but this was going to be her first grown-up trip. She would be able to practice her driving.

The next morning, before mother and daughter left, Anna hugged Eddie. "I know you don't like working at the post office, but it got us more gasoline than most, with all this rationing."

"Yeah, a little over eight gallons. Should be enough to get you there one way."

"Thank you, Eddie."

"Did you pack the ration card for another fill up for the ride home?"

Anna checked her purse. "Got it."

Eddie watched his family pull away from their house.

In the kitchen, he opened the ice box for a drink, but there was none. Quietly, he climbed the stairs to the middle bedroom, which was rarely used. He wondered how long he could keep his stash of alcohol a secret from his wife.

No visible second door in the middle bedroom was evident to the casual eye. Not even Anna was aware of this secret room within a room. He pushed on the wall near the outside wall, and a door opened to reveal a long, closet-like space under the eave. On the floor sat a dozen bottles of alcohol. Maybe he should fess up and tell her about them? But he was drinking less and less. No need to make her angry now. He promised himself he would curtail his drinking even more.

Still feeling guilty, he thought of a surprise for Anna. She had put up with a lot from him. Maybe it was time for him to change. He really loved her and would hate to lose her from his life. He closed the opening on the secret room and stepped back to look at the smooth wall. He reassured himself that finally sharing this unique aspect of their house with her would be a good idea.

Tonight, he was on night shift again and thought he had time to start a new project for her. A nice redo of this unused bedroom would be nice. After locating some old paneling in the basement, he began his labor of love.

By late afternoon, only one wall was finished. Eddie stopped to clean up and then ate some dinner before he left for work. He'd continue the paneling on the other walls tomorrow.

Anna and Kathleen wouldn't be home until later. He thought this would be great for storage and maybe for Christmas decorations. She will like it.

Kathleen and her mother shared the duties of driving all the way to Brewster. Kathleen was cautious as a new driver and drove slowly. Anna drove faster and concentrated on the road as she imagined the different scenarios of what she would be walking into at the Briar Lane house, along with the decisions that might need to be made.

They arrived later than usual. The first words out of Louis's mouth upon Anna's opening the front porch door were, "I can't take off from work."

Kathleen followed in behind her mother and was shocked at her Uncle Louis's behavior. The young girl knew he was usually grumpy whenever they visited, but never like this. He didn't even say hello.

Anna brushed by her brother without a word and headed straight to her mother's bedroom. At first, the shock of seeing her mother lying there, with a slight distortion of the right side of her face, took her by surprise, but then other matters settled into her thoughts. Louis was correct, he needed to work, but who would care for their mother while he was away during the day?

A knock on the front door interrupted her ruminations. "Kathleen, can you come sit with your grandmother? Someone's at the door."

"Yes, Mother."

Evelyn Paine from down the street greeted Anna. "So nice to see you. How's your mother doing?"

"Won't you come in?" Anna stepped aside for the neighbor, who was carrying a bowl filled with chicken salad. "She's resting or sleeping, I'm not sure. I've never cared for anyone who had a stroke." Anna twisted her hands together.

"Well, I'm glad I stopped by." She walked into the kitchen and put her salad into the icebox. After peeking in on Rosalia, she returned to the parlor. "I might be able to help you."

Anna sat down to listen.

"I have a niece visiting. She was at Pearl Harbor the day it was bombed."

"How terrible."

"Yes, she was a nurse at Schofield Hospital. Only been there for a few months before the attack." Mrs. Paine sat at the kitchen table. "Anna, please call me Evelyn."

The two women were silent, suddenly lost in their thoughts of what war was really like.

Evelyn continued, "After working amid all the death and chaos for another six months, Betsy couldn't take it anymore, so she came home."

"Where's home for her?"

"Pennsylvania."

"Oh, I see." Anna poured some tea.

"She came to Cape Cod for peace and a place to heal."

"Is she looking for work?"

"Yes, I think so. Taking care of your mother might be just what she needs."

Anna perked up. "Oh, that would be wonderful! Louis can't do it all by himself. He really needs the help."

"Betsy is very kind. Shall I send her over to meet you and Louis?"

"Could she come over tomorrow? Or later today, after dinner?"

Evelyn stood up and reached for the doorknob. "I'll leave right now and talk with her."

"Thank you so much, Mrs. Pai— I mean, Evelyn."

During dinner, Anna explained to Louis what Evelyn had offered.

"Not sure I like a stranger coming into our house."

"You really don't have a choice. As you said, you need to work." Anna began to clear the dishes.

Louis left the table to sit by the fireplace in the other room and mull over his thoughts. His sister was right. He had no other choice. At least one problem would be solved, though, with this Betsy person taking care of Mother.

61

MOLLY CARRIED A PAIL filled with warm water and good old Murphy's Oil Soap up the stairs to the middle bedroom. It was the one room that was delegated for later, among all the other chores that needed to be done, after moving in. The floor was covered with dust.

She could hear Peter outside cutting wood that had been gathered from the back woods in preparation for the coming winter. The approaching summer days would cure most of the cut wood for their fireplace.

After adjusting her ear buds and selecting her favorite playlist from her iPhone, Molly began vacuuming the ceiling and three of the four walls. She wondered why only one, an inside wall, had wood paneling, while the other three were painted. Strange, she thought, but kept going. As she reached for the pail of water, the scent of Murphy's reminded her of home.

Molly began to tackle washing the window's framework. Out of the corner of her eye, she noticed a long line that didn't fit the pattern of the paneled wall. She'd never noticed it before. She walked closer to touch it then ran her finger along the faint line from top to bottom. Molly stepped back to take another look. She could barely see it, but there it was… A break in the wall.

Instinctively, she pushed the palm of her hand along both sides of the line. After several pushes in different places, she heard a click, and then the edge of a door that had been cut into the wall popped open. Tossing the washrag back into the pail, she took her earbuds out and slowly opened the mysterious doorway.

It was dark inside and smelled musty. Her iPhone's flashlight lit the black hole and revealed crude, open, wooden shelves built under the eave of one side of the house's roof. Molly spotted a long chain for a light and pulled on it. The room lit up with a yellow glow.

She hurried to the bedroom that faced the back yard, leaned close into the open screened window, and waited until Peter's chain saw fell quiet. She called down to him, "Peter!" He still had his headphones on so he couldn't hear her. "Peter!"

He took the ear covers off and cocked his head to listen.

"Peter! I'm up here."

He looked up. "What's wrong?"

"I found a secret door! Come on! Upstairs."

At first, Peter couldn't find Molly. "Where are you?"

"I'm in the middle room. Come look."

"Wow." He walked over to the opening and found her near the back of the closet-like room.

"This is so cool." Molly waved her phone's flashlight over the shelves. "Too bad there's nothing in here."

"I guess they must have used it for storage." Peter stuck his head close to the wall to see behind the shelves. "I think I see something way down, near the floor."

Molly kneeled down and tapped the flashlight again. She bent over. "You're right. It looks like a small book." She reached in under the bottom shelf.

Peter knelt next to her. "Can you reach it?"

"Got it." Molly pulled out a small leather book. She knelt upright to open its pages. "Peter! It's a journal."

Peter still had wood chips on his plaid shirt as he leaned in to see the handwritten pages. "This is a great find, Molly."

"I can hardly wait to show it to my mom." She flipped to the first page; the date of October 1924 was written at the top, along with the name Anna Horvath Wallace. "Oh, my goodness, do you think this has been in here since 1924?"

"Probably."

Sunshine slowly disappeared from the small bedroom. "It's getting late. You finish up outside, and I'll start dinner. We've got some great reading ahead of us."

Peter kissed her on the cheek. "Just like your mom."

Molly slowly closed the secret door, moved the vacuum to the corner, and then carefully carried the found journal to a desk drawer downstairs for later. She would finish cleaning the bedroom floor tomorrow.

Later, after dinner of hot dogs and French fries, Molly returned to the old desk to retrieve the journal. Her phone pinged, reminding her they had planned to meet some new friends for a movie at the renovated old theatre in town, The Elm.

"Darn it. Peter, I forgot we were supposed to go to a movie tonight with Tom and Mary. You think we can still make it?"

He looked at his watch. "It's not far from here. Let's go."

"Okay. I guess the journal will have to wait until tomorrow."

62

IT WAS ALMOST TIME for supper. Tommy's stomach rumbled as he closed the door of the shed. He walked into the house, looking for Max.

"Hey, boss, where are you?" He called out again. "Max?"

Upstairs, he could hear sounds of furniture scraping against the floor. He double-stepped up the wooden stairs. Max was struggling with an old trunk.

"Gimme a hand, will you?"

Tommy helped Max push the trunk, almost hitting an old bed frame. "What's in this thing?"

Max stopped pushing and stood taller. "Okay, that's far enough. I want to see it in a better light from the window."

Tommy watched his boss walk around it and run his hands over the top. "What's the matter? Can't you open it?"

Max yelled back, "No! I can't open it. The damn key doesn't work."

"Let me take a look at it." Tommy took out his phone and turned on its flashlight. "The key turns in the lock, but it doesn't open. Weird."

"That's right. There's got to be something important in there and a way to open it." Max moved the bed away from the trunk.

As Tommy took his turn walking around the trunk, he stepped back a distance, and his foot fell onto a soft spot in the floor. "Are we safe up here? The floor is squishy."

Max looked over to him. "What do you mean?"

Tommy pointed to a floorboard. "This board looks different. It's sunken in."

Max bent over to feel the floor. "You're right."

Tommy took his Swiss Army knife from his pants pocket and opened it to the flat screwdriver. "Here, use this."

Within seconds, Max had lifted the loose board and had his hand inside the black hole. "This has got to be where the treasure is." He reached in as far as he could go then swirled his hand around. "Shit. There's nothing in here."

"What are you looking for? Maybe I could help more, if you told me what's going on."

A knock on the door downstairs stopped both men from looking any further.

Tommy asked, "You expecting someone?"

"No."

"You want me to take care of them?"

"Yeah. Don't let them in. Tell whoever it is, I'm not here."

"Okay, boss."

Max sat on the trunk and stayed quiet.

He heard the downstairs door fly open with a bang against the wall. Tommy was yelling. "Who are you? What do you want?"

There was a scuffle. Max closed his mouth and tried to control his nervous breathing. He heard, "Tell Appleton he's got two days."

Someone fell against a table or a chair, a car started its engine outside, and then there was quiet.

63

Present Day
BREWSTER

AFTER DINNER, THE ID on my cell phone read *Tony Gomes*.

"Nancy here." I quickly walked over to my desk in the front of the house and picked up pad and paper. "Okay, Tony. I'll be waiting for you." I tapped my phone closed.

I noticed Jane was standing in the dining room by the open door of my office. I waved and pointed to an extra chair by the bay window.

Jane quickly asked, "What'd he say?"

"Tony is coming over to collect the bones, so he can send them to the state's OCME." I looked over to her as she scooted to the edge of her seat to listen. "From the photographs he sent to Boston, Tony said the medical examiner suspects they're human."

"Wow."

"He'll be here soon."

"Aunt Nancy, what does OCME stand for?"

"Office of the Chief Medical Examiner."

Jane sat back. "Huh."

"Well, you can't say your visit hasn't been exciting."

She gave me a big smile.

We moved to the kitchen to wait for Tony's arrival.

Within the hour, Tony, Jane, and I were standing over the location of the remains of someone from the past.

After he had gathered what was needed, Tony announced, "I'd like to take a look at that old suitcase."

"Okay, follow me." I led everyone into the garage.

Paul joined us. "Hi, Tony. How've you been?"

"Just fine, Paul."

With eyebrows raised, my dear husband said, "I see my wife has found herself in another mystery."

I knew Paul cared about me and was very accepting in all that I did, so his candid remark didn't bother me. That's why I love him so much.

I held my hands in the air. "What can I say?"

We all watched as the contents of the case were inspected. "If you don't mind, I'll take this in and mark it as evidence."

"No problem." I didn't smile this time, hoping Tony would catch my hint about being careful with what Jane and I had found.

He understood and looked straight back at me. "I'll take good care of these items."

"Thank you."

"And I'll keep in touch with you, if anything else is discovered."

64

July, 1942
BREWSTER

LOUIS STOOD QUIETLY at the base of the stairs and watched from the front parlor as the new hire prepared his mother's morning tea. He noticed how comfortably she stepped around the kitchen, as if she'd always lived in the house.

Rosalia's eyes followed Betsy's every movement, at least what she could see from her bed's position.

Louis walked through the kitchen and into the bedroom to say goodbye to his mother. "Everything okay, Mom?" He sat on the edge of her bed. "I'm going to go now." He gently took hold of her weak right hand. "Don't want to be late for work."

Rosalia reached with her left hand to squeeze Louis's arm. She smiled a crooked smile.

"I hope you'll be okay through the day." He glanced over his shoulder to Betsy in the kitchen and then back to his mother. "I gotta go."

When he exited the bedroom, he was handed a thermos of coffee and a packed lunch from Betsy. He cautiously took it in hand. "*Uhhh…*, thank you."

Rosalia saw it all, then closed her eyes with a look of contentment on her face.

On the drive to Orleans, Louis decided that Betsy would work out well, taking care of his mother. He also thought she was quite an attractive woman.

Hours later, toward late afternoon, Betsy stood in front of the little pantry with paper and pad, jotting down the groceries that would be needed for the rest of the week. She heard Louis's boots on the front porch. Without turning around, she called out, "How was your day, Mr. Horvath?"

Louis put his thermos in the sink. "Fine. How was my mother's day?"

Betsy kept jotting down a few items. "Ask her yourself. She's in the bedroom."

"I will." He found Rosalia in her rocking chair. "Mom! You're sitting up."

The rocker moved a little faster.

Louis leaned in for a hug. Rosalia's eyes grew wide, and with one arm, a solid embrace was returned.

Louis took it as a signal that his mother was going to get better. He sat on the edge of the bed and smiled.

After dinner, Betsy rinsed out a can of Spam and gathered the eggshells for compost. "I'm pleased you liked what I cooked for dinner."

"Spam and eggs are my favorite." Louis wiped his mouth and headed for the front porch with a bottle of another of his preferences, the "Old World Style" beer from Pabst Blue Ribbon.

As the clock ticked closer to 8:00 p.m., Betsy prepared to leave for the night. She closed the door on Rosalia's bedroom door and turned the overhead kitchen light off.

Louis came inside. He reached for the grocery list and began to write a few things down.

"Did I miss something?" Betsy leaned over the kitchen table.

"I know my mom would like some stuffed cabbage."

"I'm not sure I know how to make it."

"I can show you." Louis looked up and waited for her answer.

A few seconds passed, and then Betsy replied, "All right."

"Maybe on the weekend?"

"That would be fine, Mr. Horvath." She started for the back door.

"Please, call me Louis."

"Okay, Louis. Good night and see you tomorrow."

65

Spring, 1946, Four years later
BREWSTER

THE HORVATHS' "VICTORY garden" looked like it was going to prove bountiful, thanks to Betsy's expert care and daily tending. All the saved compost fed the seedlings with nutritious nutrients. Rosalia loved to sit on the back steps in the sunshine and watch this beautiful young woman do the things she had enjoyed doing herself. So did Louis, whenever he was home.

Betsy checked her watch. "Rosalia, it's time for your nap. Louis will be home from work soon, and I need to start supper." She carefully assisted the frail woman up by her left elbow, so they could both walk into the house.

Rosalia's arm was warm from the sun. She smiled up at Betsy and said, "Fresh air… sunshine… Makes one feel better."

The two friends carefully climbed the three steps into the kitchen and then to Rosalia's bedroom. "Thank you, Betsy. You're a good friend."

By 4:00 p.m., Louis had arrived home. "Hello?" The back-porch's screen door slammed against the doorframe.

Betsy exited Rosalia's bedroom. "Shhh. Your mother is sleeping."

"She's usually up by now. Everything all right?" His thermos landed in the enameled sink.

"I think so. We were outside a lot today. She's tired." Betsy resumed cutting up the cabbage for everyone's favorite meal.

"Any mail for me?"

"It's on the mantle in the parlor. I also picked up a big envelope for you and put it on the floor by the fireplace."

Louis left the kitchen, only to return for a paring knife to open one end of the package.

He spread its contents across the table, separating two AAA TripTiks from other papers.

"Where you going?"

"Nowhere yet. At least, not until the war is over." He sat down to browse through the information. "I've heard it will be only a few more years for this damned war."

"Maybe so. I'm pretty content to stay put."

Louis looked over to her. "Yeah. I guess you've seen enough to last a lifetime." He came up behind her. "Need any help?"

"Sure. You want to fill the pot with water and get it boiling?"

He grabbed the round aluminum pan, filled it halfway with water, lit the stove, and waited for the next directive.

Betsy turned to him. "That's it for now."

He returned to his road maps.

She leaned over the table. "Anything fun?"

He shrugged his shoulders.

"You're a good son, Louis. I've never met such a kind man as you, and you deserve to see the world." She looked at the title words on the spiralbound little booklet, reading, "'See the United States: Cross-country travel at its best.' At least you'll see our country first."

Louis grabbed a drink from the icebox and returned to the table.

Betsy joined him. "How's your work going?"

"Busy. The roads always need fixing, and we're starting to plan the highway extension into Hyannis."

"Really?"

"Yes. They've been talking about it, but now the details and timing are coming together."

She stood to stir the cabbage.

"Betsy, I've been thinking."

"What about?"

"Mostly about you."

She stopped stirring and slowly put the ladle on a plate beside the stove.

Louis noticed her hesitation. He stood up near her. "I'm sorry. I shouldn't have said anything. Sometimes, my thoughts spill out too quickly."

"It's all right. I've been thinking about you, also."

His eyes opened wide. "You have?"

"Yes."

Ninety miles away, Anna was in the secret room upstairs. She carried another installment to add to her collection of journals, which she had diligently kept up to date since moving into this wonderful old house. The middle shelf held the small books, stacked on top of each other, in three piles. On the opposite side of the little closet were all the Christmas decorations and some of Kathleen's elementary school-day memories.

Anna turned to the books and slid the first one out from the bottom. The journal was labeled *1924, Moving Day*. She recalled it was a crisp, autumn day. She touched her slim stomach and remembered how fat she'd felt in her eighth month of pregnancy on the day they had moved to Millbury from Eddie's parents' home. She had missed her mother during that stressful time. Rosalia had never learned to drive, and the trip was just too far for quick visits. A phone call to her would be in order, when she got downstairs.

Within the hour, Anna sat by the small desk that held the phone and dialed the Horvaths' number.

Back in Brewster, the phone rang.

Louis answered. "Hello?" He watched Betsy leave the kitchen to check on Rosalia. "Hi, Anna. I just got home. Mom seems to be doing well."

"Can I speak with her?"

From the bedroom, Betsy's voice called out. "Louis. Come quick!"

"I have to go. Betsy's calling me. I'll call you later." He hurried toward the kitchen.

He found Betsy kneeling by the bed, whimpering and holding his mother's hand in hers.

Louis bent over to check Rosalia's wrist. There was no pulse. He touched the side of her neck. Again, nothing.

He sat on the edge of the bed to hold his mother's hand. With his free arm, he circled it around Betsy's back, while they both cried tears of sorrow.

66

TOMMY WAS STUNNED but managed to get himself up off the floor and onto a chair in the kitchen. He wiped blood from the corner of his mouth.

Max cautiously descended the steps and looked around downstairs. "Tommy?" He caught a glimpse of his cohort sitting at the kitchen table, supporting his head with the palm of his free hand, while the other held a paper towel against his mouth.

Max came closer. "What happened?"

"That's what I'd like to know." Tommy got up to get some more ice.

"Sorry, man. I didn't think they'd find me." Max sat opposite Tommy.

"Well, they did. Whoever they are." He stared at his boss. "What're you going to do about it?"

"What do you mean?"

"I'm getting out of here, unless you tell me what's going on and how much I'm going to get from whatever you're looking for."

Max hesitated, but then he began to realize he really needed this guy. He couldn't do this by himself anymore. He stood to get a beer for both of them and started to explain.

Tommy's face was bruised red and starting to swell up. "You're telling me there's really some kind of treasure around here?"

Max nodded.

"And it's enough to get these guys off your case?"

"Sure hope so. It's all I got." He leaned back in his chair and began to scrape the paper label off his beer.

"Okay. Then we better get some protection. These guys mean business."

"I don't have a gun."

"Leave it to me. I know where we can get a couple."

Max leaned over the table. "I don't know."

"Well, I know. I'm the one who got beat up." Tommy headed for the bathroom. He smiled and thought of how all his practice and sharpshooter awards would finally pay off. He secretly hoped his marksmanship would be needed. "Let me clean up, and then I'll get going."

"Where to? Hyannis?"

"Yarmouth. Why? Want me to pick up something to eat?"

"I have a taste for some DJ's Wings."

"You got the money?"

"Hold on." Max pulled a fifty out of his wallet. "I want the change back."

Later, as the two men licked their fingertips from all the BBQ sauce, Max's phone rang.

"It's my wife." He wiped his fingers, walked toward the back door, and answered the phone outside.

67

May, 1946
BREWSTER

FOLLOWING A SHORT SERVICE by Herbert D. Nickerson, the funeral director in Orleans, Rosalia Horvath's funeral mass was held at Immaculate Conception's Catholic Church in Brewster.

Louis, Anna, Eddie, Kathleen, and Thomas filled in the front pew during the Mass, with Betsy in between Louis and Anna. It was an acknowledgment to Betsy for all her care and love toward Rosalia.

After the church service, Eddie held his wife around her shoulders as they walked to their car. His parents were still alive. He hadn't experienced the loss of a parent, as all children will at some point in their lives. The only thing he could do, he thought, was to be there by Anna's side, like she was for him throughout their married life.

Neighbors had brought casseroles filled with savory foods, cookies, and various desserts for the grieving family. Evelyn had left the service early to prepare the house for the wake's reception. She made coffee and placed several bottles of alcohol on the side buffet.

Louis reached for the vodka. He turned to Eddie and held the bottle in the air.

Eddie looked over to his wife and shook his head toward Louis.

"You sure, Eddie?"

"I'm good." He sat next to Anna and held her hand.

Louis shrugged his shoulders, as if he thought Eddie was crazy to refuse a drink.

Anna looked over to Eddie and smiled. Deep in her heart, she wondered if her mother had given her daughter a parting gift. Her husband had returned to her with more love than ever before. The past several years had been wonderful, since he'd stopped drinking. She felt she could face the grief of her mother's death now that Eddie was by her side.

The Horvath house was empty by 7:00 p.m. Anna, Eddie, and Kathleen were the last to leave. Anna leaned down to hug her brother, who was sitting in a chair by the fireplace. He smelled of alcohol. It didn't bother her. She understood.

"Get a good night's sleep. I'll call you in the morning."

He looked up, squeezed his sister's hand, then emptied his glass again.

Betsy joined them in the parlor. "I'll make sure he's okay before I leave." She gave Anna a deep hug.

Within the hour, the kitchen was clean. Betsy went to find Louis to say her goodbyes.

His chair was empty. "Louis?" No answer. She went upstairs to the second floor. She found him whimpering and curled into a fetal position on his bed.

Maybe she should leave him alone, she thought. But the need to comfort him overwhelmed her. She sat on the edge of the bed and placed her hand on his shoulder. His trembling hand grasped hold of it. The need to console grew stronger inside her. He's such a good man. No one should be alone at this time.

She quietly moved to the other side of the bed and positioned herself against his back, holding him close to her breast. Within a few minutes, his body calmed. Betsy pulled the blanket over the two of them, and both drifted into a peaceful sleep.

The phone rang at 9:00 a.m. and woke Betsy as she lay next to Louis. He was still asleep. She gently shook his shoulder.

"Louis, wake up." She sat up on the edge of the small bed.

She felt the soft touch of his hand on her arm.

Louis quietly said, "Betsy, thank you for staying with me."

"The phone's ringing. You should get up. I need to go home now."

He did as he was told and hurried down the stairs to answer the phone. "Hello?" He sat at the small table and raked his fingers through his hair, trying to wake himself up. "Oh, hi, Anna. I just got up." He watched Betsy close the rear door as she left the kitchen. "Can I call you later?" He walked over to the front window to see Betsy walk onto the road for home. "Thanks, Anna. We'll talk later."

Over the following days, Louis drifted from one task to another, never completing anything. He was alone for the first time in his life and was left with worrying only about himself. Nothing made him smile. He couldn't bring himself to go into his mother's room. He knew he had to but didn't want to. He kept calling in sick at work and everyone understood.

Betsy finally appeared at the Horvath house and knocked on the screen door.

Louis opened the back door. "Betsy. Why are you standing outside?"

"I'm not sure. Things feel different now."

"Please come in. I've made some coffee." He quickly pushed papers, food containers, and mail over to the side of the kitchen table.

She entered, took her hat off, and cautiously sat down.

He placed a cup on the table near her. Neither of them spoke.

Louis broke the ice. "I've missed you." He kept his head down as he sipped his drink.

Betsy looked over to him. "I've missed your mother, I've missed my routine, and I've missed you." She placed her hand over his.

He raised his eyes to her face and smiled.

Her shoulders dropped, and she returned a smile.

The tension from before was broken, and after a few sips of her coffee, Betsy stood to clean the dirty dishes. Louis watched her for a few minutes and then stood next to her, grabbed a dishtowel, and began to wipe the dishes dry. Neither spoke through the quiet clinking of the simple task of cleaning. The silence was comforting.

Throughout the day, they slowly opened their hearts to each other and talked, not holding any feelings back. They finished the evening with a glass of wine.

Louis looked deep into her eyes. "Will you come tomorrow?"

"Yes."

He took Betsy in his arms and gently kissed her good night. "Shall I walk you home?"

"No. I'll be fine. Thank you."

He watched her disappear into the dusky evening.

Over the following week, Betsy returned to help Louis get his mother's papers in order and go through her clothes. By the end of the week, the last two boxes were sorted into a giveaway and a keep pile.

After the small legal file box was gone through and then closed, they made stuffed cabbage in honor of Rosalia. The evening slowly turned into a bittersweet occasion. Dinner grew quiet as each pondered the emptiness in their lives and their future, possibly with each other.

Betsy stood to clear the dishes. Louis took her hand as she reached in front of him. He looked at the woman he wanted to spend his life with from now on. She didn't pull away. He stood to embrace her. She melted into his arms. He picked her up and carried her to his bed upstairs.

68

Present Day
MILLBURY

AS MAX DROVE ALONG Route 495 toward Millbury, he couldn't stop thinking about what his wife had wanted to talk about in person. She sounded nervous and wanted him to come home. It must be important.

He texted his ETA to Roberta and finally pulled into their driveway at around 10:00 p.m. The house was dark. Strange, he thought. His wife was a night owl. He tried to use his key to open the front door, but it was deadbolted. He went around to the back and made his way through the kitchen door using only his key.

"Roberta?" It was dark, but he could hear the TV in the back room. "Roberta? It's Max." He took a few steps in and noticed her shadow crouched behind the island, holding a baseball bat. "Roberta?"

She stood up, ready to swing.

"Hold up. It's me." Max cautiously took another step toward her.

Roberta lowered her weapon and leaned against the counter with a sigh of relief. "I've been so frightened."

"About what?"

"I'm scared someone is going to break in here, looking for you."

"What do you mean?" He slowly took the bat from his wife's hands and leaned it against the door jam.

"Since those two guys came by, I just get the feeling that they're watching me. I don't like it."

"Is Stevie home yet?"

"No, he took a side trip to drive his roommate home to New Hampshire. He said he'd stay a couple of days up there." Roberta rubbed her arms to help her stop shaking. "Right before I called you, I was taking the trash out to the garage and found some footprints in the mud under the kitchen window."

"Maybe you should go stay with your mother up in Maine for a few weeks."

Roberta sat at the counter with her hands folded. "You'd better tell me what's going on. Right now!"

Max quickly checked all the doors in the house while Roberta silently waited in the dark kitchen. He switched on the dimmer lights under the cabinets, poured himself a glass of wine, sat opposite her, and began to explain everything, including the $100,000 he'd borrowed from the Mica brothers.

Halfway through, she poured herself a glass of wine. "So, you think there's actual treasure on the Cape somewhere?"

Max nodded.

"And you can't find it?"

He swirled his wine and shook his head.

"What's your plan?"

"First, you need to go to Maine. Text Stevie to meet you there. I don't want anything to happen to either of you."

Roberta kept her eyes down in silent agreement.

"Tomorrow, I want to get into Grandma's old house to check if there's anything there that I may have missed when it was liquidated. I'll make sure, before you leave for Maine, whoever's spying on us will see that I'm still here. They don't want you. They want me."

"Did you clean out our bank accounts?"

"Most of them."

69

August, 1946
BREWSTER

BETSY AND LOUIS began to spend more time with each other, at least when they could. She had found a part-time job as a caregiver to an older woman near the Brewster/Dennis border. Louis returned to his work. But each evening and on weekends, they were together. People who knew them thought it was sweet that they were a couple.

Near the end of August, Betsy called Louis to say she wasn't feeling well. She told him it must be a bug or something. She stayed home from work for a few days, but by the third day, she wasn't any better. Over the week, the urge to vomit became part of her morning routine.

Her Aunt Evelyn suggested she see their family doctor. As she dressed for the office visit, her favorite skirt felt tighter than usual. She glanced at her figure from the side in the mirror. Her stomach puffed away from her otherwise slim figure.

The doctor told her the results of her urine test would take a few weeks and nothing was set in stone. She left the address of her parents in Pennsylvania for any future correspondence.

The doctor's diagnosis was not what Betsy had hoped for, so she kept the news to herself when she arrived at her aunt's house. She told her aunt she was just a little run down. Evelyn agreed and didn't question her niece. Betsy hoped the doctor's promise of confidentiality would be honored.

Her queasiness never went away. As she walked home from work the following day at around noon, she passed Brier Lane but couldn't bring herself to stop in like she always did. Then, in an instant of spontaneity, she turned around and walked toward the Horvath house. She had to tell Louis that she might be pregnant. She respected him and loved him too much for him not to know.

The back door was open, as usual. She took a deep breath as she entered the kitchen to calm herself, thinking she could start dinner for him. Her appetite had been minimal, and she'd had to force herself to eat anything.

The papers across the kitchen table stopped her in her tracks. She fingered the AAA packets of roads and places where one could stay travelling across the country. She sat down and carefully pushed one map on top of the others, skimming all the information. Her heart began to beat faster, and at that moment, she realized what her condition would do to the man she loved. He'd always dreamed of travelling. Her news would mean he'd have to change everything he planned to do.

Betsy looked away to stare out the window. She loved him too much to do this to him. He deserved more in his life. She decided to leave the Cape as soon as possible. If she hurried, she could catch the last bus off Cape for the train station in Boston.

Before Betsy left Cape Cod, she called her mother to tell her she was coming home.

"I'll call Frank. He'll pick you up at the station."

"Oh, Mother, can't Father come?"

"He's working late. I know Frank has missed you. I'm sure he'd love to pick you up."

Betsy watched the trees fly by through the grimy window of the train car as it sped toward the small town of Altoona, Pennsylvania. By the time she arrived, it was after midnight. The station was empty save for a lone ticket seller inside. She hovered under the platform roof and against the outside wall.

A car drove up with its headlights on, illuminating a light mist that drifted within their white glare. A tall figure got out of the car. "Betsy?"

"Frank? Frank Adams?"

The last time she had seen Frank was when she'd left for her assignment at Pearl Harbor. It had been a sad day for him, but she remembered she was excited for a new adventure. A memory crept into her head of the horrific images of the wounded and badly damaged men who had crowded Schofield Barracks Hospital, in the days after the bombing. She shook her head, trying to make it disappear.

"Ahhh, Betsy. It's so good to see you." Frank embraced the only girl he had ever loved.

The weary traveler accepted his hug.

They talked as they drove to Betsy's home, with Betsy listening more than contributing to the conversation.

Frank looked over to her. "Are you okay? You're so quiet."

"I'm sorry. There are a lot of things going on."

"What kind of things? We've been friends since grade school. You can tell me anything."

She placed her hand on his. "You know, I've always felt guilty…, leaving you when I went off like that. I wish I could have known what awaited me as a nurse in the army."

Frank pulled to the side of the road. "When I heard what you had gone through and seen, I was mad at myself." He shook his head. "I should have married you, right then and there, and convinced you to stay in Altoona."

Betsy sniffled but kept her eyes down.

He took his handkerchief and dabbed her eyes, then handed her the cloth to wipe her nose.

They sat quietly for a few seconds.

Frank twisted toward her, grabbed her shoulders, and turned her to face him. "I know this may sound crazy, but… Betsy, will you marry me?"

She was stunned.

"I have a buddy who's a justice of the peace. I know he'll do me the favor. He lives close by." Frank patiently waited. "Oh, Betsy, what do you think?"

"I can't, Frank." Betsy turned away, holding his handkerchief close to her lips.

"Why not?" He leaned over to see her face. "I don't understand. I know we once loved each other."

"I'm afraid I've gotten myself into a situation."

"Well, whatever it is, I'm sure it's nothing we can't handle together."

Betsy whispered, "I'm pregnant."

Frank straightened his back and stared at the steering wheel.

"Don't you see, I can't marry you without you knowing the truth about why I came home."

He remained quiet.

Betsy adjusted her skirt and wiped her eyes. "It's okay, Frank. I'll be fine."

With no words, he started the car and pulled back onto the road.

Betsy stared through the side window. She couldn't bring herself to look at him. She whispered, "I'm so ashamed."

The next ten minutes felt like an eternity to Betsy as they travelled in silence. All she wanted to do was climb under the covers in her old bedroom and disappear.

Frank turned into the Paines' driveway and switched off the car. He gently took her hand in his. "Betsy Paine, will you be my wife?"

She looked over at him. "I can't marry you, Frank. It's not fair to you. I—"

He pulled her close to his chest. "I love you, Betsy, and always have. I love who you are and everything you'll bring to our marriage, including whoever is inside you."

"I need to think, and I'm so tired." Betsy opened the car door.

Frank got out, grabbed her suitcase from the back seat, and whispered, "I love you, Betsy Paine."

That night, as she lay in bed upstairs in her old bedroom, her thoughts ran the gamut of love to fear and back again to love. Was it possible to love two men at the same time?

She remembered how much she had cared for Frank. He had been her best friend. And yet Louis came into her life after the war, when she needed someone to remind her that the world was still a loving place. Now, Frank seemed to be her safe haven. Could she learn to love him again?

Betsy still had feelings for Frank, and maybe with time, she hoped, they would grow into a deeper love. Her hands settled on her belly and gave it a gentle rub. Finally, she closed her eyes with the comfort that she'd made the right decision.

70

August, 1946
BREWSTER

WHEN LOUIS ARRIVED home, he washed up then sat at the kitchen table to resume planning his trip. By 5:30, he wondered where Betsy was. When the clock struck 6:00, he called her.

"Hi, Evelyn. Can I speak with Betsy?"

"I'm sorry, Louis, she's not here. Her uncle drove her to the bus stop in Hyannis."

"What? Where is she going?"

"To Boston. She said she was taking a train home, to Pennsylvania."

"She's gone? Did she say why?"

"No. I'm sorry, Louis."

"Did she leave anything for me?"

"She did not. I don't know what else to say to you, except that she's gone."

Louis hung up. He sat by the small table until dark, trying to figure out what to do.

Later, he drank himself to sleep.

Two days passed before a letter arrived in his mailbox. Louis recognized Betsy's handwriting. He tore open the envelope as he walked into the house.

My Dearest Louis,

By the time you receive this letter, I will be safe and at home with my parents. I couldn't bear the thought of saying goodbye to you in person. We need to follow our dreams, and maybe someday, we will see each other again under different circumstances. For now, we need to go our separate paths. One day, you'll understand. This is the best solution for both of us.

I have asked Aunt Evelyn not to tell you where I am. Please don't follow me.

Love,

Betsy

He read the letter over and over, trying to figure out why she had left him. There was no return address. Pennsylvania was a big state. He called Evelyn several times but got no answer. By the fourth call, he walked over to her house. No one came to the door.

He stood outside and yelled, "Evelyn! Please. Talk to me."

Sad and alone, Louis went home. Once more, he drank himself to sleep.

The rest of the week dragged on for Louis. His vacation time had been used up during his mother's death, so he was forced to keep going to work.

Another few weeks passed, and Louis's love for Betsy slowly turned to self-pity. He blamed himself. He must have been the reason why Betsy left.

He threw his AAA TripTiks in the garbage and scolded himself for being selfish for not wanting to care for his mother and always resenting his role as her caretaker. He didn't deserve to travel. If it wasn't for his job forcing him to leave his home, he would have isolated himself. Looking for Betsy was not an option. She deserved a better man than he could be.

Each night, before he closed his eyes, Louis would ask himself what Betsy ever saw in him.

His question always went unanswered. The cloudiness of too much drink blurred his senses.

71

A Sunday in June, 1965
BREWSTER

THE SIXTIES WERE A tumultuous time for the United States. There were riots, protests, and a general unrest across America, but Louis didn't care. Cape Cod was a secluded place, so life on the peninsula remained comparatively calm.

Louis went to work, saved his money, and kept to himself. At fifty-nine years old, he looked forward to his retirement. His state pension would be all he needed to live out his days of solitude and maybe do some fishing.

He grumbled to himself as he flipped the month on his calendar to June. He didn't like the yellow pollen that saturated and clogged everything, making his asthma worse. He struggled to breathe in and out as he closed the windows and doors to keep the thick dust out of the house.

Louis made some coffee and sat at the kitchen table to read last week's newspapers. When he heard a knock on the front door, he shook his head.

The neighbors next to him had only bought the house to enjoy it for three weeks in the summer, yet they were always trying to get to know him better. Well, he thought to himself, he was not going to have anything to do with that notion.

He peeked behind the blinds but couldn't see anyone. Another knock. Annoyed, he quickly opened the door. "I wish you'd leave me…"

He was taken aback by the presence of a young man with a backpack on his shoulder. He was tall, of average build with dark hair. Louis was shocked at how much he resembled Betsy.

"What do you want?"

The young man stared at Louis.

"I said, what do you want?"

"I'm looking for a Louis Horvath."

"Well, you're staring at him."

"My name is Martin Adams."

Louis stared back.

"I was wondering if you knew my mother, Betsy Paine?"

Louis hesitated for a second. "What about her?"

"I have something for you, from her." He reached into his jacket pocket and pulled out a wrinkled letter addressed to Louis Horvath, Brier Lane, Brewster, Massachusetts. He stretched his arm with letter in hand toward Louis.

Louis stood, looking at the creased envelope. He felt his heart racing. Martin pushed it closer to him.

Louis took a step back in the doorway.

The boy finally placed the letter on the wicker rocker to his right. Then, he turned to leave.

By the time Martin reached the grass of the small front yard, he heard a voice behind him.

"Wait!"

He stopped and looked toward the house. The man was holding the letter.

"Come back." Louis sat in the rocker and slowly began to open the message.

Martin kept his distance, taking a seat on the top step of the porch, wondering if he was looking at his real father.

Louis recognized Betsy's handwriting. He silently read it.

Dear Louis,

If you are reading this letter, then I have passed away. Don't grieve for me. I've had a wonderful life with my husband, Frank, and that also included you and our special time with each other on Cape Cod.

I hope Martin is with you. He's a good boy and oftentimes reminded me of you and your kindness. I think he resembles you. I instructed my mother to have Martin give this to you, if anything would happen to me. I also wrote a letter to Martin, explaining all about you. I never had the courage to tell him or you, myself.

You're not obligated to recognize him as your son, but maybe one day, you will. I want both of you to know the whole story. Give our son a hug from his mom.

Betsy

Martin patiently remained quiet as Louis read his mother's letter several times over. Louis finally leaned back with the letter dangling between his fingertips.

"I don't know what to say."

A long silence passed between them before Louis stood up, opened the screen door, and turned toward Martin. "You hungry?"

The young man twisted around toward Louis. "I could eat."

"Well, come on in.

Martin's steps were uneasy as he went into the house.

The darkened rooms took Martin by surprise, but he still kept following this stranger to the kitchen.

All Louis had to drink was beer, so he offered his visitor cold water and leftover pizza from the night before.

"Sorry for the meager offerings. I'm not used to company."

Martin offered a half-hearted smile. The cold pizza filled an emptiness in his stomach. The bus ride had been long, and he didn't have much money on him.

He slowly began to explain what had happened. About eight months earlier, his parents had been in a car accident with a train.

They had been killed instantly. "I really don't like to talk about it," Martin said, pushing the hard pizza crust around on the plate.

"I understand." Louis rose from the table and reached for a box of cookies stored over the kitchen sink. With his back to Martin, he gripped the counter's edge and then reached for his handkerchief to wipe his nose and dab his eyes. As if nothing had bothered him, he turned and placed the opened box on the table in front of Martin, then sat opposite him.

The young man took one cookie. He nibbled at it. Quietly, he asked Louis, "Did you love her?"

"How old are you?"

"I turned eighteen in April."

"You're too young to know what real love is."

"But did you love her?"

"Yes, I did love her." Louis pushed his chair away from the table and stood, once more, by the kitchen sink with his back to Martin, head hung low.

Martin reached for another cookie. "After the accident, I just wanted to stay home. Couldn't even go to my graduation. Not without my parents."

Louis turned to face him. "Well, at least you graduated."

"I guess so. Everyone pitied me. I hated that." Martin stood to put his plate in the sink. "Grandma gave me your letter. I knew I had to find you. To let you know..." He sat back at the table.

Louis joined him again, and the two men sat quietly for a long time.

Louis spoke first. "It's getting late. You got a place to stay?"

"No, sir."

"You can stay in my mother's old room." He pointed to the bedroom off the kitchen.

"Thank you kindly. I will leave tomorrow."

Louis nodded. "The sheets and blankets are in the dresser."

Louis locked the doors, paused before the stairs, and said to Martin, "I'm very tired."

No goodnights were uttered between these two strangers, each one questioning their role in this new relationship, if there was even going to be one. As Martin entered the small bedroom, he noticed the pictures on the wall above the bed and small dresser.

An older woman sitting in a rocker with a much younger Louis by her side was framed in a large, oval frame. On the dresser top was a small easel frame that held a picture of the older woman again, but this time, he recognized his mother standing next to her, cradling a basket filled with vegetables. He knew his mother was an expert in growing delicious tomatoes and peppers in her garden.

Upstairs, Louis shut the door and crawled into his bed but couldn't fall asleep. So, this is what people complained about, not being able to sleep. Their heads filled with worry and stress.

Building roads had always been back-breaking work, so he usually fell right to sleep. Tonight felt so different. He could not believe that he has a son. Why hadn't Betsy ever told him? Why couldn't he have been strong and brave enough to go after her? His life would have been so different.

The rattling of a few pans and the smell of coffee woke Martin the following morning. He sat on the edge of the bed, thinking about what his next move should be. It didn't feel like he would be asked to stay. He was okay with that. Showing up like he did must have been a shock to the old man.

He stuffed his dirty shirt into the backpack and pulled out a clean one for the bus ride back to Altoona, a place that offered nothing for his future.

"Morning," Louis greeted his son. A few pieces of toast sat on a plate with a knife next to a jar of peanut butter and a small glass container of strawberry jam. "Help yourself." Louis sat down, grabbed a slice of bread, slathered on the peanut butter, and spooned a tablespoon of jam on top. "Coffee?"

"Yeah."

"Then help yourself. I'm no waiter."

Martin smiled as he poured himself some coffee. The two ate in silence. They didn't seem to mind the quiet, each man comfortable with only a few words.

He noticed that Louis had a slight grin on his face, too, but couldn't decide what the expression meant. Either way, his mission to deliver his mother's letter was complete.

Louis stood to rinse his plate and cup. Without looking at Martin, he asked, "Are you handy?"

Martin nodded. "I helped my dad with his home remodeling business. It was only part-time for both of us."

"What else did he do for work?"

"He was the night watchman at the railroad station."

"I was wondering if you might be interested in doing some work for me. I'd pay you."

Surprised, Martin said, "Sure. I could stay a while and give you a hand. I'd appreciate the cash."

"Let me show you what needs to be done. Then, I've got to leave. I can't be late for work."

Martin followed Louis up the stairs to a back corner of the top floor.

"Over here, under the plastic, is the problem." Louis twisted, pointing to a hole in the roof.

Martin looked under the covering.

"Do you know what you're doing?"

"I can fix that."

"Good. You'll find some plywood and shingles over there." Louis pointed to the repair supplies stacked against one of the walls. Then, he stared down at the floor for a few seconds. "Okay, I gotta' go."

As they headed downstairs, Martin glanced around the sparse bedroom. He noticed an old trunk in the opposite corner. "That looks cool. What's in it?"

"None of your business. Besides, I don't remember how to open it."

Martin shrugged. "Okay. I'll get started right away."

Louis stopped at the bottom of the stairs. "Listen, there are some tools in the shed outside. I know where everything is in this house. Mind your own business, and don't get too snoopy. I won't tolerate it. Understand?"

"Yes, sir."

Martin was lonely. He desperately wanted Louis to like him. He measured and cut the plywood, but it didn't fit the hole. He measured again and trimmed. Still no luck.

Martin took a deep breath and repeated his process. "Son of a bitch!" He threw the third piece of plywood across the room. It slammed against the wall and dropped onto a table, knocking over a small lamp.

After he witnessed the additional damage thanks to his temper, he wanted to punch something but couldn't find anything to vent his anger onto.

He went downstairs to look for a beer. At this point, he didn't care what Louis thought of him. He needed a drink. The beer brought a small semblance of calm over his body, but his brain was still fuming about his inadequacy.

"Get control of yourself," he whispered.

This was exactly what had gotten him into trouble back in Altoona. If it wasn't for his grandparents convincing the judge that he was upset about his parents' deaths, he would have landed in jail for sure.

The roof remained unfinished by the time Louis arrived home. Martin had hidden the empty beer bottle at the bottom of the garbage pail.

Louis yelled, "Martin?"

"I'm up here."

As Louis got to the top of the stairs, he saw Martin sitting on the floor beneath the hole. "What's the matter?" He glanced at the open hole in the roof.

Martin kept his eyes down. "I'm having trouble."

Louis came closer and examined the pieces of ill-fitting wood scraps. He took each one and held them up to the hole. "Well, you're off just a little on this piece."

Martin stood next to him.

"I think this one will do fine. It overlaps just right. By the time you get the tar paper and shingles over it, the roof will be good as new."

Martin swiped at his dripping nose.

"Besides, you should be outside on the roof to do this kind of repair."

Martin recalled how his father back in Altoona had spoken in the same kindly way to him, when he made a mistake.

"Get your hammer and this piece of plywood. Set the ladder up, and I'll be with you in a minute."

He did as he was told and followed the man who was possibly going to give him a second chance.

72

1970
MILLBURY

ANNA SLEPT IN A little longer on this early morning. She ran her hand across the sheets on their bed. Eddie must be already up and downstairs. She grabbed her robe and went down the stairs to join him for some coffee, then called out, "Eddie." No answer. She called again. Nothing. As she rounded the corner toward the bathroom, she found him on the floor and screamed, "Eddie!"

Anna sat next to her husband of almost fifty years in the ambulance as it drove to the hospital. She couldn't bear the thought of losing him. She clutched his hand as she prayed that God wouldn't take him away from her.

Kathleen drove behind them. She knew her father had a weak heart and was worried that ten-year-old Max would not remember his grandfather, if he left them too soon.

Max sat up front in the car next to his mother. He watched her quietly crying, and he wondered if he would ever see his Grandpa Eddie again.

Two days dragged on with no good news. Eddie's heart was weak, and the doctors had not given a hopeful diagnosis. Anna stayed by her husband's side until he finally took his last breath.

Kathleen drove her mother home that night. "Mom, do you want me to stay a while with you?"

"No, dear. I'll be all right."

Anna put the kettle on for some tea. "You're just as tired as I am. Go home to your family." She sat down at the kitchen table.

"Are you sure?" Kathleen leaned over to give her a hug.

Anna reached to caress her daughter's hand.

Kathleen walked to the door. "I love you. See you in the morning."

"Okay. We have a lot to do tomorrow. I'll need your help. Get some rest."

Anna listened for the door to click shut before she sat in Eddie's wingback chair by the fireplace and dropped her head into her hands. Tears flowed until she couldn't breathe.

Tilting her head back, she ran her hands over the armrests, trying to feel his presence again. The teapot whistled, separating her from her sorrow and forcing her to get up and face the reality that she was alone.

Her hand trembled as she added a bit of honey to her tea. She wondered what was next for her, now that Eddie was gone. Would she be strong enough to continue?

Her chamomile tea was soothing. After the teacup was rinsed and put away, she turned the lights out and softly climbed the stairs to the middle bedroom. A quick push on the secret door allowed her to enter the hidden room, where her stack of journals sat on a shelf to her left.

She took the most recent book and sat at a small desk that faced the windows. With pen in hand, she wrote, *"Today, we lost my Eddie..."*

The funeral was small and quiet. That was fine with Anna. She wanted to be alone with her thoughts. What was left of the Horvath family arrived the day of the wake and departed the same day.

It was good to see her brother, Louis. His son, Martin, had been welcomed into the Horvath family but with reservations. Martin was rude and had a temper.

Anna couldn't understand why the young man didn't appreciate what Louis had done for him. Outwardly, he was never grateful. He kept to himself most of the time, and even Max thought something was off with his new cousin.

Louis, at sixty-four years old, and Martin, a young twenty-three, looked almost identical in their habits, except for Martin's temper. Both enjoyed their fishing, but neither one of them had any kind of a social life.

Anna decided it was not her problem. She had to concentrate on what her next step in life was going to be, even if she only had a small number of years left.

A week after Eddie died, Anna received a letter from Martha Deering. As she walked the long driveway from the mailbox back to her house, Anna read Martha's condolences but had to stop in mid-step to go over the last few sentences.

Martha was asking Anna if she would be interested in returning to work at the Deering household. By the time Anna reached the porch door, she was thinking it might be a good idea. Keeping busy was always the best medicine for grief, and she was in need of something to boost her well-being.

She called Kathleen and presented the idea of her going back to work.

"Are you sure?" Her daughter sounded concerned over the phone. "Maybe you should take some time for yourself. You don't need the money, do you?"

"No. Not really." Anna sat down at the kitchen table. "Martha said it would involve just being a companion to her and her mother."

"How old is Martha now?"

"I believe she's in her late sixties. Her mother is almost ninety." Kathleen was quiet. Anna continued, "Martha never married, and I guess her mother is not doing well."

"Will you have to do any nursing?"

"I don't think so, not according to the letter. Maybe I'll drop over and speak with her."

The Deering Mansion, on Riverlin Street in Millbury, was surrounded by over 175 acres of woodlands and secluded from everyone, at the end of a long, wooded driveway. A far cry in stature compared to Anna's little home on Burbank Street.

Anna knocked on the door of the front porch. She heard dogs barking in the background. Unsure if anyone was home, she worried her unannounced visit might prove to be futile.

A nurse opened the door. "May I help you?"

Relieved to see a medical professional, Anna replied, "I was hoping to speak with Martha. She sent me a letter offering a position."

"Come in, please. I'll see if I can find her."

The grandeur before Anna took her breath away. It was the first time she had ever been to the Deering's Riverlin house.

She stayed put as she watched the woman ascend one of the two curved staircases that flanked the ceiling-high stone fireplace. The stone structure was the central focus of the elegant but rustic room. Her eyes darted across as many items as she could see in the short time she waited, finally settling on the little shelves built into the walls alongside the stairs that were filled with curios.

After another quick glance across the entryway of the first floor, Anna noticed all the rooms had arched doorways above the closed doors, which only added to the mystery of what could be behind them.

"Hello?" a voice came from upstairs.

Anna looked up to see the nurse leaning over the painted wooden railing that curved around the upstairs balcony. "Come on up. Martha will see you now."

Anna walked slowly up the stairway, so she could see what interesting items were housed on the small shelves.

"Hurry up. I must tend to Mother Deering."

"Yes, ma'am."

"Martha is down that hallway." The nurse pointed in the opposite direction to where she was going.

"Thank you." Anna had no indication as to where she should go. All of the four doors in the hall were closed.

She started with the first room. The door opened, and she peered over multiple boxes stacked against the door, blocking her entry. Beyond the boxes, the room was stuffed with clothes, shoes, hats, and several unopened boxes. She moved on to the next room. This time the door opened, and she saw Martha at her desk, surrounded by more clutter.

"Hello," she said, stepping into the room.

Martha turned around. "Anna, it's so good to see you after all these years." She rose to hug her old friend. "How are you?"

"Well, I just lost Eddie, but I'm keeping busy."

"So sorry to hear." She turned back to her desk. "That's very sad."

"How is your mother?"

Martha continued to check a list of items on a yellow pad of paper. Without looking up, she continued, "I see you've met Nurse Jane. She's been a big help. What with me volunteering at the hospital and," she added, turning once again toward Anna, "my shopping."

Anna was quiet as she observed all the furs, clothes, and jewelry, wondering what this woman could possibly need with them all. Out of the corner of her eye, the edge of a grand piano peeked out under piles of dresses.

Martha moved a stack of shopping catalogues to one side of a silk divan, to put her shoes on. "No one knows how long Mother will be with us."

Anna picked up a lovely cashmere sweater and started to fold it.

"Never mind that, Anna. I like everything just the way it is."

Anna wasn't sure what to do next.

Martha took the lead. "Now, if you'll excuse me, I have to get dressed for a shopping trip with Gary."

Anna stepped toward the door. "Oh, shall I come another day?"

"Yes, that would be better. I assume you're going to take the job of a companion for my mother and, of course, occasionally for me?"

"Yes. I think I will."

"Fine. It may involve picking up some things that have been special ordered for me at various stores."

"That would be no problem."

"You may show yourself out. See you tomorrow around 9:00 a.m.?"

"Of course." Anna took one more look around the messy room and headed for the balcony and the top of the stairs. As she slid her hand over the smooth balcony railing, she remembered the secret shopping trips for the glamour magazines that teenage Martha would send her on. She smiled and thought to herself, she could handle this.

That evening, Kathleen paid a visit to Anna.

"Hi, Mother. Did you talk with Martha?"

"Yes, I did."

"Tell me everything." She sat at the kitchen table.

"The house is magnificent but strange."

"How so?"

"It's a combination of elegance and hunting lodge."

Over tea, Anna described the fireplace and the clutter throughout the rooms, at least the ones she could get into.

Kathleen grabbed a cookie from a tin cannister. "I've heard she wants to decorate each room according to the fashion decades."

"Well, she's off to good start." The two laughed.

"Will you take the job?"

"I think so. I know she inherited a lot of money from her Aunt Mary, and I suppose more will come when her mother passes."

"Martha Deering is quite eccentric, and she's a big spender."

"Kathleen, I feel sorry for her. She never married. Buying things must fill an empty void. Perhaps it even makes her happy." Anna held her daughter's hand. "I wouldn't trade you for all the money in the world."

Two Years Later

Anna could not get warm. She wore a thicker sweater over her thin, aging body. At seventy-seven years old, her stamina had slowly begun to fade. The doctor had mentioned poor circulation. She took her pills faithfully but would become out of breath after climbing the stairs from the basement with the laundry.

It was time to quit her job with the Deering household. Martha's mother, Georgia, recently had passed, so there wasn't much for Anna to do anymore.

A cup of coffee warmed her hands. As the steaming drink slowly moved through her body, she decided to call Martha and then Kathleen.

"Hi, Mom. How are you today?"

"Oh, I'm all right. I wanted to let you know that I just called Martha and told her I won't be in today and that I might be leaving."

"Mom, that's good to know. I've been wanting you to quit for a while now."

"I guess it's the right thing to do. The house is packed with things Martha will never need. It just bothers me to see all the wasteful spending."

"She is quite a shopaholic."

"God only knows how much more she'll buy after her mother's estate kicks in. Most of the dresses still have their price tags on."

"How about I bring you over one of those new burgers from McDonalds?"

"I'd enjoy that. I do need a distraction. Every time I think of Martha and her foolishness, it makes my blood pressure rise a little."

"Well, just relax. I'll see you around noon."

Anna climbed the stairs to her favorite room. She pushed on the secret door, grabbed the latest of her journals, and sat at the desk under the window.

By the time it was 10:30 a.m., she felt she had written enough for today. Kathleen would be there soon, and Anna wanted to bake some cookies for their special lunch.

She gazed at the stack of journals with pride. All of her dreams, hopes, and joys had been written down for her family to enjoy and, hopefully, understand the what and why things happened the way they did. Her writings served as her solace through times of sadness and were pleasurable when times were joyful. Her favorite was the first journal from 1924. She reached for it.

A sudden uneasiness hit her. The whole side of her body felt numb. Her head began to spin, and she grew nauseous. She tried to put the old journal back on the open shelf, but her weakened hand pushed it off the back of the shelf. Anna slumped onto the wooden boards while the journal fell behind and wedged itself under the bottom board.

Kathleen arrived around 11:30 a.m. and came in the back door by the kitchen. "Mom? Where are you?" She placed the bag of warm burgers on the table and went into the living room. "Mom?" She went halfway down the basement steps and called again.

She climbed the stairs to the bedrooms and kept calling out, "Mom!"

Kathleen found her mother lying on the floor in the middle room, inside the house's secret hiding place.

"No!" She fell to her knees and felt for a pulse. It was faint, but her mother was alive.

She ran down the stairs to call for an ambulance.

A few weeks later, Kathleen was driving home from the hospital. The stroke hadn't been fatal, but it was debilitating. Her mother's memory remained erratic, and her balance became more unstable.

She needed home care, and Kathleen was ready to step in as much as she could. Her husband couldn't help, because he already worked two jobs, but maybe, with Max's help and summer approaching, the situation would be bearable.

Her young son could carry boxes, take the garbage out, bring the laundry up or down from the basement, and keep a watchful eye on his grandmother. Yes, she could cope with the situation, for a while, at least. In Kathleen's eyes, a nursing home was out of the question.

By the end of summer, she decided to find a live-in nurse's aide to stay at the house. Max was with his mother when she greeted the first female candidate.

After a few minutes, he finished his snack in the kitchen and then went to sit with his Grandma Anna. She appeared to be agitated, gesturing that she wanted to show him something.

73

Present Day
MILLBURY

THE NEXT MORNING, Molly and Peter slept in, soothed by the steady rhythm of the rain outside their bedroom windows. By 10:00 a.m., they finally got out of bed. After breakfast, Molly cleaned up the kitchen and prepared to test out a new microwave dessert she'd found online, while Peter started the laundry in the basement.

The doorbell sounded. Since no one was expected or had ever used the old bell, it startled Molly. "Peter, someone's here. Can you come upstairs?"

"Sure. I'll be right up."

Within seconds, Peter could see a black SUV behind Molly's Toyota. "Who's that?"

They both walked toward the front door. Peter opened it to a nicely dressed, middle-aged man. "Can I help you?"

Molly stood behind Peter.

"Yes. My name is Max Appleton. I was wondering if you could help me. My grandma used to live in this house. She's gone several years now, and I'm going to be moving to the West Coast. I was hoping you'd consider letting me in to take a look around, for old time's sake?"

Peter looked to Molly.

The stranger quickly added, "I won't be long. I just have so many memories of her. I miss her."

Molly smiled, and Peter caught her signal that she was okay with it.

"Sure. Come on in." Peter stepped aside as the stranger walked onto the enclosed porch.

"I really appreciate this. I used to stay overnight a lot." Molly led them into the main house and as they walked past the wooden stairway, the stranger said, "I remember sliding down those stairs in a big laundry basket."

She steared them into the kitchen. "Has it changed much?"

"Not really. It's very comforting to see everything." He glanced into the back yard. "Nice to see the old pear tree is still going strong."

"Yes, we hope to harvest some pears this summer. It looks very healthy." Peter followed close behind the man as the stranger slowly scanned the downstairs rooms.

"I guess I should be going. I really want to thank you for letting me snoop around. It means a lot to me."

As they passed the stairway to leave, he stopped and asked, "Do you think I could take a peek upstairs? I remember there was a tiny bathroom that you had to step up into."

"Yes, it's still there." Molly heard the microwave sound. "Of course, go ahead upstairs. I've got to check this new dessert I'm making."

"Thank you. I really appreciate it." The man started up the stairway.

Molly left for the kitchen, and Peter felt safe enough to check on the laundry in the basement. After a few minutes, she returned to the living room. The man was not in sight. She walked over to the stairway, and before she reached the third step, he appeared at the top of the stairs.

He quickly descended the stairs. "Sorry, I just really enjoyed looking around."

Molly backed away.

As he passed her, he said thank you and hustled out the front door.

Peter appeared next to Molly in the living room. "Did he leave already?"

"Yeah. I couldn't find him at first, but then he came down the stairs, and with a big smile, he thanked me again and was gone."

"I guess no harm was done."

"Agreed. I remember one time, when we visited Ohio a few years ago, my mom showed us the house where she grew up and asked the people if we could see inside. She was so happy when they let her in."

Molly started for the stairway. "I'm going to go up and see if everything is still in its place. You never know."

Before Peter reached the kitchen, he heard Molly call out.

"Peter!"

He ran upstairs.

She was in the middle room, staring at the floor.

"There's an extra set of footprints on the dusty floor, and they seem to be coming out of the secret room I found."

74

I WAS UP EARLY, thinking about who belonged to the bones next door and how they got there in the first place.

Jane met me in the kitchen. "I couldn't sleep." She reached for the orange juice in the fridge.

"Neither could I." I grabbed some coffee and sat next to her at the table.

"How did those bones ever get there, Aunt Nancy? Do you think he was killed?"

"That's a good question, and I don't know if we'll ever know." The two of us sat in silence, lost in our own thoughts.

My cell buzzed with an incoming call. It was Tony. "Hello?" I waited to listen to my friend's every word. "Oh, that's good to know." I saw Jane's face go from surprise to quizzical.

"Okay. Yes, we'll be home this morning. Bye."

"Well, the bones were human. They date back to 1900 or earlier. It was an older man. No foul play was evident from the bones that were brought in."

Jane spoke up. "So, why was he there? Was he homeless?"

"He could have been."

"Do we get the suitcase back?"

"I think so. Tony said he'd bring it by in a week or so, after the bones are tested for their DNA origins."

"Does that mean I... I mean, we can keep that old compass?"

"There's a possibility you'll be able to claim it. Unless we do some more research with those initials and find out who the man was and see if there's any family left."

"Okay. I'm going to get dressed."

As Jane skipped up the stairs in anticipation of reaping something from her adventures, I couldn't stop speculating about the how and why of this man's death. Not finding any real details about the man was a little frustrating and having to wait longer made me impatient.

Later, we both huddled over the computer. I input the initials, E.S.P., from the suitcase, added Cape Cod and 1900.

Jane leaned in closer. "There are a lot of hits about Cape Cod 1900."

"Look at this one." I opened the link. "It's an article about an exhibit at Cahoon Museum featuring scrimshaw and a female pirate. That doesn't help us very much."

Jane sat back in her chair. "Do you think E.S.P. could have been a pirate who settled in the woods to hide, along with all his treasure?"

"It's possible. Remember, we found out that the inscription on the back of the compass, *Bully 1860*, referred to the pirate Bully Hayes? Well, he is recorded as being a real pirate up until around 1877. The suitcase looks like it's from 1900. That's only around twenty years later. This E.S.P fellow could have sailed with Bully."

Jane appeared lost in her thoughts, then she said, "I kind of knew he was a pirate."

"I had the same thoughts."

"I hope I can keep the compass."

"We could look some more, but I honestly think we're going to come up with nothing. I'd say it was a *yes* for keeping the contents of the suitcase. It's like looking for a needle in a haystack."

Jane jumped up and hugged me. "Thank you, Aunt Nancy. I'm so excited. Do you think it's valuable?"

"Very possible."

She jumped up and ran to tell her sister and Uncle Paul.

While we were eating lunch with Paul, my cell phone rang. It was Danny, calling from L.A.

"Hi, honey." I put my cell on speaker.

"Hey, Mom. I've got some good news."

"Great. I've got you on speaker with your dad."

"I'm coming home tomorrow."

"That is good news. What's the occasion? You miss us?"

"One of my buddies from high school is getting married and asked me to photograph his wedding. So, I thought it would be nice to spend a few extra days with you, and yes, I miss you guys."

"Now you tell us you're coming home?"

"I've been really busy."

"It'll be good to see you."

"I better go now. Traffic is finally moving."

"Okay, Danny. We'll talk more when you get here."

"I'm taking the redeye. Landing at Logan around seven tomorrow morning. I'll catch the 9:00 a.m. bus to the Cape. Can you pick me up in Hyannis?"

"Absolutely. Text me your flight number. Love you."

Jane reached for some more chips. "I haven't seen Cousin Danny since he left for L.A., before Covid."

"He hasn't been home for a few Christmases."

"Is he still doing photography?"

"Yes, and he's very successful at it. Mostly freelance."

"What does that mean?"

"He doesn't work for one company or production studio. He gets paid for each assignment or job. Apparently, he's secured contracts with a lot of companies."

Paul wiped his mouth with a napkin. "We're very proud of him. Making his own way in the creative world."

I placed my hand over Paul's. "Just like his father."

The sky grew dark, and the heavens suddenly opened into a rainstorm. Jane looked disappointed.

"What's wrong?"

"I wanted to go back to where we found the bones and the suitcase. I thought we might find something else."

I stood to load the tray with our dirty dishes. "Maybe Danny will come with us tomorrow, if the ground isn't too wet."

Jane grabbed the pitcher of lemonade. "That's a great idea. He could take some pictures, so I can show my mom what we've been doing."

"I think he might be interested in capturing some images."

As I was cleaning up in the kitchen, Molly texted.

Have time for a quick zoom? I've got something to tell you and show you.

I grabbed a glass of water and opened the Zoom app on my office computer.

Molly's lovely face appeared before me. "Hi, Mom."

"Hi, honey. What's up?"

"You wouldn't believe what's been going on. I found a secret room upstairs."

"A secret room? You're kidding!"

"Yeah. And inside, this was tucked under the bottom shelf against the back wall." Molly held up the small brown journal.

"What's in it? Wait. What do you mean, a secret room?"

"The other day, I was cleaning in the middle bedroom, the one we don't ever use, and found a secret room. There was a thin line going from top to bottom within the wall that has wood paneling. I pushed on it, and it opened."

Peter peeked over Molly's shoulder. "Hi, Mrs. C. Your daughter's a real sleuth."

"What's inside the book?"

"I haven't read all of it, but the woman who wrote it was Anna Horvath Wallace. The first entry was made in October, 1924."

"That's awesome. What else?"

"Besides living in this house, she connects herself to Brewster on Cape Cod."

"Brewster?"

"Yeah. And there's a mention about treasure, a map, and the name of Wilkins. But then her writing is smudged, like she dropped some liquid on the pages, and that's it. The writing stops. Maybe there were other journals and this one got lost behind the shelving."

As Molly spoke, I scribbled the names and dates she was telling me on a small notepad. I sat back to think. Too coincidental, I thought. It can't be. As I listened to Molly, I began to doodle and underlined the woman's middle name, *Horvath,* with a question mark.

"Mom? You okay?"

"Yes. I'm fine. It's just that Wilkins is the same name as the owner of the property next door. You know, the big property between us and Mrs. McPhee. Really weird. And that name *Horvath* sounds so familiar."

"Well, you've always told me, life is a series of coincidences."

"You're right. Never doubt the power of fate and how we're all connected in some way or another."

"Then yesterday, some guy came to the house. He told us his grandma used to live here, and he asked if he could take a peek around, for old time's sake."

"Did you let him in? Was Peter with you?"

"Yes, and yes. Remember when we were in Ohio, and you wanted to show us where you grew up? They let us in."

"Yes, I remember. But I'm glad Peter was with you. Did he stay long?"

"No. I left him for a minute to check on an apple dessert I was making. When I went back into the living room, he was gone. When he first came in, he mentioned something about the weird bathroom upstairs, so I assumed that's where he went. I started to go upstairs, and that's when he reappeared, at the top of the stairs, muttering that he had wanted to check out the bathroom."

"Well, I'm glad you were careful, and Peter was with you. I think that, nowadays, people are bolder."

"Everything worked out. The only strange thing was that, after he left, I went upstairs, just to check things out. I saw his footprints in the dust, coming out of the secret room, which was odd, because I had closed the secret door the day before."

"Maybe, as a kid, he went into that room? Anyway, don't let anyone else in the house again."

"Yeah, I probably won't. I just thought you'd like to hear about what had happened."

I drew another big circle around *Horvath*.

Jane joined me in my office. "Hi, Molly."

"Are you having a good time on Cape Cod?"

"For sure. Your mom is really cool."

Molly laughed. "She absolutely is, and that's why we love her."

I heard something drop in the background. "Everything okay?"

"Oh, Peter must have dropped his hammer. He's repairing the back door. I better get off now and see if I can help him."

"Okay. Bye, Molly."

"Love you, Mom."

After I explained to Jane what Molly had discovered, she couldn't believe it.

"You know, I wouldn't think that would happen, but after being with you for the last week or so, I'm a firm believer that anything is possible."

The name *Horvath* stuck in my head. I couldn't connect it to anything, but I knew it was important.

75

Present Day
MILLBURY

MAX PULLED AWAY from his Grandma's old house and drove back to Worcester, all the while wondering where his mother had put all of Grandma's things, when they sold the family home. He thought there were some journals but couldn't be sure, because he'd never seen any of them.

By the time he got to his house, it had started to rain. He ran to the back door, used his key to unlock it, and then felt a hand on his shoulder. He spun around to face the one guy he had never liked: Benny Paulson.

"What're you doing here?"

He pushed Max into the house. "We need to talk."

The door slammed shut behind the two men as Max landed hard against a chair. He faced his old business cohort. "Look, Benny, you don't have to get rough with me. We go back a while. You know I'm good for the money."

"The Micas want their money. They're getting very impatient. Remember when you were late in delivering those vending machines?" Benny slowly reached into his pocket and pulled on some thick, black-leather gloves.

Max raised his hands, palms up, to protect himself. "Hold on, Benny." He recognized Benny's trademark of violence: Sap gloves, the knuckles filled with lead for a deadly punch. "I'm looking for treasure. I've got a lot of clues. It's worth a lot of money."

"What do you mean, treasure?"

"It's all connected to my grandma. There's a map. Everything leads to Cape Cod… and something valuable. I just know it"

Benny took one glove off. "Tell me more." He took one step back.

Max explained about the dead body, the map, suitcase, and the trunk they couldn't open. "I know there's something there, maybe enough for all of us." In the back of his head, he thought, if he could convince this jerk that he was on to something big, he might have a chance to get more time.

Benny inched closer to Max, leaned into his face, and said, "Because I've known you for a while, I'm going to give you another twenty-four hours."

Max relaxed.

As Benny straightened up, he quickly punched Max in the gut with his gloved hand. Max doubled over. His attacker smiled at the pain on his victim's face.

As he left, he turned to calmly whisper, "Twenty-four hours." He straightened his jacket and pocketed his gloves. "Say hello to Roberta when she gets home."

Max rubbed his stomach and tried to take some deep breaths to regain his composure. After several minutes, he was finally able to stand and groaned, "Oh my God, it hurts."

His cell went off. It was Tommy, back on the Cape. Out of breath, he whispered, "Yeah, what do you want?"

"Hey, boss. You sound terrible."

He sat back down at the table. "I'm okay."

"I got that trunk open."

"What?"

"I opened that trunk upstairs. Guess what I found?"

"Don't play damn games with me. Just tell me what you found!" He rubbed his stomach again.

"A map."

Max sat a little straighter. "I'll be there in a few hours. Make sure the doors are locked and those guns are loaded."

"Okay, boss."

Dreading the long drive back to the Cape, Max occupied his mind by thinking about that secret room. No one had ever known about it except for his mom, Grandma, Grandpa Eddie, and himself.

He remembered, at the time of the sale, how rushed his mom had been to get the house ready to sell. She was hoping to close on a new house for the family and didn't talk much about Grandma's house with the realtor. His mother had concentrated on getting rid of their house first and all the paperwork for their new house. He figured she had never mentioned the room to anyone, for fear it would trigger some more inspections or something to slow the sale down.

Max turned onto Route 495 South toward the Cape, unaware of a car with Benny and another man inside, following a few cars behind him.

76

Present Day
BREWSTER

BENNY'S CELL SOUNDED through the car's audio system. "Benny here."

Jimmy kept driving and listened to the one-sided conversation. He and Benny had been partners for over ten years now. The Micas liked the way the two worked together. The old good cop, bad cop scenario always reaped results.

"We've got him in sight now. Jimmy's a good driver. We're not going to lose him."

The driver smiled as he sipped his coffee.

Benny disconnected the phone from the car and continued talking to his boss in private. "We're headed for the Cape." He looked at his watch. "Not much traffic, so we should be good."

A few seconds of silence passed as Benny listened, then he continued, "This guy has got some cockeyed scheme of finding treasure to get you your money."

He looked out the passenger's side window. "No matter. We'll do whatever is needed to finish the job." He ended the call.

Jimmy put his sunglasses on. "Do you think Appleton is going back to that old house on Brier Lane?"

"Probably." Benny closed his eyes. "Wake me when we get to Hyannis, unless he changes his route."

"Will do."

77

AS PAUL DROVE THE CAR into the driveway, I hurried down the deck to meet them halfway, happy to see father and son together again. It was so good to give Danny a hug. Zoom is great, but nothing can replace the feeling of holding your child in your arms, no matter how old they are.

"Did you get a chance to sleep on the plane?"

"A little." Danny threw his backpack across his shoulder and followed his dad up the deck to the house.

Walking behind them, I noticed a few stray weeds popping up amongst the garden beds. I had neglected my gardening in all the excitement since the girls' arrival.

Once indoors, I instructed, "Go wash up and get out of those travelling clothes. The girls are staying in your old bedroom. You can settle in the front one."

I went into the kitchen to make some fresh coffee. Jane and Madeline were finishing setting the table, then Madeline made a beeline for the TV.

Jane stayed in the kitchen. "Aunt Nancy, I'm having such a great time with you. I don't want to go home."

"That's good to hear, except the part about not wanting to go home. Don't you miss your mom and dad and your friends?"

"To be honest, I don't have that many friends. I'm sort of a loner."

"I understand. I was like that, too."

"You were?"

"Yes, and I turned out okay." I threw a smile at her as Danny and Paul walked into the kitchen.

Paul filled his mug with more coffee. "Nancy, don't forget that Madeline and I are driving over to Falmouth after lunch. We probably won't get back until quite late."

"Okay. You'd better remind Madeline. She's watching TV."

Danny grabbed a soda. "So, what's been going on?"

Jane and I looked at each other, waiting to see who would start talking first.

Danny noticed the looks on our faces. "Somebody better tell me."

I started by explaining all about how Jane was the first one to find the coins, and how we'd stumbled across the suitcase, the remains of what appeared to be a real pirate, and then the map upstairs, in the hidden box.

Jane chimed in with, "Don't forget about the journal in the secret room that Molly found at her house."

Danny shook his head in disbelief but then quickly asked, "Can we go see next door?"

I grinned at Danny. "Let's go."

Jane stood, ready to go outside.

Before we got to the laundry room's screened door, I turned and asked Danny, "Would you mind bringing your camera?"

"Not at all. Just like in the movies."

We waited for him to rejoin us.

As we walked a little farther away from the house, Danny appeared cautious at the sight of the yellow tape. "Are you sure we're allowed to go through here?"

I repeated that Tony had said it was okay for us to go back on the property, but if we found anything more, we were to let him know right away.

Danny was quiet as he viewed the scene. Then, he raised his camera and started capturing anything that looked interesting. Jane and I watched him crouch for lower angles and then bend over for others. He looked so professional. I was proud of him.

Jane stood a short distance from us. "This is where your mom and I found the bones and suitcase."

I walked closer and pointed to the remnants of the old iron bed. "Yes, the bones were right around here."

Danny took a few more shots and then stood up to look around from where he was standing. "How's our neighbor, Mrs. McPhee?"

"Well," I said, "she seems to be doing okay. Jane baked her some cookies, so we took them over to her. We thought it might be a good idea to have a little chat with her."

Jane stood up. "Yeah, I don't think she liked the cookies much, and she was pretty grumpy."

"She ate quite a few when we were over there." I focused back on the potential crime scene. "We had caught her looking at us through her binoculars. That's when she told us she knew all about the suitcase we'd found."

"Did you tell her about the bones?" Danny reattached his camera to a large strap on his shoulder.

"Yes, but it didn't seem to faze her. She just grabbed another cookie."

Danny laughed. "Good ole' Mrs. McPhee."

Jane reminded me, "She did tell us about a man, around 1900, coming and going from these woods." She crouched closer and began to push the dirt around.

Danny looked toward the McPhee house. "Did she tell you anything else?"

I took my boot and dug into the dirt with my toe. "I think she might be hiding some information, but I don't know for sure. Just a hunch." After another quick scan of the forest floor, I turned toward the house. "Nothing new here." I stood straighter to leave. "Let's get back. You hungry, Danny?"

"I could eat."

"While I'm making some sandwiches, will you upload those pictures to my computer?"

"Sure. We can blow them up to highlight any details we might have missed with our eyes."

"Great. Just like in that sixty's movie, *Blow-Up*, about a photographer who takes random shots in a park and then happens to come across evidence of a murder in the images."

Danny stomped his shoes off in the laundry room. "That was a real classic. Then, the photos are stolen, and the photographer wasn't sure what was real and what might be in his imagination."

As I prepared lunch, I watched my youngest son sit at the kitchen table, going through the images on his camera.

"I'll make a file for the photos I just took, then I'll download them onto your laptop."

Jane came in and sat opposite him.

I put plates out and caught a glimpse of some of the images he had taken a few months ago.

"Wow! Those are awesome." I stared at a fantastic image of the Milky Way over a mountaintop, his lit car/camper glowing under the nighttime sky. "Where did you take that? And how did you catch that?"

Jane stood behind us to see. "You took that photo?"

"Yup. On my last camping trip to the Alabama Hills in Lone Pine, California. Pretty neat, huh?"

"Did you have to stay up all night to capture it?" I was concerned about his safety, all by himself in the middle of nowhere.

He smiled at me. "Almost all night. Those are the Eastern Sierras."

"Well, I can't wait to see the pictures you just took outside. We've got a few minutes while the sandwiches are heating in the oven. Can we upload them now?"

"Sure. Lead the way." Danny followed me into my office with Jane in the rear.

It took less than a minute for them to load. Danny got up so I could sit to see them closer.

"Mom, this might take a while, if you want to blow each one up for details."

"Yeah. I guess so." The buzzer went off in the kitchen. "Let's go eat."

"The rehearsal dinner isn't until around six. We could look at them after lunch. Right now, I'm starving."

Lunch on the back porch was delightful, just like years ago, when everyone was home. The table was filled with laughter and smiles.

Danny's phone went off. "I gotta' take this. Sorry." He left the porch.

He returned halfway through our meal. "I need to leave in about thirty minutes. My buddy asked if I could come earlier, to take photos at the beach. It's getting close to high tide. I need to go."

"What about your sandwich? Want me to wrap it up for you?"

"That would be great. I'll get my gear together." He turned to give me a parting hug. "Mom, thanks for letting me use your car. I really appreciate it."

Paul finished the last of his sandwich. "Nancy, you okay with no car?"

"Of course. Jane and I will be just fine all by ourselves."

78

Present Day
BREWSTER

MAX CROSSED OVER the Sagamore Bridge and had only forty-five minutes left before he'd get to Brier Lane.

He made a call to Tommy. "Just crossing the bridge."

"Okay."

The miles flew by. The closer he got to Brewster, the more curious he became. He spoke into the car's audio, "Call Tommy."

"Hello?"

"That map… What's on it?"

"Not sure. I can identify the Old King's Highway, and it looks like the foundation of a house above the lines of the road."

"That's all?" Max sounded exasperated. "Anything else?"

"You wouldn't believe whose name is on the map."

"Christ, just tell me!"

"It's Wilkins. And on the bottom is the name Anna."

Max's heart skipped a beat. He sped up but eased back when he passed a state patrol car hidden inside the dense middle section of the highway. He kept glancing in his rearview mirror, checking to see if the police car had followed him. He relaxed when he didn't see a cruiser. He did notice another car that looked familiar, though. Was that Benny?

Max hit the gas, so he could get in front of a big semi. He made a quick right at exit 79B and then took the short cut to Brewster, down Airline Road. Hopefully, Benny hadn't seen him turn off. He should have enough time to meet up with Tommy, get the map, and then hustle over to a bayside beach, where they could plan their next move.

Tommy's car was parked in the driveway. Max pulled past it and drove toward the back of the Brier Lane house. He jumped out and double-stepped into the side door. "Tommy!"

A voice came from upstairs. "I'm up here."

"Bring the map and those guns. I'll get my papers." He heard Tommy's heavy feet clunk down the stairs.

"What's the rush?"

Max was ramming all his papers and notes into his briefcase. "Gimme the map."

Tommy handed it over.

Max shoved it in next to the papers. "We'll take your car. Get a couple of shovels and a flashlight from the shed and some duct tape. Hurry up!" In the rush, he never noticed a scrap of paper fall to the floor and slip under the table.

Tommy hustled through the door.

Within five minutes of Max pulling into the driveway, Tommy was driving them down Lower County Road toward Breakwater Beach. The short ride was quiet. Max took a deep breath, reached for the mysterious map, and then began to examine the markings.

Mrs. McPhee's binoculars dangled from a thin, black-plastic strap against her ample bosom. She couldn't decide if she should call that Appleton guy and tell him about someone taking pictures next door.

She pulled her phone from her apron pocket and began to punch in Max's number. Another fifty dollars would be nice, she thought.

Mrs. McPhee slowly made her way back across the cluttered porch and into her house. She took the binoculars off and picked up her kitty. "What do you think, my little Penelope?"

She finally pressed the red button to make the call.

"That Caldwell lady and her niece are nice people. Maybe I should just shut up about anything else I see."

After three rings she hung up, then she walked over to her chair, carrying her companion. She scratched Penelope around and under the kitty's collar as she ate the last of the delicious cookies.

79

Present Day
BREWSTER

TOMMY BACKED INTO the upper parking lot, beside a picnic table. About five cars were already parked in the front lot, near the entrance to the beach. "We should be okay back here."

Max heard Tommy speak but was too interested in the map to pay attention to what he was saying. His thoughts traveled back to 1972, his Grandma Anna, and the day she had told him about the family treasure. He felt for the leather pouch in his jacket pocket.

Tommy leaned over to Max. "I noticed the name Wilkins on the map right away."

"It's got to be the same Wilkins that my grandma talked about." He placed his finger on the Old King's Highway road. "That has to be Brewster."

"How do you know for sure?"

"I just know it." Max added, "It also has my grandma's name on the bottom, Anna, written upside down."

Max's phone rang. He recognized the number. It was Mrs. McPhee. "Great, it's the old lady. Maybe she's got some more info for us. We're going to need all the help we can get in the short time we have to find anything." During the third ring, it stopped.

Tommy laughed. "Maybe she had a heart attack."

"Christ, Tommy, don't be such a smart ass. We'll be over there in a few minutes. We'll find out what's going on." None too soon, Max thought. Benny's on my trail, and I want to get whatever there is to find before he does.

Tommy eased back into the seat. "So, what do you want to do?"

"See all those Xs? We're going to find us some treasure."

After several minutes, Tommy pulled into Mrs. McPhee's driveway. "I hope that stupid cat isn't around," he hissed.

"Keep your temper to yourself. We might need her. She knows stuff."

"Do you think we've been followed?"

"No. We left no clue at Brier Lane about where we were headed. We should be okay for a while. The guy who followed me isn't the smartest guy."

Mrs. McPhee looked out her window. "Damn it!" She reached to open the door but hesitated. She wondered if she should let the two men inside her house. She secured the chain on the door jamb to talk to them from behind the door before opening it. "What do you want?"

Max leaned in closer to the narrow opening. "You called me?"

"No, I did not."

"I saw your number. Got some news for me?"

Tommy stood tall and peered into the house, looking for the cat.

Mrs. McPhee saw his blond hair and stared back at the cat-hater. "I don't want you in here."

Max lifted the back of his hand in front of Tommy's face to stop him from doing something rash. He knew Tommy had a temper. In a condescending tone, he added, "Come on, why don't you let us in? I have another fifty in my pocket." Max guessed this woman was hiding something that might help him. He needed to know what that was.

Mrs. McPhee thought for a moment and then replied, "I don't think so." She started to close the door.

Within seconds, Max had wedged his hiking boot between the door and the door trim. Tommy mistakenly took his boss's cue as a call to action and gave the door a hard shove. The old wooden trim cracked, and the door flew open. The shotgun was knocked to the floor.

As the old woman fell backward onto a small sofa, she screamed, "I'm going to call the police!" She tried to stand up to reach for her favorite weapon and saw Penelope scooting into the kitchen.

Tommy rushed inside behind Max and gave her a backhanded slap. "No, you don't." This time, as she fell, her head smacked against the wooden trim along the back of the sofa, and her eyes closed.

Max leaned over her to check for a pulse. "Tommy, what the hell did you do?"

Tommy stood wide-eyed. "I hardly touched her."

After a few seconds, Max said, "Well, you're lucky. She's alive."

"The old broad was gonna kill us." Tommy started to look around the room. "Where's that damn cat?"

"I don't know." Max went into the kitchen and found Penelope crouching under the table against the wall. He looked over to Tommy. "She's not going to bother you." Max checked his watch. "Get the shovels. We've got some digging to do."

80

Present Day
BREWSTER

AS JANE HELPED CLEAN up after lunch, she grew more curious by the minute. "Aunt Nancy, can I please go and look at the photos that Danny took?"

"Of course. I never closed the screen down."

"Thanks."

"I'll finish up here and then I'm going to check on our neighbors on the other side. I heard them talking earlier. They put in a new pool, and I want to see if it's up to code. I caught them draining the pool into our woods a few weeks ago. They're also supposed to have a fence around it, according to the law in Massachusetts."

Jane left for the office and the computer. After opening up several of the images and magnifying them, she didn't find anything unusual. There were two images left to look at. She opened one of the them, selected the magnifying glass in the tool bar, and then began clicking to enlarge it.

The photo was of the iron bed frame, or at least what was left of it. She took another look. Something stuck out from inside the top of the bed's tubing. Whatever it was had scratches on it, but she couldn't figure out what it was. She magnified the image a little more. The small, narrow piece looked shiny, like gold.

Jane didn't remember seeing that on the iron frame in the woods. She'd better head back out for a look—maybe it was something valuable. In her haste to go look again for treasure, Jane stuffed the map she had found upstairs in the metal box into her pocket, but it didn't fit all the way in and stuck out of her jeans.

She called out to her aunt from the office. After a few moments of no reply, Jane grew impatient and headed to the woods alone through the laundry room door.

Halfway into the dense woods, she arrived at the yellow police-tape barriers. She knew the area well by now and walked closer to the bed springs and the iron bed. She reached for the rusty bar. As she tilted it up, whatever was inside slid down a little and out of sight. Jane took the bar and tried to tilt it the other way, hoping to dislodge whatever was inside.

From behind her, a voice called out, "What are you doing here?" She dropped the bar and quickly turned around.

The man standing before her was holding a flat piece of paper. The younger guy behind him was carrying two shovels and had a menacing glare on his face.

"Just looking around."

"This is private property. What's your name?"

"Jane."

"Well, Jane, do you live around here?"

She pointed to the Caldwell Gallery. "I'm visiting my aunt and uncle, next door."

"My name is Max, and I'm interested in buying this property. Do you know anything about what's going on here?"

"Not really. I should be going now." Jane took a few steps back from the men.

The guy holding the shovels slowly walked between her and the gallery.

Jane saw the men look at each other. She took it as a signal that they might harm her. She slowly moved to the side, hoping to run. She quickly decided her aunt's house was out of the question, so she bolted toward Mrs. McPhee's house, remembering the shotgun. Jane knew she could outrun the two men. Afterall, she was a cross-country winner. The green of the foliage turned to a blur as she took off.

Tommy dropped the shovels and ran after her.

Max was slower. After only a few seconds, he stopped to catch his breath. He noticed a piece of white, folded paper on the ground. He picked it up and recognized it as almost identical to the map they already had.

"Tommy, stop! Let her go."

Jane could see an old Volvo parked next to another car in Mrs. McPhee's driveway. Her head turned to see the blond guy circle back. She kept running until she flew up the stairs of the porch. The door was half-open.

Jane found Mrs. McPhee sitting on the sofa, stroking Penelope and rubbing the back of her head.

Jane blurted out, "I need help."

Mrs. McPhee looked up to see Jane panting in front of her. "My dear girl, come in. As you can see, there has been a situation here, too."

Jane collapsed into the chair by the window. "Two men were chasing me." She looked toward the shotgun on the floor. "I thought you could help me. I can't find my aunt." She leaned forward to explain more but stopped when she realized her pocket was empty. "It's gone!"

Max handed Tommy one of the maps. "Since they both look pretty much the same, let's split up."

The two men stood in the woods between the old foundation and the yellow taped-off area, trying to get their bearings. Max identified the map's drawing as the foundation of a house, then he looked at all the Xs.

"It's the old house back there. Get the shovels."

Tommy said nothing as he jogged back to the yellow tape where he'd dropped the shovels. On his return with tools in-hand, he kept asking himself, did he even need Max? There were two maps. He could find treasure by himself. He wasn't stupid. He touched the gun hidden on his back, under his waistband.

81

Present Day
BREWSTER

JIMMY TURNED RIGHT onto Brier Lane. "I forget, where's this house again?"

Benny looked and then pointed to the tiny half-cape. "There it is. Pull in and go real slow."

"Okay."

"Cut the engine."

"Isn't that Appleton's car?" Jimmy pointed toward the back shed.

"He must still be here." Benny pulled his gun out of his shoulder holster. "You take the back. I'll go in the front way."

He looked through a window next to the door, then he opened the screen door and listened. He tried the door handle; it was locked.

Jimmy appeared behind him. Benny signaled with his free hand to pick the lock. Jimmy withdrew a little tool, and after about ten seconds, he heard a click and the door opened. Quietly, Benny grabbed his gun with both hands, aimed in front of him, and pushed the door wider with his foot.

Seeing no one nor hearing any other sound besides themselves, Benny whispered, "What a mess." He gestured for Jimmy to go upstairs.

"No one's up here, Benny."

Jimmy came back down and stood by the table. He began lifting papers up to find anything that looked important. A thought crossed his mind: he didn't know what he was supposed to be looking for. "Now what?"

"I don't know. We've got to find him. He's around here somewhere."

"Remember there was another guy with him when we came looking for him the last time?"

"You're right. There were two cars parked in the driveway." Benny sat in one of the chairs by the table.

Jimmy sat opposite him. He leaned down to scratch his ankle. "Damn this mosquito bite. I can't stand it, it's so itchy." He spotted a small, folded piece of paper on the floor. It looked like a Post-it® note. He picked it up, opened it, and handed it over to Benny. "Look what I found."

Benny read, "*Caldwell Gallery.*"

Jimmy looked it up on his phone. "Got it. It's at the other end of Brewster."

82

Present Day
BREWSTER

THE CLOSER I GOT to where the new pool was being built, on the other neighbor's side of our house, the louder the talking became. I used the old paths I'd carved into these woods, years ago. They were still clearly marked.

Up ahead, I could see the clear-cut area and the large cement hole for the pool, with all of its drains and pipes exposed. I was not a fan of pools, but it was my neighbor's property, so I knew they could do with it whatever they wanted, as long as they followed the rules.

Approaching the property line, I noticed the pool guys were moving toward their trucks, then they left. I looked around to see there was no fence yet. There was also no evidence of water puddling in the woods from possible illegal dumping. Things appeared to be status quo, so I turned and walked back to the house.

When I entered through the back porch, I headed toward my office. "Jane?"

No answer. I called up the stairs, waited a few seconds, then glanced into the kitchen and ended up in the laundry room. The thought ran across my mind that she might have found something in the photos and gone to look for it. I decided to go look outside.

The sun was still shining as I crossed over the property line and passed the oak tree. "Jane?" No answer.

I walked toward the back and high-stepped over the ivy and branches for a good distance, but I still couldn't see anyone. Finally, I spotted the yellow tape. I noticed the iron bed had been moved, so I stepped closer. As I leaned over to pick it up, I heard rustling behind me.

I stood tall, ready to confront whomever or whatever it was.

A man broke through the underbrush. He called out, "Hello!"

I greeted him with a hesitant but curious, "Hi."

"Sorry to bother you, but my friend and I were just looking over this property with the hopes of buying it." A younger man appeared behind him.

"Oh, I see." I immediately recognized him as the guy from Brier Lane. "I'm looking for my niece. Have you seen anyone else in these woods?"

He looked over to his younger friend. Both shook their heads. "No, can't say we have."

It was time for me to leave. "Okay."

"Say, what's with the police tape?"

I needed to find Jane, so I quickly explained, "Oh, that? I use police tape to mark where I find rare wildflowers."

An awkward silence ensued.

"I guess I'll be going. My niece probably has her headphones on and can't hear me calling her in the house."

The older guy called after me, "Good luck finding her."

I left the men as they walked away from the yellow-taped area. I called Paul as soon as I got inside the house.

"I can't find Jane. I've looked all over. Will you ask Madeline if she knows anything about where she might have gone?"

I heard Paul ask her, then he replied, "She doesn't know."

"Paul, I'm worried."

"Take it easy." I could hear Madeline say something in the background. Paul repeated, "Madeline says her headphones are noise-cancelling. She probably can't hear you calling for her."

"All right. I'm going to go look again. I'll call you back."

"Okay, love you."

"Be safe, Paul. I love you, too."

This doesn't make sense, I thought. After searching each room upstairs again, I checked my office, looked out the laundry room door, and then walked around the outside of the house to Paul's studio and workshop in the back. I even crawled up and into the hayloft. Nothing. She wouldn't just wander off and leave the property. She's too smart for that. Besides, what was the guy from Brier Lane doing on the property next door?

A little over ten minutes passed before I hurried back into the main house and went straight to my office to get a look at the photos. Maybe I could get a clue from them as to Jane's whereabouts.

I turned the corner to enter the office, and my heart went through the roof. The two men from the woods were hunched over my computer, looking at the photos.

How had they gotten in? I recalled the laundry room door was unlocked. We never lock the doors in the back of the house when someone is home.

"What're you doing in here?" I demanded to know.

"Sorry, lady. I think we can stop with the what and the why. According to these pictures and these," he held up two maps, "we're looking for the same thing."

"Who are you?"

I watched the Brier Lane guy walk toward me and then stop halfway, by the piano, which was a few feet from me. "Did you ever find your niece?"

The blond one kept looking at the photos.

My hands started to perspire at thoughts of where Jane might be and whether these men had harmed her.

"No, I didn't. And I'm very worried about her." I put my hand inside my pocket, next to my cell phone, and then moved past him, closer to the computer. I looked at the blond guy seated at my desk. "Do you mind?"

The man holding the maps nodded his head and the blond guy stood up. I sat down, hoping to shut the computer off, but within seconds, the blond grabbed my elbow and pulled me up and out of my chair.

"Leave it on," he hissed.

I calmed myself, recalling that I had been in worse situations than this one before.

"My name is Max, and this is Tommy. We've met, haven't we? Over at the Brewster house. What was your name?"

"Nancy." I decided to play along with the nice game, at least for now.

"Well, Nancy, why don't you tell me what you know about the Wilkins's property next door."

I was taken aback at hearing that name again, but I tried to hide my awareness as much as I could. I had to cooperate with these guys for Jane's sake. "I already knew a Wilkins owned the property next door."

"Okay, what else do you know about Anna Horvath Wallace?" He held up the paper I had scribbled her name on, when I was talking to Molly.

"Wait. Were you the guy who walked through my daughter's house?"

"You mean in Millbury? I guess I was. What a coincidence. Your daughter? And here we are."

Tommy let go of my arm and took a wide-legged stance by my side. "Hey, Max, I was looking at those pictures. There was one that looked important."

"How so?" Max asked without taking his eyes off me.

The young guy sat back down. "I didn't get to see it real good, but it looks like something is sticking out of that old bed frame."

"What do you mean?"

He pointed to the image on the screen and then magnified it. "See? At the end of this iron bar, there's something sticking out. There should be a rounded cap on it, but this one is missing."

I was determined to find Jane, so I offered, "If I help you, will you tell me where my niece is?"

"Of course, Nancy. I'm a nice guy. A family man. I have a son in college. Just interested in finding some treasure… at all costs."

Max stopped to look around at the walls that held all my exploits from the past. "It sure looks like I've found the right person to help me find my treasure. What else can you tell me?"

"My niece found a map in our house."

He held up one map. "We know that. And we found an identical map at that Brier Lane house." He held up the second one.

I silently prayed, *God, please let Jane be okay.* "Where did you get Jane's map?"

"We found it in the woods."

Another worry entered my head. "I'm not saying anything else until I see Jane. And she had better be okay."

Tommy stood to grab my arm again.

Max put his hand up, signaling him to back off.

He let go.

I breathed a little easier.

Max added. "Let's go outside and see what's in that iron bar."

"Can I take another look at the map?"

"Here. Look at it while we walk."

Max pushed me first in line as we walked toward the yellow tape. I tried to think of how I could stall for more time. At least, until I could figure out how to get help.

83

BENNY AND JIMMY pulled into the Caldwell Gallery's empty parking area.

Jimmy looked around. "Looks like nobody's home."

"Perfect."

The two men walked up the deck and jiggled the door. It was locked.

Jimmy peered inside the glassed door. "I don't see anyone."

Benny stepped back. "Let's go around back."

They walked around the house, then, as they turned the corner on the screened porch, Benny held his hand out to stop Jimmy from going any farther. He raised a finger to his lips.

The men silently watched two other men and a woman enter the woods. One of them carried shovels. Benny whispered, "I think that's Appleton." After a minute or two, Benny and Jimmy followed their path into the brush.

84

Present Day
BREWSTER

WHILE WE WALKED, I asked Max, "Have you found anything at those X spots?" I hoped they hadn't.

"No. That's why you're with us. You must know a lot more than we do."

I wished I did know more. As we walked deeper into the property, I glanced at the map several times. "What does Anna Horvath Wallace have to do with all this?"

"She was my grandmother," Max replied. "I have to figure out how she's connected to Wilkins and this map."

I thought for a second and then asked, "The same Anna who lived in the Millbury house?"

"Yes."

I kept quiet about Molly and the journal she'd found.

A random branch behind me slapped Tommy in the face as I made my way through the thick woods.

"Watch it, lady."

Deep down, I was pleased that he got smacked. I smiled and said, "Sorry."

As I looked for another branch to possibly whack him with, I was also aware I needed to be careful. We were now all on this hunt together, only they were looking for treasure and I was looking for Jane. Max didn't seem to be a real bad guy, but Tommy was a whole different animal. I hoped my instincts were right about Jane and that she was safe somewhere. But where?

The yellow tape lay up ahead. Two maps, I thought. Based on the dates, Anna from Millbury and Ellsbeth from Brewster somehow knew each other, but what was their connection to Wilkins? He must have made the maps for each of the girls. But why?

"I see the iron bar!" I hurried across the brush toward the rusted bed springs.

Tommy followed close behind me.

Max stood where he was, about eight feet from us, looking at one of the maps.

The blond lifted the bar and tried to look inside. Then, he shook it.

"Wait, something's sticking out." I reached to touch it.

Tommy swatted my hand away.

I held my palms up and backed away. Let him go. No need to make this kid angry.

I watched him slowly pull a long, rectangular, brassy-looking piece out of the hollow bar. He dropped the bar and sauntered closer to Max. "I told you there was something in there."

He handed it over to Max. "What are those markings?"

"I don't know." Tommy wiped his dirty hands on his jeans.

I walked closer. "Let me see." I took the piece from Max and lay it on my palm. "These look like coordinates."

"Like on a map?" Max leaned closer to me.

From behind us, I heard Tommy say, "Hand it over."

Max turned around. "What're you doing?"

Tommy was pointing a gun at the two of us. "Just getting my fair share."

"Take it easy, Tommy. I was always going to give you a cut." Max slowly began to take a few steps toward a shovel lying on the ground. "Put the gun down man."

As Max lunged for the shovel, Tommy shot him.

Max grabbed his bleeding arm. "Christ, Tommy!" He squeezed his arm. "Why'd you do that?"

"I want all the treasure."

"You'll never get away with it. Those guys who were following me are going to find you."

He stared at Max. "I can handle them." He pointed to an old tree stump. "Sit down and don't move."

Then he looked at me.

"You! Come here. Can you read those numbers?"

"I think so. I need my phone to find out where the numbers point to." I took a step toward Tommy. "My phone's in my pocket." I started to reach inside. "Okay?"

"Yeah. Go ahead. Don't try any funny stuff."

"I won't." I pulled the phone out, opened my Google maps, added the numbers, and then waited.

"What's taking so long?" Tommy sounded impatient.

"Reception may not be so good back here." I secretly hoped I was right.

As I looked at the whirling symbol, I heard some movement behind me. I turned to see two other men appear in the woods. They also had guns drawn.

One of them yelled, "Appleton!"

They headed toward Max.

I dove to the ground.

Tommy fired two more shots. Both men fell behind the massive trunk of a fallen tree. Then silence.

85

Present Day
BREWSTER

IT TOOK A WHILE before Mrs. McPhee felt stable enough to stand up. "Whew, that son-of-a-bitch pushed me hard. I must have hit my head on the wood."

Jane's breathing calmed as she moved to the old woman's side. "You sure you're okay?"

"Yes. I'm fine. I've been through a lot worse than this." She waved Jane away.

Jane looked toward the open door and the shotgun on the floor. "Should we call the police?"

"Nah. Don't need anyone else coming onto my property." She straightened her paisley shirt over her wide-legged acrylic pants. "Hand me my shotgun."

Jane hesitated but brought it to her anyway.

"Don't you worry. You'll be safe here." Mrs. McPhee reached down into a small drawer on the coffee table. It was filled with bullets. She grabbed several, stood up, opened the shotgun, and filled the empty chamber.

Jane stood still, watching the woman closely.

"Go get my Penelope and put her in my bedroom. Then, get my binoculars from the window, over there."

Jane gently picked the cat up, shut the door on her, and returned to hand Mrs. McPhee the binoculars.

The old woman stood tall, holding her gun like a pro. "Now that my darling's safe, put those specs around your neck. We're going to have a look-see before we call anyone."

They went onto the porch side that faced the empty property.

A gunshot rang out.

Jane jumped.

Mrs. McPhee stopped halfway to the end of the porch. "Stay back."

Jane started shaking.

Mrs. McPhee turned toward the young girl. "You stay here. Now you can call the police. Use my landline."

"But what about Aunt Nancy?"

"That's what I'm going to find out." She carried the shotgun at her side as she stepped into the dense brush.

Another two shots echoed through the woods. Mrs. McPhee continued walking ahead.

Jane ran into the house. As she frantically searched for the phone, she whispered to herself, "Please, God, take care of us. Don't let anyone hurt us."

86

Brewster
PRESENT DAY

I LIFTED MY HEAD up and saw Tommy standing with his gun pointed at where the two men had gone down.

He flicked his weapon at me. "Get up, lady."

I slowly stood up, brushed myself off, and then picked up my phone from where I'd dropped it.

"Start walking to the foundation."

"Don't you want me to see where those coordinates will send us?" I had a strong hunch that the real treasure was wherever this location was and not at the foundation at all.

"I want some distance between me and those guys."

I glanced over to Max. He must have fallen off the tree stump when Tommy fired at the two other men. He was lying motionless on his back, still breathing and holding his injured arm. I moved deeper into the woods, followed by Tommy.

After a few minutes, he yelled, "Stop!"

I turned and obeyed his command.

"Put those numbers into the phone again."

I typed them in and watched the gear begin to whirl. "No luck." I lowered the phone and looked to Tommy for my next move. I wasn't going to take any chances with this kid. I had to stay calm.

We both stood silent for a few seconds, as if Tommy didn't know what to do next.

From behind him, Max appeared from out of the woods.

He held up the maps and said, "Don't you think you'll need these?"

Tommy twisted around. "Give them to me."

Max tossed them on to the ground, took a step back, and then stood with one hand raised. His other arm showed some blood.

Tommy reached for the maps, stuffed them into his pocket, and then ordered, "Get over there. Next to the lady." He used his gun again to direct us. "Both of you walk slowly toward the foundation near the road."

I looked behind me a few times as we walked forward, single file. I thought I saw a glimpse of Mrs. McPhee in the woods, but I wasn't sure. Soon, we reached the foundation.

Tommy looked at the map. He walked over to the side that was closest to Mrs. McPhee's land. He pointed to me. "Get in there and dig in the middle."

"With what?"

"Your hands. Just dig."

He pointed at Max with his gun. "You, too. Go look on the other corner. There's got to be something here."

I knelt down and started to scratch away at the black dirt. Max did the same on his side.

Out of the corner of my eye, I saw Mrs. McPhee walk out of a clearing holding her shotgun aimed directly at Tommy. As happy as I was to see her, I couldn't stop thinking about where Jane was.

"Put your gun down, you cat-hater."

Tommy didn't move. He just stared at the old woman.

I've never seen a standoff before in real life, only in movies. I was ready to lay flat on the ground to avoid getting caught in any crossfire.

Mrs. McPhee moved the shotgun tighter to her shoulder in a determined stance. "I said drop your gun, punk."

Tommy raised his gun higher, aiming it right at Mrs. McPhee's heart. "I'm a pretty good shot, lady. I won't miss."

"We'll see."

I heard a slight rustling behind Tommy, but before I could catch a better look, a shot went off. I dropped to the ground and buried my face in the leaves. There was a slight thud and then silence.

I looked up to see Tommy squirming on the ground and holding his upper thigh. I quickly turned my head to see Mrs. McPhee still standing, her shotgun now by her side.

A familiar voice yelled out, "Everyone all right?" Detective Tony Gomes walked out of the woods from McPhee's property.

Four more policemen followed behind him.

One of them checked on Tommy. "You have the right to remain silent..."

Those were the happiest words I had heard in a long time, besides Jane's voice. She appeared behind the last policeman. "Aunt Nancy!"

Tony helped me up. "You okay?"

"I'm fine."

As Tony put his gun back into his holster, I watched the second policeman walk over to Mrs. McPhee and carefully take her shotgun from her. The third policeman helped Max up to a standing position, while Jane came toward me.

With a big hug, she said, "Aunt Nancy, I was so afraid for you."

Mrs. McPhee sauntered over to Tony, Jane, and me. "Glad you could make it to the party, Detective Gomes."

"Nice to see you again, Mrs. McPhee. How's your porch looking?"

"Well, pretty clean, at least in my eyes."

Mrs. McPhee put her arm around Jane's shoulders. "Jane, you did well."

A big smile grew across my niece's face.

I looked to my friend. "Tony."

He turned to look at me.

"You should find two other bodies, over by the yellow police tape, that this guy shot." I pointed to Tommy. "Do you want me to show you where I believe they went down?"

"Jane, you stay with Mrs. McPhee," Tony ordered. "I'll go with your aunt."

After confirming that his men had things under control, he signaled to the fourth policeman to follow us.

87

Present Day
BREWSTER

WE HURRIED THROUGH the woods only to find the two men were gone.

"I know they were here." I pointed behind the fallen tree trunk. "They were right there."

The sound of a car door slamming came from our house's direction.

Tony pulled out his gun. "Nancy, stay behind us." He and his officer started to jog through the brambles.

I followed his order, all the while trying to see what might be going on ahead of us. I was pleased I was able to keep pace with them, from a safe distance.

As we approached the rock wall that surrounded our back screened porch, I heard a second car door slam and noticed a few drops of blood on two stones.

When the police reached the grassy lawn behind Paul's studio, the officers took off. I quickly followed. We rounded the corner toward the parking area. Ahead of us, I saw an unfamiliar car turning around.

The officers kept running with their guns drawn. They were both yelling, "*Stop! Stop the car!*"

My heart stopped when I saw Paul had turned into the driveway, with Madeline in the front passenger seat. "Oh, my God."

The car idled at the edge of the berm, blocking anyone from coming or going. I wanted to go to Paul but stayed put.

The police cautiously walked over to the driver's side of the stranger's car with guns drawn. The car windows were open, and the men had their hands in the air. "Get out of the car. Keep your hands up."

The men did as they were told.

Feeling safer, I ran onto the front grass and sprinted over to Paul. He looked about three shades pale.

He opened his window. "Nancy. What the heck is going on? Where's Jane?"

Within the hour, there were several police cars in our driveway, along with two parked on the side of the road, in front of the empty lot between our property and Mrs. McPhee's.

Our brave neighbor stayed at her house to give her statement. Jane and I went to our back porch to give ours. Paul, with his arms crossed, stood in the doorway of the house, watching and listening. Every once in a while, I noticed him shaking his head.

By the time the property was clear of police cars, it was time for dinner. From the looks of everyone, eating wasn't really on their minds. I knew we had to eat something, though, so I sent Paul down the road to Cobie's Clam Shack to pick up some comfort food. Hot, crispy, and salty fries always felt good going down to me.

We started eating in silence. As our bellies filled, we began to chat.

"Well, it's been quite a day." I was halfway through my bowl of chowder.

Jane smiled as she added more ketchup to her plate.

I glanced over to Madeline, who was finishing her burger, and asked her, "Does it taste good?"

With a mouthful, she returned a smile.

"Jane, I'm sorry you had to go through all of this."

She wiped her mouth with a napkin. "It was okay. I was scared at first, but when I finally saw the police pull onto Mrs. McPhee's driveway, I felt better."

Madeline piped up, "Glad I was with Uncle Paul."

Paul put his arm around her shoulders.

"I sometimes get too involved in figuring things out. I'm sorry, I guess I can't help myself when I get the curiosity bug."

Paul stared at me with a slight smile on his face.

As we cleared the picnic table, I commented, "Jane, Madeline, you've only got a few more days before you'll be leaving us. I hope you'll want to come back."

Jane emptied the tray into the trash then gave me a big hug. "Aunt Nancy, this was the best vacation I've ever had."

"Really?"

"Yeah. I mean, we solved a mystery and found real pirate treasure. Do you think I can still keep that compass and what about the coins I found?"

"Pretty sure. If you don't get to take the compass home in a few days, I'll send it to you, along with the coins."

"You're going to call my mom and explain everything to her, aren't you?"

"Of course. I think I'll Zoom. That way, I can see her reactions and carefully choose my words. It's always better to drop news like this in person, but Zoom is better than a phone call."

After the girls went to bed, Paul and I sat on the couch together, watching a repeat of an old sitcom.

"I've been thinking."

Paul hit the pause on the remote. "I'm listening."

I placed my hand on his leg. "What do you think about buying the property next door?"

"Are you serious?"

"Yes. I've been thinking about it for a long time, even before Jane and Madeline came. I don't think I could stand to have someone come in and clear-cut the trees to build a new house. Even when we first moved here, I wanted more land around us."

"You're right. I've thought about it, also."

"I've saved a lot of money from all my escapades. Maybe we could sell some of the jewelry from the pirate treasure?"

"That's a thought. It is your money."

"I know, but we're still partners. What do you think?"

"I say, yes."

"Great!"

Paul selected play on the remote.

After a few minutes, I announced, "I have such a good feeling about those map measurements on that piece of brass."

He pushed pause again. "What did you say?"

"I think the biggest treasure is located wherever those map coordinates take us."

"So, you're surmising, if we own the land, everything found on it belongs to us?"

"Exactly."

"You're going to start looking deeper into buying the land and put the map on the back burner?"

"Yes. I'll call the town as soon as the girls leave."

Danny came home at around 10 p.m. He found us in the living room, half asleep. He stood in front of us and asked, "Did you and Jane find anything cool in those photographs I took?"

Paul and I looked at each other and started to laugh.

"What's so funny?" He sat opposite us.

Paul lowered the sound of the TV and looked at me.

I took a deep breath. "Not sure where to begin, but here's what happened…"

88

Present Day, Six Months Later
BREWSTER

FOR ALMOST HALF a year, I worked on the details of acquiring the land next door to us. Success came a little before Christmas.

Paul and I sat by the fire, watching old home movies, with our decorated Christmas tree twinkling behind us. In between switching out the discs on our old DVD player, Paul returned to his seat next to me.

"I guess you finally got your wish."

"I guess I did. That property now belongs to the Caldwell family. No clear-cutting, no houses. Nothing but green and open ground to protect the Cape's sole source aquifer."

"I'm proud of you for curtailing your curiosity and not searching for whatever treasure remains on the land."

"It's been tough. Every time I walk past those woods, I want to jump in and start hunting."

"When do you plan on resurrecting the search?"

"I'm going to wait until Jane and Madeline return in June. I owe it to Jane. She worked just as hard as I did and experienced much the same emotions."

"You're a good aunt and friend to her. Of course, I'm surprised your sister will let them come visit again, after all Jane went through last summer."

"Oh, we're all good. She knows I'd protect them with my life."

Another six months passed

By lunchtime, Paul had returned from the bus station with the girls.

"Jane, it's so good to see you." I hugged my niece. "Come here, Madeline. So happy to hug you, too."

I watched Jane run upstairs with her backpack and return with the brass compass engraved with *Bully* in her hands. "When can we go searching?"

I started laughing. "Slow down. We'll get to it as soon as we eat and decide on a plan."

Madeline laughed all the way up the stairs to put her backpack away.

"I've got lunch set out on the back porch." Everyone followed me outside.

Sandwiches, chips, pickles, and soda were quickly dispersed.

"I didn't think I would be hungry, but everything tastes delish." Jane wiped her mouth with a napkin. "Aunt Nancy, I've been studying old compasses. They're really cool! I'm so excited to test out what I've learned."

"Yes, I've been waiting very patiently for you to come back, so we can go on this hunt."

"I was wondering, whatever happened to those two guys, Tommy and Max?"

"They both plea-bargained and got lighter sentences. Tommy got five years and Max, three. The courts are so bogged down, plus the lawyers were pleased because it made their jobs easier. Even Benny and Jimmy cooperated. They are going to testify against the Mica brothers in a tax-evasion case."

Jane reached for the ketchup. "Breaking the law is something I would never do."

"Hold onto that thought for the rest of your life."

About fifteen minutes later, as we cleared the picnic table, I noticed Jane was looking toward the woods. "Everything okay?"

Jane piled the empty plates together on the tray. "Just thinking about how far people will go to get more money, or whatever else they want or think they need."

"Jail is a scary place." I hugged her again. "Remember that poor man my friend found last summer, at the Brier Lane house?"

"Oh, yeah. Do you think that had something to do with that guy Max?"

"I thought so, but the man's death was ruled natural causes. My theory that Max had killed him to get the house and whatever treasure was inside was debunked."

"Aunt Nancy, I bet he did it."

"We'll never know."

"You ready for another adventure?"

"Absolutely. I'll get my compass."

Before we entered the dense green of our newly acquired plot of land, we met on the back porch once more. I placed the old piece of brass on the picnic table.

"Uncle Paul cleaned it up and lightly brushed some stain over the markings, so we can read the numbers better."

I began to put the coordinates into my Google maps app. After I pressed *search*, we both stared at the blue-green circle that would indicate where we needed to explore.

Jane pulled out the old compass. "I read that most real old compasses are set to magnetic north. Not as accurate as modern-day GPS."

"I've also heard that. My iPhone will probably set it at true north. If we get the general location, we'll be good to go."

I handed Jane a piece of paper with the old coordinates written on it. "Let's see how good your compass is."

The sun broke through a few clouds as we made our way into the woods.

"I left the yellow tape up, so we can find the spot easier."

I knew we might lose phone service, so I was glad Jane was using her compass.

We slowly moved along the forest floor. When my iPhone dropped service, I noticed Jane kept walking on ahead. I put my phone away and followed her.

After a few minutes, we both stopped. We were in between the foundation and the yellow tape.

Jane looked up at me. "I haven't reached those coordinates yet."

"Can I take a look?" She handed the compass over to me. It took a while for it to settle. Finally, I said, "Almost there."

From behind us, sounds of someone walking grew louder. "What's that?" Jane asked.

"Not sure who it could be."

We both looked in the same direction.

"Hello there." Mrs. McPhee came bursting through the brush.

"Mrs. McPhee!" Jane ran to give her a hug.

"Why Jane, how have you been?"

"Fine. Just anxious about what might be hidden out here. What about you?"

"Doing okay." Our neighbor looked at me. "Nancy. Been up to anything interesting?"

"Well, maybe. We're trying to follow those markings on the copper plate."

"I remember you mentioning them to me. What are you looking for?"

"We don't know yet."

"That certainly is interesting."

"I think we should put away the compass and start looking around. Our coordinates are only off a few degrees."

Jane started to kick away some of the leaves and broken twigs with her feet in semicircles.

I followed suit, trying to clear the ground. Mrs. McPhee joined in. Jane occasionally stopped to pull out the compass and check her bearings. Then, she would take a few steps and change her position. I looked up and noticed that, this time, she hadn't moved.

"You found something?" I walked closer to her.

"Aunt Nancy, the bearings point to right where I'm standing." She looked down.

I looked to the ground. Mrs. McPhee sidled up next to me and stared at the dirt in front of us. All three of us looked at each other. Then, we all took a big step back.

I slowly said, "Let's do some digging."

Jane and I had brought trowels with us.

Mrs. McPhee added, "I guess I'll lend my moral support to you two ladies and just watch."

Jane knelt down. "It feels just like when we were looking for those gold coins."

The dirt slowly turned darker as we twisted the small tools in, up, around, and deeper into the dirt, looking and hoping to find something. Five minutes passed, then ten minutes. At the fifteen-minute mark, I leaned back to survey what, if anything, we had uncovered. Jane followed my actions.

Mrs. McPhee turned toward her house. "Got to feed Penelope. Keep me posted, ladies."

As Mrs. McPhee's brightly colored blouse disappeared from view, I scanned the area once more. I honestly thought Jane and I spotted it at the same time.

On the edge of where we were searching, there was an odd-looking bump sticking out of the dirt. We both stood to get a better look. Next to the raised lump was a blackened, thin piece of leather-like string lying across the forest floor. I touched it with the tips of my two fingers. I looked up to Jane.

"Do you want to pull it out?"

Jane slowly knelt down, reached for the string, and gently loosened it away from the ground. Whatever it was, it had been protected for many years, nestled under the forest floor.

The leather pouch was released from the dirt's hold. Jane handed it to me.

"You want me to open it?" I asked her, surprised.

She replied with a big smile. "We're a team, remember?"

I carefully loosened the top then shook the pouch upside down over Jane's open hands.

Out dropped one gold coin.

"Only one?'" Jane looked disappointed.

I picked it up to inspect it closer. "This is no ordinary coin. I believe this is a Brasher Doubloon."

"A what? Is it worth more money than the gold coins we found before?"

"If I'm correct, it's worth a lot more money." I closed my fingers around the coin that displayed special markings. "Jane, let's get home. I think we have a winner."

89

September, Present Day
BREWSTER

CASEY'S SPECIAL DAY had seemed so far away back in June, when Paul and I had enjoyed the sights and sounds of spring from the gallery porch. We'd talked about our full life and asked each other if we were ready for another wedding.

We sat on the porch again, each in our oak rockers, this time enjoying the changing autumn leaves. I sipped my coffee.

"We are so lucky that Casey, ever the professional, planned her wedding to perfection."

Paul turned to me. "An intimate back-yard celebration was perfect for the two of them."

"I was so honored to have been asked to marry them, just like I officiated the wedding ceremony for her brother."

I thought about all the gifts that had come rolling in from September to mid-October. And not only for the wedding. Word had also come from Sotheby's about the coin we'd found. It was authenticated as one of the seven coins minted by the New York silversmith Ephraim Brasher, in 1786. The oval stamp of *EB* was imprinted on the left wing of the eagle, a sure sign it was a Brasher Doubloon.

"I can't believe Jane and I found the missing seventh coin!"

Paul was gazing up at the clouds.

I stopped rocking. "I'm still flabbergasted by its potential worth."

I recalled the day Sotheby's called. The man on the other end had mentioned the possibility that it might be a substantial sale, based on the last coin selling for a record $9.36 million, in 2021.

Paul shook his head. "I'm absolutely amazed by the value. You sure you heard those Sotheby auctioneers correctly?"

"I did."

"What's your plan for the coin?"

"I'm going to sell it." I sat quietly for a moment. "Jane will be a part of the first disbursement of monies. Then, of course, our children. And finally, I can't forget the bravery of Mrs. McPhee."

Paul grinned. "That's quite a windfall."

"I'm going to insist that we remain anonymous. No information about us or the location of where the coin was found will be publicized."

"Agreed." Paul reached for my hand.

A beautiful silence passed between us as our rockers settled into a gentle rhythm with each other.

I looked over at my soulmate and lover. "Want to go on a travel adventure?"

"Maybe."

I squeezed his hand. "Let's go see the world, together."

THE END

AUTHOR'S NOTES & ACKNOWLEDGMENTS

THERE ARE TWO ACRES of woods that surround our old 1890 home on Cape Cod. Within them are interconnecting paths that I've carved out of the brush and thorny ground cover since we moved from Ohio, over thirty years ago. These rustic byways were my solitude, when I needed to be by myself.

I mention these little roads in all of my books, and they actually became character-like in my fifth novel, *The Old Cape Map*. On the front cover is a snapshot of one of these paths that separate the grass's edge from the green wall of dense woods. You have to really look to find these passageways. I love walking in the woods.

The kernel that inspired me to write another novel was provided by my youngest daughter, Annie, and her husband, Eric. When they bought an old 1880 house that was originally a barn in Millbury, Massachusetts, I was as excited as they were. Its crooked floors, windows, and hidden rooms sparked my imagination and resulted in some twists for the story.

A connection to Millbury's history came from Karen Gagliardi and her fascination with the reclusive Martha Deering. Her collection of memorabilia about the Deering family and the Ivy Corset Company opened up a world of Worcester commerce, family secrets and the real truth about the Deering Empire. Thank you, Karen.

Other sources for information came from Anne Marie Murphy and her research about Worcester, *City of Corsets.com*, and Sara Acheson from the Town of Brewster's Assessor's Office.

As always, my writing group came through with many edits and helpful suggestions. Thank you, Anita, Iris, and Catherine. I'm especially grateful to my daughter, Heather, for her advice and grammar checks. Once again, Nicola Burnell, my editor, was extraordinary, and my proofreader, Kathryn Flynn Galán from Wynnpix Productions, also proved professional.

Finally, I'm grateful to my two granddaughters, Casey and Madison, up in Alaska, who inspired me to include the characters, Jane and Madeline, in the novel. And to all my children and my husband, Tim, for letting me be me. I intend to remain adventurous and will always ask, "What if?" Or wonder, "It could happen."

ABOUT THE AUTHOR

INTERNATIONALLY BEST-SELLING author Barbara Eppich Struna is a storyteller at heart, who bases her tales on the history, myth, and legends of Cape Cod, along with her own personal experiences. She created a contemporary character, amateur sleuth, Nancy Caldwell, who is the vehicle that moves her novels between time periods in alternating chapters.

Her suspenseful historical novels, part of her *Old Cape Series*, have won numerous literary awards and accumulated thousands of reviews. Her books include *The Old Cape House, The Old Cape Teapot, The Old Cape Hollywood Secret* and *The Old Cape Blood Ruby*. She also cowrote the memoir, *Family, Friends, and Faith,* with her late sister, Sister Barbara Eppich O.S.U.

Barbara is President of Cape Cod Writers Center; a member of International Thriller Writers; a Member of Sisters In Crime, National and New England. She also writes a blog about the unique facts and myths of Cape Cod.

Find Barbara here: barbarastruna.blogspot.com
          Facebook: B.E. STRUNABOOKS
          Instagram: @barbara_struna
          TikTok: @beswrites24_7
          On X: @GoodyStruna

ALSO BY BARBARA EPPICH STRUNA

The Old Cape House

The Old Cape Teapot

The Old Cape Hollywood Secret

The Old Cape Blood Ruby

Family, Friends, and Faith

www.ingramcontent.com/pod-product-compliance
Lightning Source LLC
Chambersburg PA
CBHW030733160325
23558CB00022B/295